GW00870412

SKIN HUNTER

Skin Hunter: Book 1

TANIA HUTLEY

For Mum & Dad.
Thanks for being the best parents ever.

Chapter One

I'm licking the bottom of my bowl to get every morsel of stew when I notice the couple coming into the shelter.

The shelter's entrance is packed with grunts escaping the downpour, shaking water out of their clothes and stamping their shoes. The din is loud enough to give a corpse an earache, as Ma likes to say. Not a good night for noticing people, but I've been watching the door, looking out for Tori, and the couple stand out like two shiny goldfish swimming into a sewer.

They're tanned, so they must be from New Triton. And they're carrying helmets, which means they're rich enough to have a motorbike, one of those fancy retro ones with no cover. The guy's coat is long, and it looks like real leather. Expensive. He runs one hand through his hair, slicking it off his face. A gold ring gleams on his finger and my stomach sinks. He's begging for trouble wearing that in here.

The ends of the girl's long hair are soaked and dripping, but her woolen coat looks dry, treated with water repellant. Not like my soggy coat, an old one of Ma's that soaks up more water than it keeps off. Hers is a beautiful blue color, so blue it makes me ache inside. Her skin is smooth and brown, and her features are so perfect, her face must be tweaked, but it's such a good job I can't tell which parts have been altered.

The girl is about my age, but nothing like me. She's my opposite: maiden instead of monster. Just looking at her makes me want to turn my hideous face away, to hide my hollowed-out cheek and scars. Not that she's looking at me. No, she's gazing around the huge room, her expression uncertain as she takes in the chaos.

It's just gone end of shift for most, and the pouring rain means nobody's game to sleep outside tonight. Food and mattresses are in short supply, and I don't know what's worse, the clamor of everyone trying to be heard over everyone else, or the stink of wet clothes and sweat.

Got to be six or seven hundred grunts in here already, jammed into this cavernous, noise-filled concrete room. A lot more will have gone upstairs to the shelter's other floors, searching for a safe place to sleep in a place where such a thing doesn't exist. Most are like me, just wanting a meal and a dry bed. But there'll be some sharks cruising, for sure.

What are the goldfish thinking? Someone needs to tell them to ride their motorbike back up to New Triton. Far better to get soaked than take their chances in here.

The guy's got the right idea, he's gesturing toward the door. But the girl shakes her head and presses her mouth into a thin, flat line. He points at the band on her wrist, but she shakes her head again, looking over to the big holo screen at the other end of the shelter. Seems they're arguing about it, but from the set of her lips I can tell he's going to lose. What show could be so important she'd want to watch it in here?

I keep thinking one of the stompers watching the dinner lines will tell them to leave, but a fight's broken out near the cluster of food machines that are spitting out the stew. At least a dozen men are piling into the fray, and the stompers are heading toward them instead.

I want to see if the goldfish do the smart thing and take off, but my band vibrates. It's Ma. When I answer it I have to shout over all the noise.

Ma's head appears above my band. Even if my cybernetic eye didn't glitch out when I tried to look at holograms, her image is so pixelated, she's little better than a blob.

"Milla, you okay?" It's Ma's way of saying hello.

Every time she asks that question, I think about answering with the truth. But what good would it do? Besides, she lives in a shelter too, the one above the factory where she works, and they're all equally dangerous, especially for a woman on her own. That's why I never ask if she's okay. I don't want her to have to lie.

"Fine," I shout. Then, feeling bad for shutting her out, I add a little truth. "Actually I'm worried about Tori. It's packed tonight, and she's late."

"She might be pulling a double shift?"

"Maybe. She got called in to see the boss." If Tori is pulling a double, I'll have to find another woman to buddy up with tonight so we can take turns in the line for the bathroom and guarding each other while we sleep. It's weird Tori didn't give me a heads-up.

"Have you eaten?" Ma asks.

I glance down at the licked-clean bowl that held lumpy

gray stew. "Steak." The word makes my mouth water. "With creamy potatoes and gravy. You?"

"Oh, I went straight for the chocolate cake and ice cream. Double portion." She chuckles, but when she draws in her breath I catch a hitch that makes my heart ache.

"I got paid today." I do my best to sound cheerful. "I was about to transfer it to you."

"Thanks, love. I'm sorry I can't talk, I'm about to start shift."

"But—"

Although I know she's already done a full day's work, I bite off my objection. It won't help if I kick up a fuss. If my cybernetic eye and my band's hologram app both worked properly, I'd be able to check whether she looks as exhausted as she sounds.

"You're only doing a double shift?" I ask instead. "And after this one, you'll get some sleep?"

"I will. Don't worry about me, love. I feel fine, and I need to take the work when it's available."

Ma and I are saving as hard as we can for a real home. Somewhere safe for the three of us, including my brother William, like we used to have when my father was alive. When I first started work at the factory, I thought we'd be able to get William back with us soon. Now I try not to keep track of how much Ma and I have managed to save, or imagine the day our dream might come true. If I think about it too hard, the shelter might somehow pollute it. The floor in here is filthy, everything covered with grit and mud. I don't want that filth worming its way into the one bit of hope I have left.

"Work safe, Ma," I say. "Don't get too tired. Make them give you a break if you need it."

"I will, love. You take care of yourself. Sleep safe."

When I disconnect, I look back to the door, but the

food line's grown and it's blocking my view. Anyway, Tori knows where to find me. Ma's right, she's probably working an extra shift.

I can't see the two goldfish either, but they must have left. They couldn't be dumb enough to hang around. Night like this, too many exhausted, pissed-on, frustrated grunts crammed into this place, they wouldn't last ten minutes. I've seen enough robbings and bashings without looking for more, and I'm beat from another long, sweaty day working beside hot machines.

"Milla." Tori's voice comes from behind me.

Shoving my empty bowl into the receptacle, I jump up and give my place at the table to a meat-sack who's jostling to get in. When I turn to greet Tori, her expression is grim. Her hair is wet from the rain and she's holding a grimy, over-stuffed bag of clothes under her arm.

My stomach turns over. Why has she grabbed all her stuff out of her locker?

"Milla, they're transferring me."

"What?" I can hear my own heart beating, as though it's suddenly dead silent in the shelter instead of deafeningly loud. "No." I step toward her to grab her arm. "You can't go."

She glances at the door. "A group of us got canned, but I'm lucky, they said there was a place at another factory for me. They gave me just a couple of minutes to grab my stuff."

"Which factory are you going to?"

"No idea." She shrugs as though she doesn't care, but I can see the pain in her eyes. "Be a change from this place though, right? Hope they transfer me to a food factory and let me stuff myself until I can't eat any more."

"Maybe I could come with you. There might be two jobs…?" My voice breaks as I hear how raw and desperate

I sound. It'd be stupid even to ask. Might get me fired with nowhere to go, which could be a death sentence for someone like me.

"Hey." Tori grabs me in a fierce one-armed hug. "Be strong, okay? I know how tough you are. You just need to believe it."

I hug her back, dropping my face onto her shoulder. Even the stink of her sweat after a twelve-hour shift smells sweet to me now. My friend is all muscle, guts, and smarts, and her grip is strong.

Her dripping hair is cold against my cheek. It gives me a reason to have a wet face on that side. On the other side, I can't make tears from my cybernetic eye.

"You won't know anyone," I mumble into her shoulder. "Who'll look out for your sorry ass if I'm not there?"

"I'll find someone. When you were transferred you met me, right? Bet I meet someone I like way more than you at the new place." She hugs me tighter, then releases me and steps back. "I'd better go. If I take too long, they'll leave without me."

I swipe my cheek dry with my sleeve before she can see it's wet. Tori's the best friend I ever had, and a hundred times tougher than me.

"How am I going to survive without you?" I don't even realize I'm asking the question aloud until I hear the words.

"Hang out with Sabbie and Ray. They'll take care of you. And watch your back, okay? Get yourself killed, and I'll kick your scrawny butt." She glances to the door. "I need to go. If they give the new job to someone else, I'm screwed."

"Then go, already." I force myself to keep my arms by my sides instead of grabbing hold and begging her to stay.

The only thing worse than losing her would be if she didn't have another job to go to.

"Love ya, slugger. Keep fighting." She holds one fist up, curled fingers facing me, giving me the salute used by the Fist, the resistance group she belongs to.

"Please be safe." The words have a hollow ring. She's anything but safe, and any chance I'll ever see her again is remote. From now on, she'll be a pixelated blob that occasionally projects from my band, just like Ma.

Tori turns and strides to the door, hitching her bag of clothes higher on her hip as she goes. Her head is lifted and she doesn't hesitate as she pushes through the grunts still shuffling into the shelter.

I stare after her for a long time, both fists clenched tight and my good eye burning. I hate this place so much, I want to scream my rage and pain at the top of my lungs, but my throat is so tight, I can't even swallow.

She'll be okay. Maybe if I tell myself that enough times, I'll believe it. I really hope we'll both be okay, but it was stupid of me to depend on Tori as much as I did. I should have learned my lesson when I was transferred away from Ma, dumped in here on my own to survive however I could. This place will never be fair.

The one thing you can count on here is that anything good won't last.

Blindly, I stumble toward the back of the shelter. The mattresses are stacked back there, and it's still early enough that there should still be some dry ones. All I can think of is curling up in a corner and covering my head with my arms so no one can see me bawl.

Most of the grunts who've finished eating are jammed in around the big holo, and I have to fight through the crowd of watchers to get to the mattresses.

Then I see them.

Two dumb goldfish.

Their perfectly tweaked faces are angled at the holo, their eyes fixed to the screen. They have no idea that sharks are circling.

I count three sharks who I know by sight and reputation. They're behind the goldfish, checking them out, sizing up their expensive clothes and the motorcycle helmets. Speculating about what treasures they might find in their pockets. One shark fingers something inside his ripped old coat and I'd bet a week's wages it's a blade. All sharks have hardware, smuggled in past the scanners.

I should go right past. There's already a circle clearing around them, people edging away, and I can hear Tori's voice in my head. *First rule is to steer clear of trouble, Milla.*

But my heart is full of so much frustration and rage, my feet stop of their own accord.

The girl's eyes are fixed to the holo, barely blinking. She's standing there as if nobody else exists, not looking behind her, like nothing could ever hurt her. Even more clueless than I was when I first arrived at this shelter, before Tori took pity on me.

In a minute the sharks will be on her.

Every good thing in this place gets ruined, and I'll never have the strength or power to do a single damn thing about it.

Unless…

I jostle forward until I get spat out of the crush of people into the empty space that's formed behind the two goldfish. This close, the girl's skin looks more polished than I can believe. It's stupid to be pretty; it makes you a target. In here it's better to look like me.

"You need to leave right now," I say from behind her, pitching my voice low and urgent. "Men are coming for you." At the same time, I reach out to run my fingers over the fabric of her coat. All my clothes are dirt-colored, and I've never seen such a deep clean blue. It's so beautiful it takes my breath away. I wish I could soak up that blue, that it was a place I could escape to. If only I could drink it up through my fingers.

She shrieks and I snatch my hand back, but she's not reacting to me, hasn't even glanced my way. "That was my name." She clutches her boyfriend's arm. "I got through. I did it! Did you hear? They called my name!"

"Was it you? Are you sure?"

"Look!" She points at the holo and we both follow her finger to the screen.

My cybernetic eye's scanning frequency is the same as the holo, so all I see is interference patterns unless I keep that eye closed. By shutting my bad eye, I can make out a short list of names, only they're too hard to read one-eyed because the letters are flashing, with fireworks bursting behind them.

"Oh my god." His voice goes high. "That's you, Rayne. It's you!"

"Five million credits!" She squeals it so loud my heart just about stops beating. Five million credits? Has she won it? It's got to be a joke. Nobody could win that much, could they? My good eye snaps back to the holo, but all it shows now is a woman's face. It's Director Morelle. She's standing in front of the Morelle scraper, looking not a day older than when I used to watch news feeds about her, before I lost my eye.

The girl's band is coming to life, a hologram of a woman projecting out of it. I catch only a glimpse before someone jostles my side. Turning, I see one of the sharks closing in on the goldfish, his blade half-drawn from under his coat. At the glint of metal, all my muscles go tight. In a moment he'll be on her, and she has no idea he's coming.

Without thinking, I reach out and shove the girl hard in the middle of her blue-coated back. She stumbles forward, dropping her motorbike helmet and smacking into a hard-faced woman who spits a swear word at her.

"Hey!" someone yells. Probably the girl's boyfriend, but I'm too busy watching the shark to glance in his direction.

The shark glares at me, his lip curled in an ugly sneer and his blade brandished as a threat. My heart's thudding. Am I crazy? What the hell am I doing?

"Get lost, freak," the shark snarls.

I hold both hands up like I'm surrendering. Pretending to give in, so he thinks I won't get in his way. But when his attention goes back to the girl, adrenaline rushes through me. I couldn't do anything to help Tori, but there's one thing I can do. If this is a way to fight back against the unfairness of this place, I refuse to walk away.

The shark lunges at the girl, and I ball my fist and punch him in the side, right in the kidney.

He doubles over, cursing. The girl stares at me, her eyes filled with horror. Whether it's from how I look or what I just did, who knows? Either way, she's about to start screaming. Good. The noise might get the stompers over here. Better a beating from them than a shark's blade in my guts.

Two more sharks close in on the boyfriend. One yanks off his fancy coat, the other goes for his pockets. He's yelping. The girl screams so loud it deafens me. Nothing I can do about the boyfriend, but with luck the stompers should be here before she gets stripped or knifed.

Time to get lost. I turn to run but the shark I punched must have a cast-iron kidney. He fumbles for my coat, grabs the back of it and holds on. I struggle, trying to pull myself out of it, but he yanks it so hard I fall over. The side of my face smacks against the muddy floor. My arms are trapped behind my back, tangled in my sleeves.

I roll over, trying to get back on my feet, expecting him to reach down and stick his blade into me. Instead he lunges at the girl and holds the sharp metal against her face. Her scream cuts off as though he sliced it.

"Five million credits," he snarls. With his free hand he grabs her wrist, gripping her band. "Transfer it to me!"

She's gasping. Her brown face has gone pale. "I don't... I just... please..."

A fine red line appears on her cheek, under his blade, like he's drawing it on with red pen. It feathers and blurs, becomes an ugly red streak that runs down and drips on the girl's blue coat.

"Give me the money and I'll let you live."

Two more sharks are holding the boyfriend back, rifling through his pockets while he struggles against them. He shouts, "Stop it! She didn't win the money yet. Don't you know about the Skin Hunter contest? Let her go!"

I scramble to my feet. Stompers are coming, their heavy boots pounding over the floor. The shark hears them too. He strips the girl's coat off, then yanks off her necklace. She's trying to pull away as his blade stabs forward and her cry of pain turns into a moan. The shark shoves her and she slams into me. I stagger backwards, but she sags against me. My hands are warm and wet with her blood. It soaks into my jeans.

The girl's limp, and though she's smaller than me, I struggle to hold her up. As she slides downwards, I see how her perfect face has been ruined. All it took was a few minutes in this place, and now I'm watching the life drain out of her. Why did she come here? If I lived where she did I'd never leave. Never.

Five million credits.

The words ring in my ears as though her dead lips are saying them again. It's a fortune. More than enough for a house for me, Ma, and William. And Tori, too. With that much money we could live together, all of us safe. No more double shifts. No more being transferred. No more shelter.

The sound of boots is closer. The girl's blood is all over my hands. Her DNA. Without thinking it'll work, I push the release button on the band around her wrist. The mechanism's fooled. It reads her blood instead of my skin and opens. Jamming it onto my own wrist, I press it closed. Maybe it's my imagination, but it seems to hesitate. I'm convinced it won't be fooled a second time, but after a moment it locks. It's a much nicer band than my plain one. A New Triton band with a golden sheen that's all but hidden under a layer of mud and gore. It barely fits.

I can't leave the dead girl with no band. The stompers will notice right away. Wiping my hand on my coat, I hold my thumb on the sensor to release my own dull, cheap band and lock it around the girl's wrist. Then I lower her to the ground.

A stomper is suddenly in front of me. Did he see what I did? He's got his gun out and I flinch backwards, my hands up, trying to make myself small.

The sharks have vanished. The crowd is pressed as hard away from me as they can get, so I'm standing in an empty circle that's bigger than I'd have believed possible. At my feet are two dead bodies, the girl and the boy. Their blood feathers across the damp floor.

The stomper grabs my hands and twists them behind my back. I gasp with pain when the cold metal of hand-cuffs bites viciously into my flesh.

Craning my head around, I see him use his band to read the ID chip in my stolen band. "Rayne Walker," he says, obviously reading the name that comes up. Though

I'm covered in the girl's blood, his lip doesn't curl until his gaze settles on my scarred, ugly face. The way I look is what disgusts him most.

"That's me." I meet his cold eyes. With a sick feeling, I realize I'm betting my life on whether he believes me.

Chapter Two

"Y̲ou're under arrest. Do you understand?"

Without waiting for an answer, the stomper pulls out a hand-scanner to give me the once over, and when that doesn't flash up any hardware, he frisks me. His hands are even harder than his face. He searches through all my layers of clothing, as rough as if he's punishing me for not having the blood-covered murder weapon tucked into my front pocket.

It's only when I see the perfunctory way he logs the ID on the dead girl's band that I let myself believe he didn't see me switch my band with hers.

Even if he didn't, I'm completely at his mercy. He can do what he likes with me. Especially if he thinks I killed the two people lying at my feet.

The dead couple's fancy clothes are gone. Covered in blood and mud from the floor, they look like ordinary grunts dead in an over-crowded shelter. Nothing we all haven't seen before, and the stompers aren't examining them closely. Why would they? Nobody's stupid enough to steal someone else's band, because without the owner's DNA to activate its functions, it's just a useless ID bracelet.

But she's Milla now, and I'm Rayne. No time for second thoughts. It's too late to change back.

I sway on my feet, my hands handcuffed behind me, as the stompers go around the crowd, asking those nearest what happened. Nobody saw anything, of course. I wouldn't expect anyone to go against the sharks, but no one speaks up to say I'm innocent either.

"*Please*," I mouth at a kind-faced woman. But she turns her head away. I can't blame her, but with a band of ice tightening around my chest and terror making me breathless, I want to grab her by her coat lapels and beg her to help.

At least the stompers can't find the blade. Without the murder weapon, maybe my fate's not sealed.

Finally, two stompers take me out into the rain, and push me, still cuffed, into a car. They ignore me the whole way to the station, then drag me inside and sit me in a small windowless room with just a cold metal table and chair. Then they leave.

The room stinks with the pungent scent of ammonia, so strong it makes my nose burn. The hard floor is stained with dark splatters, and I try not to look down in case they're what I suspect. Craning my head to stare at the closed door, all I can hear is my own panicked breathing and the blood pounding in my ears.

Time ticks by, stretching out into an agony of waiting that I'm sure is intentional. The cuffs dig into my flesh and my arms ache from being held behind my back. My throat and chest hurt too, from gulping down ammonia-filled breaths. I'm trying not to make a sound because I don't want to attract attention, but I feel like I'm suffocating.

Tori's voice is in my head. *So stupid, Milla. What the hell were you thinking?*

Dropping my forehead onto the table, I close my eyes. I wish I were back in the shelter, my mattress next to Tori's, laughing quietly at how loud she snores while I take my turn lying awake to guard against sharks.

Stealing someone's identity is a bad enough crime to be locked away for. And if the stompers decide I killed those two goldfish, they'll never let me out. As bad as the shelters are, I've heard prison is worse. There are no bands in prison, just ID chips buried deep enough in your flesh that they can identify you when you're dead, no matter how messed up your body is.

By the time two of the stompers come back, I'm sobbing with the pain of vicious cramps shooting through my shoulders and arms. They pace around, asking questions. I try to watch them both, but my cybernetic eye is playing up, my vision glitching out on that side. At first I try to hide how scared I am, but I can't stop shaking and my throat's so sore it's hard to swallow.

I answer their questions in a scratchy voice, wishing for a drink of water. The girl fell against me. She was already dead. Three men did it. No, I don't know their names and didn't see their faces. They wore long coats. They had knives. I don't know who they are. I didn't do anything. Really, it was them. Please believe me. Please.

The stompers don't say anything about Rayne's name being announced on the holo. Guess they either didn't see it, or they haven't made the connection. I leave that part out and when they punch me I don't change my story. Not even with pain exploding in my ribs, or when they hit me so hard my jeans flood with warmth and sharp-smelling urine dribbles onto the floor. For a while after that I can't talk, only groan and pant. The pain sucks all the air out of the room.

The stompers act disgusted that I've pissed myself, but it's the last thing I care about. The warm liquid soaking my legs isn't as bad as having Rayne's blood all over me while she died in my arms.

When I can force words out, I beg them to stop. I swear over and over that I'm telling the truth. They tell me I'm lying and call me filthy names. Then one of them punches the side of my head and reality disappears. The world swirls violently as I gag up some thin liquid that must have once been stew. My ears ring, the sound unbearably loud. I feel like I'm falling sideways, though when my eyes manage to focus again they tell me one of the stompers is holding me onto the chair.

The other stomper's face is close to mine and his mouth is moving, but I can't hear what he's saying over the ringing. Another wave of dizziness and nausea hits, and what's left in my stomach burns its way up, dribbling down my chin.

Faces twisted with contempt, the stompers pull me roughly to my feet. Standing, straightening my body, hurts almost as much as their punches did. I still have that sickening, falling sensation, like I'm spinning sideways, about to hit the floor.

As they drag me into the hallway, a single terrified question cuts through the fog of confusion like a bucket of icy water. *Will they kill me or lock me up?*

Then we're through the front door, and fresh air blows against my face. After the harsh white light of the room I was in, my eyes can't adjust to the dimness of the New Triton street. When I blink, dozens of lit-up signs and banners advertising tiny stalls all run into each other, painting bewildering streaks.

The cuffs loosen from my flesh, and my arms are suddenly free. It feels like someone's stabbing my hands with hundreds of knife cuts as the blood rushes back into my fingers, but the relief of being able to move my arms is so intense I don't care about anything else.

They're letting me go.

My brain shies away from the suggestion. *Too much to hope for. It could be a trick.*

Then the stompers push me down the steps of the police station. My broken body collides hard with the sidewalk and reality disappears into pain.

I don't know how long I lie moaning, too sore and disorientated to move. But eventually my thoughts straighten out into some kind of coherent order. First priority is to get as far away from the stompers as I can.

Forcing myself up, I manage to stagger only a short distance before collapsing again. But at least now I can lie tucked against the side of a building, eyes closed, pressed into as small a space as possible. Hot tears spurt from my good eye, so much force behind them that they burn. I'm so desperate for water to soothe my burning throat that I angle my face to make my tears run down to my lips. It takes a while, but the ringing in my ears gradually fades, and the dizziness, the feeling that I'm falling sideways, does too.

I'm alive, and free. They let me go.

But if they notice me lying here, they might change their minds.

Get up, Milla. Focus.

Wincing, I try to work out where I am. I don't recognize this street or its ramshackle stalls, but Old Triton is an immense city, overflowing with millions of people. Our streets are always dark because New Triton sits over the top of us and blocks most of the sky. Their walkways are like a giant spider web overhead, and their scrapers loom over our streets.

Trickles of sunlight do manage to get through. Right now, narrow shafts of light are slanting in, hitting the sides of the buildings, and catching the laundry that's been hung from windows around twenty stories up and higher. The sun's angle means it must be early morning. Just before day shift, judging by the number of people on the street. And if I'm right, Ma will be getting off night shift. I need to call her.

My hand goes to the band on my wrist before I realize I can't. Unless the band's sensor detects Rayne's DNA, it's effectively dead. I can't operate it. I can't call anyone, or connect to my account.

I have no money.

Desperately, I rub the bloodiest bits of my clothing against the sensor, trying to get it to read Rayne's blood, now dried and stiff. *Nothing*.

What the hell have I done?

I squeeze my eyes shut, cursing myself. Stupid! Why didn't I think about what I was doing before I gave away my band? This one may be prettier than mine was, but unless I can fool the DNA sensor again, it won't even let me open it to take it off.

Rayne's body will have been taken for disposal, my band on her wrist. Everything I had, gone. It wasn't much, but enough to keep me alive. And for what? Some girl said the words five million credits and I grabbed at it, not even knowing if it was true. Did I really think that by taking her band I could swap my world for hers, somehow transport myself to a better, fairer place?

I can't get my band back. What's done is done. Better stop whining about it and get up. If Rayne's name is all I have left, then I'll try to use it. The Morelle scraper was on the holo. How far away?

My hand goes to my band before I remember I can't look up where the scraper is. All I know is that it's somewhere in the city above, in New Triton.

Before I go anywhere, I need a drink of water. Perhaps I should find a shelter so I can sleep and recover. I'll have to ask someone where the nearest shelter is, except everyone's hurrying past without more than a glance in my direction. The way I look, I can hardly blame them.

A woman comes by. Her tired, sagging face says she probably just finished night shift. Just like Ma. Even looks a little like her, in the gloom anyway. I wish it were Ma. I'd give anything to have my mother here with me.

"Excuse me." I make it onto my feet without staggering too much, and amazingly, the woman stops. I've got blood and puke and piss all over me, and I must stink. My face is always an ugly mix of cybernetics and scars, and after the beating I took, it'll be an even worse mess.

Bless her, she doesn't run away screaming.

"Yes?" Her voice is wary and my ears are still ringing, so I need to strain to hear her.

"My band's glitching. Could you tell me where the nearest shelter is?"

She doesn't need to look it up. "There's one along that way, a thirty minute walk."

Thirty minutes. Shit. I'm still dizzy, so even standing still without swaying takes effort.

"Do you know how far it is to the Morelle scraper?" I ask.

She doesn't get too close, but looks it up then holds out her arm so I can see the map, a glowing 3-D projection emerging from her band. Closing my cybernetic eye to read it, I see the Morelle scraper's quite a distance away, close to the Deiterran wall. I'm too weak to walk that far. The shelter it is.

"Thank you."

The woman's nice enough to wish me luck, and that small bit of kindness makes me want to grab hold of her and not let go. I stare after her, wanting to beg for help. But from her patched coat I can tell she hasn't got enough for herself, let alone to offer comfort to a stranger.

Besides, haven't I learned the hard way that it's a bad idea to rely on others? The only kind of help that sticks is the kind you scrounge for yourself. If I can't survive on my own I won't survive at all, and if I want to make it to the shelter, I'd better start putting one foot in front of the other.

I don't walk so much as shuffle. My head swims, and with every step, sharp pain shoots up my side. The stompers must have cracked my ribs, and my throat feels raw from throwing up. All night in the station without a drink has made me so parched that each time I pass a hawker selling drinks, it gets harder to swallow.

The seething city crowd keeps clear of me. Nobody tries to hustle me or sell me the latest pirated band app. I struggle along past hole-in-the-wall stores, black market tech traders, and ramshackle fried noodle stalls, with vendors tossing noodles in frying pans over flaming gas bottles set up on the sidewalk. The bright blue light from their gas flames is all the signage their stalls need, and the smell of frying noodles makes me salivate.

The main streets of Old Triton are always crowded, but there are hundreds of dark, narrow side streets where most people don't linger. I get to the base of a scraper, and the rough concrete wall seems to go on forever. High overhead, the scraper soars up into New Triton. Up there, it's probably filled with fancy apartments. Down here, the Old

Triton base of the building holds a factory. Light shines from its windows, illuminating the graffiti scrawled underneath it. There are lots of drawings of a stylized fist, and the Fist's slogan, *What's buried will rise*. But there are other slogans too. *Two cities, one people. Underneath & overlooked. The strongest fighters grow in the dark. NT Sucks.*

Some of the graffiti is so old that mold has grown over it. Leave anything for too long here, and it'll go black. Sunlight never reaches down this far, not even at midday, and the darkest parts of the sidewalk are dangerously slippery.

Once I'm back on the main street, cabs centipede past, flowing soundlessly in endless, joined-up strings, like beads on a necklace. Occasionally one pulls away from the string and stops to let someone off or on. I wish I could get in and stretch out on one of the comfortable seats, but without a working band I can't get one to stop, let alone pay for it.

Just ahead, the base of a massive New Triton walkway forms a roof over Old Triton that covers several blocks. Underneath it'd be pitch black, except the stalls that line the sidewalks are lit up with colored lights. Puddles of blue, red, and green reflect onto the sidewalk, glitching out my bad eye and making my dizziness worse. The stall's owners call out to the people walking past, urging them to buy a bottle of street brew, or a sweet snack. None of them call out to me.

There are public bathrooms here, and I think longingly of gulping down some water from the faucet, until I see the line of people waiting. The shelter will be quicker.

But when I finally reach the shelter, I realize how bad a mistake I've made. It's well past the start of the working day, and inside there are only night-shifters, already fast asleep. Not like when Rayne turned up at my shelter on a rainy night at dinnertime, when the doors were jammed open and there were too many grunts coming in for the scanners to work.

I'm desperate enough to try Rayne's band on the scanner anyway, swiping it again and again, pushing uselessly against the locked door until the stomper inside snarls at me.

Nowhere to go, but back to the public bathroom. Every step I retrace is agony. Then I face a very long wait in a slow-moving line until I finally get to gulp down handfuls of water from a rusty faucet.

I need to rest, but I can't lie down here. Under the overpass, away from the stalls, it's black as night. Every available corner is filled with rough sleepers. They rustle on plastic sheets, smash their empty bottles, and cough up phlegm from damaged lungs. A man with a matted black beard leers at me and fingers his crotch.

Sleeping outside's too dangerous. At least in a shelter if you scream loud enough the stompers might rouse themselves. If I stick around here and can't get into the shelter tonight, what then? Where will I sleep?

Stumbling out from under the overpass into gloom rather than darkness, I let myself sit down, leaning against the side of a giant cable that's anchored into the sidewalk, stretching up into New Triton. My guts are arguing against the water and I have to fight to keep it down. My ribs ache and I ease my shirt up for a glimpse of the bruised skin underneath.

No, don't look. It won't help.

Exhaustion drags my eyelids down, but I can't rest. I've got to get up. Just because it's mid-morning and the city is filled with grunts doesn't mean I'm safe.

Forcing my eyes open, I see a red bug crawling along the cracked sidewalk. A ladybird. I push it onto my finger, then lift it to eye level. Seven black dots on a shiny red body. Lovely but fragile, and already missing two legs.

"How'd you get here?" I say aloud. I haven't seen a ladybug for years. Lots of insects are extinct now, and in dark, plant-free Old Triton all we get are cockroaches, spiders, and mosquitos. The ladybug must have fallen from New Triton.

There's no way it'll survive down here. And neither will I.

Lifting my finger above my lips, I gently blow it up, trying to help it fly back up to New Triton. That's where we both need to go. I'll follow the hope that Rayne's band will magically let me into the Morelle scraper. Her name must have been on that list for a reason, and maybe it's a reason that'll keep me alive.

Would I bet my life on it?

When I fastened on Rayne's band, that's exactly what I did.

I pull myself back onto my feet, and drag my aching body to the bullet station. When I reach it, the bullet is at the top, dropping down from New Triton. It's a glass bubble that holds up to fifty people, but there's only about fifteen other people waiting. It glides down to ground level and the door slides open. I let the others board before staggering in.

"Ninety credits." The door doesn't close and a mechanical voice repeats, "Ninety credits."

Fifteen weary pairs of eyes swivel to me. Damn, I forgot about the fee. Ninety credits is a day's wages, too much for most sinkers to waste on unnecessary trips to New Triton.

I lift Rayne's band to the bullet's payment terminal. When the terminal asks me to confirm the payment, I press my finger against my band's DNA sensor in the crazy hope it'll work. Of course nothing happens. It's so frustrating I feel like banging the band against the terminal, but I could beat my arm bloody and it wouldn't do a bit of good.

The others in the bullet stare at me with varying levels of distaste. By their lined, pale faces I can tell most are sinkers headed up to New Triton for work. Housekeepers, janitors, and dishwashers, doing the jobs the floaters don't want. And pressed against the back of the bullet, as far away from the sinkers as possible, are two floaters. They're dark-skinned teenaged boys in expensive clothing, wearing sunglasses to hide their eyes. They have matching expressions of bored arrogance.

Sinkers can get a free bullet ride if they're traveling up for work, but obviously Rayne doesn't qualify. The only way I'm getting up to New Triton is if somebody's willing to pay for my trip.

Unlikely.

I'd better get off the bullet.

There's a public stairwell next to the bullet that costs forty credits to get into, but I can't even pay one credit, and even if I could, there's no way I'd be able to climb twenty-eight floors.

One sinker makes a show of checking the time on his band. When his gaze lifts back to me, I meet his eyes. "Sorry, my band's glitching. It won't let me pay."

"Then get out."

"I need to go up."

He clicks his tongue in disgust. "You're making me late for work."

A woman with sunken eyes speaks up, agreeing with him. The angry murmurs build as I stand my ground, waiting. Hoping for a miracle. My desperation must be written across my face, as plain as my scars.

Finally, one of the floaters pushes off from where he's lounging against the back wall of the bullet. "Fucksake," he mumbles, swiping his band to cover my fee.

I try to thank him, but he moves back to his friend and turns his back on me. The door slides shut and I brace myself as the bullet shoots up to New Triton.

At the top, the door opens onto a paved square. I blink and squint against the sudden brightness. My cybernetic eye's supposed to filter out sunlight, but instead it whites out, leaving me half blind.

New Triton is a much newer city, though its scrapers start down below, in Old Triton. As each towering scraper thrusts up through the New Triton street, it changes its character completely. Down in Old Triton, the scrapers' bases are rough concrete shells crammed with factories and the overcrowded shelters the corporations are forced to provide. Up here, the same scrapers soar into the sky, filled with luxurious apartments and office buildings.

And New Triton streets aren't like the ones in the city below. There are no fried noodle vendors, pickpockets, or vendors selling drinks from ramshackle lean-tos. Instead, New Triton's bright, wide sidewalks are lined with fancy stores with big windows, filled with clothes and appliances I could never afford. The city smells fresher, and there's plenty of sunshine to grow plants. Scanning the windows, it seems almost all of them hold a potted flower or shrub.

There are no factories or shelters in New Triton, and no rough sleepers. Rumor is that if you try to sleep rough up here, the stompers will throw you off the edge. I can believe it.

My feet drag as I force them onwards, and I can't even summon the energy to peer over the barriers that line the edges of the walkways to catch glimpses of Old Triton far below.

The sun lifts, and the higher it gets, the less shade is cast by the scrapers. After a while, the heat's almost as bad as working with super-heated machines in the factory, but if I take off my coat, I'll either have to carry it or leave it behind. All the glass and steel up here bounces the light around so I'm squinting, almost blind. My lips are so dry they're swollen and split. When I lick them, they sting.

At least I'm going the right way. The Morelle scraper is by far the tallest building in New Triton, and it has a distinctive glass roof that intensifies the sunlight, making it way too bright to look at. It's like a giant lighthouse that towers over the other buildings. But no matter how far I walk, it doesn't seem to get any closer.

I'm not used to being in the sun. It's burning my pale, sinker face. It saps what little energy I have, and my head is so hot it's pounding.

As it gets even harder to shuffle one foot in front of the other, I imagine how easy it would be to lie down by the side of the road. Nobody would stop. Not the cabs whizzing past. Not the floaters hurrying past me on the sidewalk. I could pull my coat over my face and fall asleep. Maybe I'd never wake up.

The only thing that keeps me going is the hope someone in the Morelle scraper will take pity on me. They won't let me die on their front steps, will they? They'll have to at least give me a drink.

My feet scuff along the ground. I'm not really walking anymore, more like falling and catching myself. The scraper's a mirage. I'm never going to get there.

But when I round a corner, suddenly it's in front of me.

Steps lead up to oversized glass doors. There are two security guards. I can tell they're not stompers because their heavy boots are shorter, lacing up to the ankle instead of mid-calf, and their uniforms are red instead of black.

My heart still plummets. I stop, feeling myself sway. My legs are weak and the pain in my head makes it hard to think. How can I get past them?

Through the mist in front of my good eye I see a woman in high heels get out of a cab and go up the steps, then everything blurs. Did she go through the door? Did the guards stop her? I blink, trying to see, but the guards are just two hazy blobs now.

No way will they let a sinker in. Only I'm not a sinker any more, am I? I'm Rayne. And if they don't let me in I'm going to fall onto their shiny marble staircase and I don't think I'll have the strength to get up again.

I barely get to the bottom of the steps before they're on me. One guard grabs me by the shoulder. His rough grip sends a jolt of pain through me so strong that I cry out. The other stands in front of me, his nose screwed up. His face is moving, swinging up close then far away. Is he swaying, or am I?

I try to talk but nothing comes out. My mouth isn't working. The guard snaps something, but his voice is jumbled. I can't see him now. Stupid blurred vision. I can't see a thing, even out of my real eye. Where've they gone?

My legs sag and I fall.

Chapter Three

I wake up in a small room, lying on a bed. When I open my eyes, there's a woman in a white coat standing over me, watching me.

"How are you feeling?" she asks. Her accent is pure New Triton. Floaters speak slow and lazy, each word like a little fat man rolling out of bed.

"Um." My voice is croaky and my vision's still blurry in my bad eye. "My head hurts."

"That should fade soon." She glances at a desk cluttered with bottles, cloths, a jug, and some other things I'm not sure of. "Would you like some water?" And when I nod, "Can you sit up?"

It hurts to move, but the woman eases me onto another pillow, lifting my shoulders and tucking in the support behind me as if she's done it lots of times. Is she a doctor? There's a needle stuck into the crook of my arm, connected to a plastic tube, and I finger it, wanting to pull it out.

"That's just electrolytes, but I think you've had enough now anyway," says the woman. She takes the needle out and sticks a tiny adhesive bandage over the single drop of blood that wells up, which is pretty funny considering the beating I took and the purple bruises on my arms. "You were severely dehydrated. And when I scanned you for nanoceuticals you came up clean, so I gave you some shots to speed up your healing. Of course, I'm supposed to get your signature on the right forms before treating you, so don't tell anyone, will you?"

She smiles, her cheeks dimpling. Her face looks older and more weathered than most floaters, with laugh lines around her eyes as though she hasn't been tweaked. She's even let her wispy hair go a little gray, and strands of it are falling out of her bun. I like her face. She reminds me of Ma, the way she looked before William was born.

At the thought of Ma, my heart contracts. My hand goes to my useless band, but I turn the movement into something else at the last minute, scratching my arm instead. Is my secret still safe?

The doctor fills a cup with water for me. It feels so good going down my throat, I can't decide whether to gulp it, or let it trickle down to ease the aching.

"I got rid of your dirty clothes," she says. "The blood was worrying, but most of it didn't seem to be yours?"

"No."

She waits for me to say more, and when I keep silent she refills my cup with more water.

"Where am I?" I ask. "In hospital?" From what I can see above the sheets, I'm dressed in a clean white smock. But I can smell myself. I stink.

"You're in the Morelle Corporation building." She sounds surprised. "I'm a doctor, though I don't normally have patients. My name's Doctor Gregory, head of the Skin development team. I was assigned to look after the competitors, but I didn't expect anyone would need medical attention so soon."

"Competitors?"

Instead of answering, she frowns. "Can you tell me your name?"

"Rayne Walker." I stare into her eyes as I say it, and when she accepts that answer I make sure not to let my relief show.

"Your date of birth?"

Uh-oh. I don't know Rayne's birthday.

I stay silent and the doctor gets a small flashlight off the desk. "Please look up." She shines it into my good eye, pulling my bottom lid down. Then she picks up a scanner and presses it against my forehead. "Did you hit your head?"

"Don't think so." The scanner starts beeping. What's it measuring? "Maybe," I say, changing my answer. If I hit my head, is that an excuse for not knowing my birthday?

"Do you know the name of our president?"

"President Trask."

"That's right. And what day is it?"

"Friday?" It takes me a while to answer, and I'm not sure I've got it right. How long was I unconscious? Is it day or night? The room has a window but the glass is opaque, its control panel set into the wall beside it.

The doctor clicks her tongue. "Your temperature is normal now, but you were in bad shape. Cracked ribs, a perforated ear drum, concussion, swelling of your abdominal organs, hematoma, severe bruising and sunburn." She shakes her head. "I should have waited for you to wake up before offering you the nanotech shots, but without them you'd be in a lot of pain."

I shift, wincing a little, although she's right about me being a lot less sore than I should be after the beating I took. Problem is, whatever she gave me has to be expensive, and there's no way I can pay.

"You should heal quickly," she says. "I'll give you some lotion to keep your skin moist while the sunburn fades. I'm concerned about your memory loss, but hopefully it'll improve after a meal and a good night's rest."

Does she mean I'll get to eat, and then sleep in an actual bed with sheets and pillows? It sounds too good to be true.

The doctor speaks into her band. "A light meal for 401. Soup, please." Looking at me she explains, "Easy to digest."

She packs her equipment into a bag, and a man in a white uniform comes in with a tray. The smell hits me first and my stomach growls so loudly that the doctor laughs. "This might be the best medicine yet."

The man puts the tray on my lap, then leaves. The soup's thick and steaming, and there's a bread roll and a sweet drink that's delicious. The doctor sits on the edge of my bed. Because she's watching, I try not to gobble the meal too quickly.

"Rayne, may I ask a couple of questions before I go?" she says. "I'm curious as to why you don't have a bag with you. Not so much as a change of clothes?"

Suddenly the bread roll is hard to swallow. "Um. I was robbed on the way here, and my bag was stolen. That's how I got hurt, trying to fight off the men who stole it."

"Oh dear. I wondered if it was something like that. You should report the theft, although it's unlikely the police will be able to find your belongings after this much time has passed."

Call the stompers? They actually *help* people who get robbed in New Triton?

I shoot her as sincere-looking a smile as I can manage. "Thanks, I'll do that."

"And would you like me to speak with your parents, to reassure them you'll make a full recovery?"

She means Rayne's parents, of course. I can hardly ask her to call Ma.

"No, that's okay. I left home a couple of years ago, and I've been working in a factory in Old Triton. My parents don't want anything to do with me." Just as she promised, my headache is gone. I feel clear-headed enough for the lies to flow easily.

"Oh dear. That explains..." Her voice trails off and she shakes her head. "You've had a run of bad luck, haven't you? Well, you're safe here. And I can organize a few things for you, like a toothbrush and some clothes."

"Thanks, but you've already done enough." I've got no way to pay for anything, so I really hope she doesn't push it.

"It's no trouble." Before I can protest again, she points to a closed door. "There's the bathroom. You can get up and have a shower, but if you feel woozy, press the red button on the wall. I don't want you fainting again."

I stare at the door. A bathroom to myself? Is she kidding?

The doctor hesitates. Then she indicates my bad eye. "I know I shouldn't ask, but that's one of ours, isn't it?"

I nod. "A Morelle eye."

"I thought I recognized it. But that eye's almost as old as I am. Do you mind if I ask how you got it?"

This time I can tell the truth. But I still speak slowly, making sure I'm not going to accidentally say the wrong thing and give myself away.

"I used to work in a Morelle factory, on the line that makes the casing for vReals. The polymer's superheated, then it's poured into molds." Raising my hand, I run my fingers over the burned-out hollow in my cheek, tracing the scars that cut my face into a jigsaw. "Something fell onto the lip of one of the molds. It didn't seal properly and the hot polymer squirted out. The blast hit me here." I let my fingers linger on the hollow place where the muscle and fat were burned away, leaving just scar tissue. My mouth droops a little on that side, because some of the muscles aren't there to hold it up properly.

"It got into my eye and splashed across my nose." I scratch the scar lines that run to my other cheek. They're always itchy, and the sunburn's making it even worse. "I was lucky it didn't take my nose off, and it missed my lips completely."

"My lord!" One hand goes to her mouth. "But surely, a workplace accident... the company could have regrown your eye so easily. Why give you an old cybernetic one? And they could have fixed those scars—"

"The thing that stopped the mold from sealing was a coin."

"A coin?"

"You know, old-fashioned money? My father gave it to me when I was little, supposed to be a good luck charm. Against the rules to have it with me while I was working, so the company wasn't responsible for my accident. I had to pay my own medical bills." I grimace, remembering how expensive it was. All the money Ma and I had saved, wiped out in a moment of carelessness. "Actually, I was glad not to lose my job. They transferred me to a different factory, and when I couldn't afford to get my eye regrown, a friend gave me this one. He'd kept it as a souvenir for years, from when he used to work in the factory that made them."

She's gaping. "You didn't even get it made in the correct size?"

"It wasn't too far off. The doctor filed my eye socket to make it fit."

"My lord." Her voice is faint and she looks horrified. We really do come from different worlds.

"Sure it's not pretty, but I couldn't afford to do anything about the scars either, so it all kind of matches." I try giving her another smile to see if I can lift the shock off her kind face. "Don't worry, I've learned to live with it."

"It's unbelievable. And to think it happened in one of our own factories! It's horrifying, Rayne. Unconscionable."

When she frowns like that, her eyes scrunch in a way that reminds me sharply of Ma. My heart contracts again and I have to glance away. "It's okay. Really."

"Well, at least you'll be getting a new Skin to play with."

I try not to look completely blank.

She gets up to leave, and on the desk she's left a bottle, which I guess is the sunburn cream she mentioned. She pauses at the door. "Not all the competitors have arrived yet, but Director Morelle's planning to start your training tomorrow. If you're well enough, of course, Rayne. For now, just get a good night's sleep."

What training? I have a million questions, but asking would give me away. As she leaves, I wonder whether I should have said something about the money and tried to get her talking about it. She called me a competitor, not a lottery winner, and the guy with Rayne in the shelter said something about a contest as well. Could Rayne have entered into a race? I'm pretty fast, but I'd be no match for a professional runner.

I wonder how many competitors there are going to be, and if they'll be sleeping in here too. This room could hold about eight people, though there's only one bed and this doesn't seem like the kind of place where people spread mattresses on the floor. But just in case I end up sharing, I'm going to take advantage of the bathroom now while I've still got it all to myself.

Though I'm still weak and sore, as soon as I open the bathroom door, I forget my aches. It's clean and shiny, like I'm the first person to ever use it. The whitest, biggest towel I've ever seen hangs on the rail. It smells like flowers.

Something makes me check all the corners for... I don't know what. A camera? I can't believe there's no catch.

When I strip off and get under the shower, nothing happens. Sensor's broken? Or do I need to use my band to turn it on? Damn, maybe that's the catch. Then I see something on the wall. It's a manual control panel. I can turn the water on myself and even choose my own temperature.

Does that mean the water will keep running until I turn it off?

There's even a bar of soap, and I love the slippery feel of it in my hands. How long has it been since I held soap? The closest I've come in years is the foamy water the showers in the shelter shoot out for the first ten seconds. Not even close.

Still, I soap up and rinse off fast, just in case I've got it wrong and the shower's going to cut off after a minute or two. When I'm clean, I adjust the water until it's so hot my sunburned face can hardly bear the sting, and let it run over me. It feels so good I groan out loud. It almost feels like it's washing away my fear and pain. If only it could.

When I finally, reluctantly, step out of the bathroom, there's still nobody in the room but me. I touch the control by the window that makes the glass transparent. It's night. I'm on probably the fourth or fifth floor of the Morelle scraper, and looking up I can see the sky. The moon looks close, and so huge I can hardly believe it's real.

The dark shape of another scraper isn't far away. My cybernetic eye's not great at night, but when my good eye adjusts I realize what I thought was another building is actually part of the one I'm in. There's an empty court-yard in the middle and the building surrounds it. The Morelle complex is enormous.

Tiptoeing to the door, I hit the button that slides it open. Outside is a long empty hallway, brightly lit but silent. Lots of doors. I should take a closer look, but what if I trigger an alarm? I'm exhausted and sore, and the bed's too tempting to risk stirring up trouble now. I let the door close, then slip between the crisp, white sheets, feeling so amazingly clean I should squeak when I walk.

What did the doctor mean I'm going to get a new skin? I have so many questions. But seeing as I've got no way to get any answers, at least for now, I'm just going to enjoy the sensation of lying in a real bed with a whole room to myself. Tomorrow I might get thrown out, arrested, or worse, but tonight I'm going to count my blessings.

I'm still alive and feeling better than I can believe, so whatever the doctor did to heal me must have used better medicine than I'm used to. I'm not hungry or thirsty. I'm not fighting sleep in the shelter, exhausted, but having to stay awake because it's my turn to keep watch for sharks.

Switching off the light next to the bed, I catch my breath at how dark it is, until my good eye slowly adjusts to the moonlight coming through the window.

Rayne's band vibrates, and I run my fingers over it, feeling how thin it is and how silky to the touch. Its golden sheen gleams in the moonlight. Is one of her friends ring-ing? Her parents wondering where she is? Even if I wanted to, I couldn't answer it, and it won't let me bring up a display to see who's calling.

Is my thick gray band going off on the dead girl's

wrist? Is Ma trying to get hold of me? She must be frantic that I haven't called. I really wish I could call her. I'd give anything to be able to talk to her and let her know I'm okay.

When Rayne's band stops vibrating, I lie still, listening to my own breathing. Amazing how quiet it is in this room. No talking or laughing. No sobs or groans. Plenty of times I'd have given a week's wages for a few minutes of quiet, so I can't believe that now I'm wishing I could hear Tori's loud snores, or even the annoying clank-clank-whirr of the conveyer belt at the factory. Anything at all. Who'd have guessed silence could feel so lonely?

One. Two. Three. Four. Five...

When Ma and I had to move into the shelter just after I turned fifteen, I was terrified. Nights were the worst, and I used to lie awake and count my breaths for comfort. I'd tell myself that if I made it all the way up to nine hundred and ninety-nine, Ma and I would be safe until morning.

But after I was burned and got transferred to a new job and a new shelter away from Ma, it wasn't the counting that kept me safe, it was Tori.

If only she were here, she'd go nuts over this place. Over that bathroom, especially.

The thought makes me miss her so badly, my throat aches. I really hope she's okay. She must be spending her second night in her new shelter, so she must have found someone to buddy up with by now.

If I still had my own band, I'd be able to call her, or at least look at a pic of her. *Shit.* All my pics are on my missing band and there's no way to get them back. Not just the ones of Tori, but Ma and Papa, and my brother William too.

Two years ago, William was transferred into a military academy. It sounded like a good deal at first. Free education and board, in return for a couple of years of service when he finished his schooling. We were grateful to finally get him out of the rundown orphanage that was the only place that would take him after Pa died. But at least in the orphanage, we could call him. Ma and I spoke to him every night, reassuring him we'd get him out as soon as we could afford a home. Since he went into the academy, we haven't been able to get hold of him.

And now if they finally let him call us, if he *needs* me, he won't be able to find me.

Turning onto my front, I pull the pillow over my head and press my face into the mattress hard enough to hurt.

I lost my eye because of an impulsive coin toss and a moment of inattention, and I should have learned from that. But now I've lost my family the same way. An impulsive action, over in a heartbeat. No matter what happens next, I have nobody to blame but myself.

Chapter Four

A knock from the door wakes me. I jerk my head up and stare at it until someone knocks again.

"Rayne?" It's Doctor Gregory's voice.

"Yes?"

I keep watching the door, expecting it to open, but nothing happens and there's a long pause. Then she asks, "May I come in?" like I own the whole room and she needs permission to enter.

"Oh. Sorry, yes. Come in."

She's hugging a tablet to her chest, and I was right, her smile is just like Ma's. "Morning. How do you feel?"

"Better." I ease up to sitting. "Hardly sore at all now."

"You didn't feel nauseated during the night?"

"No."

She sits on the side of the bed and hands me the tablet. But when I touch the screen, nothing happens. "It's a mind-pad," she says. "You haven't used one before? Then you won't have an implant. Here, I'll switch it to manual so it responds to touch." She doesn't reach for it, but writing appears on the screen. "These are the forms I mentioned.

They're mostly insurance waivers and permission forms. There's one for the medical procedure involved with the Skin transferal."

"Medical procedure?"

"Don't worry, it's minor. It was described in the info pack we sent when you applied for the contest."

"Oh. I, um..."

"Never mind. I know it was a lot to take in, especially when you hadn't been chosen yet. You can read through it while you have breakfast."

After she leaves, I stare at the forms. Rayne's date of birth is right at the top. She is—*was*—nineteen. The same age as me.

As I scroll through pages covered with tiny writing, my cybernetic eye starts to ache. If there are answers to my questions in there, I'm going to struggle to find them.

Zooming in at random, I read: *"...whether or not the COMPETITOR is in breach of any one or more of the aforementioned CONDITIONS (sections numbering 1.2 – 9.0 inclusively), then the CORPORATION shall be entitled, at its sole discretion and under no obligation, to dismiss said COMPETITOR from the CONTEST and to entertain no further legal, moral or financial liability with respect to said COMPETITOR or any person or entity affiliated with..."*

The door opens. It's a guy in a white uniform with a steaming bowl of oatmeal, and I've never seen a better excuse to give my eye and brain a rest.

Doctor Gregory comes back in as I'm finishing, and this time she's carrying a doctor's bag. She examines the bruising on my torso, then asks, "Do you remember your birthday now?"

"November twelve, two thousand and fifty-six."

"And, let me see, how about the year the Welcon baby boom started?"

"That's easy. Two thousand and fifty-eight." The year William was born.

"Very good." She dimples at me. "And with such a healthy appetite, the prognosis is that you're going to be fine."

"Can I get up?"

"Absolutely. But first could you sign those forms? I'm sorry to press the point, but the President's dead against this contest, and he's looking for any excuse to shut us down."

"Why is he against it?"

"You haven't been watching the feeds?"

I shrug.

"Okay, well, I think it's that such an advance in technology can be frightening at first. And you know there's tension with Deiterra. President Trask is worried the Skins will violate the weapons clause of the peace treaty, which is clearly ridiculous."

Triton used to be a single mega-city of several million people, surrounded by a little usable farmland. Deiterra had lots of smaller cities and more rural areas that weren't contaminated by fallout from the food wars. Triton and Deiterra built a giant wall between them, and signed a treaty agreeing that both sides would limit weapon manufacturing. Only stompers are allowed to have guns.

Deiterrans blamed destructive technologies for the warming temperatures, and food and water shortages. People say they developed ways to keep growing their own food instead of manufacturing it. The only person in Triton who knows for sure is the Deiterran ambassador, because it's been decades since the wall was built and anything could have happened since then. But it's easier to feed less people, and Deiterra used to have fewer than us, even before the Welcon disaster pushed up the birth rate and exploded the population on our side of the wall.

Triton now has more than fifty million people crammed into both its cities, one built on top of the other. It's hemmed in by the Deiterran wall, the sea, and the fallout zones, so the only direction we can build is up.

According to rumor, Deiterra still has farmland. I don't believe it myself. It's way too hard to imagine that farms could still exist.

"President Trask allowed Director Morelle to build the Skin prototypes, but he doesn't want her to start a full-scale manufacturing operation and sell to the public," says Doctor Gregory. "Of course that's exactly why she's holding the contest. The publicity from the contest draw alone was beyond even the most optimistic predictions. Director Morelle says she's going to create such a demand for the Skins, the president will be forced to let her go into production. Obviously not in the form you'll be using them, but a more palatable, mainstream version."

I'm dying to ask what the Skins are, but it must have been on the holo, so Rayne would probably have known.

"Advance orders of the Skin Hunter game are a hundred times what we'd normally get," the doctor adds. "It's very promising."

A game? If only I could come up with a way to ask some questions without making her suspicious.

Doctor Gregory hands me a scribe. "Would you like me to leave while you finish reading, Rayne?"

I look down at the mind-pad. "Do I have to sign?"

"If you don't, you won't be able to compete. The lawyers wouldn't allow it."

"And if I don't compete?"

"Well..." She seems confused by the question. "That's why you're here isn't it? It's why you entered? If you don't want to compete, I suppose you'll go home and the director will select someone else."

Here's a way out. If I don't sign the forms, I leave. And then what? I can't get my band back. Maybe I could find someone to hack Rayne's band and recode it, but the guys who offer those services are seriously bad news, not to mention that they charge a fortune. And if I was caught recoding a band... I don't want to think about that. Anything's better than getting arrested again.

Besides, there's the five million credits to consider. If that really is the prize money for the contest, I might have a shot at winning it. After all, working on the line has made me stronger than I look.

Although, what if it's not a physical contest at all, but some kind of intellectual test? New Tritoners go to school until they're eighteen, at least. I had half that amount of schooling, so if the contest needs any kind of book learning, I'm screwed.

"Take your time, Rayne. Read the forms and make sure you're comfortable with them. If you want to pull out, that's fine. The director will replace you."

"I'll sign." I scrawl Rayne's name every place the highlight tells me to, hoping they don't know what her real signature looks like.

"That last one is a confidentially agreement. Make sure you read it closely. If you speak to any outside party about the contest or your training, you'll be disqualified. And I'm afraid they'll be monitoring your calls while you're here."

I stare at it for what I judge is enough time to have read it, then sign.

"That's it," she says with a smile. "Now, make sure you download all the forms to your band, so you've got copies for yourself."

"Uh, sure." I hold the mind-pad up so it blocks her

view while I pretend to do a transfer to Rayne's band. But the doctor bends anyway, getting something out of her bag. When she straightens, I see it's a hypodermic needle.

"Nano transceivers," she says, as though I'm supposed to know what that means. "They'll bind with your neurons to make you receptive to the CTU."

"The what?"

"Consciousness Transmission Unit." She swabs my arm, then slides the needle in and pushes the plunger. "This is the first stage of the procedure."

"Could you give me the version of that explanation that's in English?" Then a wave of nausea hits and my skin prickles all over. My vision does something weird, and the room expands, all four walls pushing outward. I grab for the mattress, balling the sheets in my fists.

"It's okay." Doctor Gregory grips my shoulder. "The sensation should only last a moment."

Sure enough, the prickling's fading, the walls settling back into place. I take a deep breath, glad that my head's stopped spinning, but still feeling unsettled. My vision's still not quite back to normal. If I move my head too fast, the walls might start moving again.

"What *was* that?"

"It'll make sense once you see the Skins and the director explains how they work." Taking her bag and the mind pad, she heads for the door. "Why don't you get up, and I'll arrange something for you to wear. I'll come back for you in an hour or so."

After she leaves, I ease out of bed carefully and treat myself to another long, hot shower. When I get out of the shower, there are three pairs of jeans, six T-shirts in different colors, underwear, and even some bras waiting on the bed, all brand new, still with tags in. There are also some toiletries, including a toothbrush and comb.

I get dressed and find that all the clothes are snugs, even the underwear, so although they're too big when I first put them on, the smart fabric is triggered by my body heat to shrink itself down until everything's a perfect size. They're insanely comfortable, clean and fresh-smelling. And the best part is, she hasn't asked me to pay for them.

I could hug Doctor Gregory. Last time I had new clothes, or even something clean to put on, was so long ago I can't remember. And now I've got so many clothes, I could change into fresh ones every day.

Most of my life I've felt like a rat at the bottom of a trash heap. Is this what it takes to make me feel human?

While the toothbrush's buzzing over my teeth, I'm feeling so good I glance in the mirror, half-expecting my face to have been transformed with the rest of me. It has in a way — the bruises and sunburn have made me even uglier than usual. I flinch. Then bend over and rinse. Looking is always a mistake.

Doctor Gregory's voice comes from outside. "Are you ready, Rayne?"

"Coming."

She brushes off my thanks, beckoning me into the corridor. "Your room number is 401." She swipes her band across the sensor beside the door. "Doctor Gregory. Authenticate."

"Doctor Gregory." The words come from the sensor.

"Authorize Rayne Walker." She nods at me. "Swipe your band."

As I lift Rayne's band up to the sensor, I rack my brain for some kind of explanation to give her in case it doesn't work. But the light glows green. I let out a relieved breath, and when I swipe again, the door opens and closes for me. All it's doing is reading my ID chip.

Thank goodness nobody uses facial recognition for

security anymore, since constant tweaking became routine for New Tritoners.

The doctor leads me down the hall. "These five doors are the other competitors' rooms. That one is your rec room, kitchen, and dining." She winks. "You won't get breakfast in bed every day, you know."

"But that's the only reason I came."

She chuckles, so my nervous joke must have come out sounding as casual as I hoped. But this place is unbelievable. Is this how floaters live?

"Some functions of your band have been blocked," she says. "You won't be able to transfer data to anyone outside the building, and your band won't work at all in the training room. It's a security measure."

That's good. The less we're supposed to be able to use our bands, the better.

I'm a little sore, especially my torso, where my cracked ribs must still be healing. But I try to keep up as we head down the long corridor. There are doors on both sides, most of them shut. Through the one or two that are open, I catch glimpses of work cubicles and a few people using holo screens. Compared to the sweaty, crammed-in bustle of the factory and shelter, it feels like there's hardly anyone around.

At the end of the corridor is a closed double door with a guard stationed outside it. Not a stomper, because his uniform's dark red, and he doesn't have a gun. His eyes narrow when he sees me and his lip curls.

I slow down. Men in uniform make me nervous.

"Are you all right, Rayne?" asks Doctor Gregory. "Are you in pain?"

I shake my head. The doctor must notice the way I'm looking at the guard, because she says, "That's Max, one of Director Morelle's bodyguards. Don't worry, he knows they're expecting us."

As we go past, his hostile stare stays fixed on me. He's a shark. He may hunt the warm shallows of New Triton instead of the deep, cold waters below, but I recognize his type. I hope I never need to have anything to do with him.

While the doctor repeats the whole authorize thing with the doors, I can't help glancing back at the guard. His lip curls and he mouths, "*Sewer rat*".

"Okay, Rayne?" Doctor Gregory calls my attention back to her before I can react to the insult. "Why don't you open it? They're waiting for us."

I hesitate, my mind still on the guard. "Who is?"

"Director Morelle. Didn't I tell you? She's overseeing the contest herself, and she wants to meet you all. This is your training room, and it's where she's going to brief you. The other competitors are already there."

"Director Morelle?"

"Yes."

"The real one?"

She laughs. "The real one."

What the hell have I got myself into? When she mentioned the director before, I assumed I might see a holo-feed. I never dreamed she'd be here in the flesh.

Director Morelle's in this room, and she wants me to walk in like it's nothing?

"Come on, Rayne. She's just a person like you or me."

Yeah, a person like Doctor Gregory, maybe, but nothing like me.

"Don't be afraid," she adds.

My gaze jerks to her. *Afraid?* I've lived with fear for so long, I've come to know it well. And I've learned where real fear comes from.

Real fear is the sizzling of super-hot polymer spurting

at my face. It's cuffed wrists and waiting for the stomper behind me to use either his fists or his gun.

Fear is waking up with a sweaty male hand clamped over my mouth and trying to jerk free. A race to see whether he can fumble my clothes aside before I can scream awake a shelter full of sleeping people.

Yeah, fear and I are old pals. And I'm not about to let one-woman make me tremble, no matter how powerful she is.

I swipe my band against the door.

Chapter Five

The room's bigger than any shelter I've seen. It could sleep a thousand people, easy. But its size is nothing compared to its height, which feels like someone forgot to put the roof on. It's got to be ten floors tall, at least.

The far wall's mostly taken up with tall windows that flood the room with light, and below the windows are racks of weights. There's a large silver circle on the floor that's several meters wide, and a black rectangle of about the same size. The wall to my right is completely silver. Ledges jut from it at irregular intervals, going all the way to the ceiling. It could be a climbing wall except it goes dizzyingly high and looks impossible to climb.

A small group of people are standing with a woman I recognize. You'd have to be from another planet not to recognize Director Morelle. She looks as perfect in the flesh as on the newsfeeds, and her skin is smooth as glass, dark and ageless. But she looks exactly the same in all the historical feeds I've seen, so she must be a lot older than she appears. The perks of being a trillionaire:

she probably has a team standing by to tweak any blemish.

The four people with Director Morelle, three guys and a girl, turn to stare at me. They look in their late teens or early twenties, and from their dark skin and good looks, I can tell they're floaters. Most New Tritoners have their skin darkened with melanin. Apparently it started as protection against the sun, but now their bronze toning is a status symbol. Even sinkers with naturally dark skin are so sun-starved they don't have the same rich hue.

The floaters' expressions turn horrified when they see my face, but I'm used to that. I lift my chin and stare back, daring them to meet my gaze.

"Ah, here's the patient now," says Director Morelle. It's strange to hear her familiar voice coming out of a real mouth instead of a holo. "Lucky last of our group of five contestants. How are you feeling, Rayne?"

"Okay." I walk up to the others, but can't bring myself to join their cozy semi-circle. Instead I stand behind them, so if they want to keep staring they'll have to turn to do it. I didn't realize Doctor Gregory was going to come in as well, until she's next to me. She stands close, as though for moral support. I'll have to remember to tell her I appreciate it. It's nice not to be standing alone.

"You seem unexpectedly well," says the director. "Were Doctor Gregory's reports of your ill-health exaggerated?"

I shrug. I'm not being rude on purpose, but I don't know what to say. She's the most famous woman in Triton, head of the largest corporation that's ever existed. It's like God stuck his head down from the sky to ask how I slept.

"Oh, she was very sick when she arrived," Doctor Gregory says. "Considering the severity of her injuries, I'm astonished how well she's recovered."

"Is that right?" Director Morelle arches one perfect

eyebrow. "In that case, we may have a worthy competitor here. This contest will require a level of determination and toughness that will push you all to your limits. Perhaps Rayne has what it takes to win."

The group look at me as though trying to measure my strength, and I wish the director hadn't singled me out. By the way one big meat-sack is glowering, I know he'll challenge me first chance he gets.

"Let me introduce you," says Director Morelle. "Rayne, this is Brugan." The meat-sack. He's a tweaker and then some. His T-shirt strains so tightly across his chest, he's probably been high-dosing growth hormone since before he could spell it. He got his chin right, it's perfectly chiseled. But his lips are a mistake, tweaked too far and too big for his face.

Right now, his fat mouth's twisted in disgust. I doubt he's ever seen anyone who looks like me. When I meet his gaze with a glare and a lift of my eyebrows, he doesn't flush like most people do. Instead his eyes narrow as though I've thrown down a challenge.

"And this is Aza." Director Morelle motions to the only other girl. Aza reminds me a little of Rayne because she's so well-groomed and fresh-looking. Her hair is vibrant red, and her skin is a deep mahogany, the darkest of the group. Her eyes are definitely tweaked. There's no way that elfin tilted-up-at-the-corner thing is real, or the blue irises that are so bright they're almost neon. Most New Triton girls go for curves, but she's gone the opposite way. She's so willowy a decent breeze could send her drifting. She's about the same height as me, but with amazingly long legs. Those endless legs make her look elegant, like she's dressed up even in snugs. I bet she turns heads wherever she goes.

Like I do, but for the opposite reason.

Her lips suck in as she studies me. A moment later she

passes judgment: her nostrils flare and her gaze drags disdainfully away. Ouch. Guess we're not going to be besties.

"That's Sentin." Director Morelle nods at a guy with neatly combed dark hair. He's wearing glasses. Glasses! Like someone from last century. Does he really have bad eyesight and not want to get it fixed, or are they a retro-cool fashion statement?

Or could he be one of those hard-liners who think tweaking is a crime against nature? I can't see anything about him that looks enhanced. He's no meat-sack. If anything, he's on the thin side. If he weren't so well groomed, he could almost pass for a sinker.

But now I look past his glasses, the way he's examining me is so intense it makes me want to squirm. Has he had his vision sharpened? He's using his eyeglasses like a scientist might use a magnifying glass. I feel like a bug squirming on a pin.

"And finally, we have Cale."

Cale's a tall guy with black hair that's a little scruffy, and he's way too handsome not to have been tweaked. His soft brown eyes might be natural, but his high cheekbones, square jaw, and dark eyelashes must be designer. At least he kept the enhancements in check more than Brugan did, especially in his body, which looks fit but not too bulging. His faded blue T-shirt isn't straining, but accentuates the toned muscles of his biceps and chest.

Funny to see a floater with a T-shirt so well-worn. Come to think of it, I've never seen a floater wearing anything that doesn't look brand new. The snug fit of Cale's shirt definitely suits him though, so maybe that's why he...

I'm staring.

Just as I realize my eyes are raking over him, judging

his good looks in exactly the way I hate people judging my ugly scars, his mouth twitches into a small grin that I totally don't expect. It looks almost friendly.

Stiffening, I jerk my gaze away. Like I'm about to trust a look like that from someone like him.

"And now you've met each other, I'm afraid I must warn you not to become too close," says Director Morelle. "You're competing for a prize that only one of you can win."

My fingernails scratch nervously at my palms. My competitors are all floaters, which means they'll be tweaked on the inside as well as out. The doctor gave me a couple of shots that miracle-glued my ribs back together, but my competitors' blood will be loaded with those nano-robot-things that give your insides a constant tune-up. They've probably had extra memory plugged into their brains, extra smarts, energy, the works. I bet not one of them has ever had so much as a cold. What chance do I have going up against them in any kind of contest?

"You all know what's at stake, but let me say it again. The contest winner will receive five million credits."

I draw in my breath. *Five million credits*. Is it an impossible dream?

"Of course, getting to use these Skin prototypes in a prize in itself. And the contest winner will star in a series of live promotional appearances. They'll be a Skin ambassador, displaying to the public just how revolutionary this technology is. As such, they'll get to keep their Skin, though participating in official events will remain a condition of ownership." Her gaze sharpens on me, a single line appearing on her perfect brow. "Rayne, you look confused. Do you have a question?"

I shake my head, changing my expression to one of polite interest. Last thing I need is to give myself away.

"Then it's time to see your Skins. And after all Rayne went through to get here, I think it's only fitting that she go first."

Brugan flashes me a glare as Director Morelle reaches for a button on the wall next to her. Now I see there's a sliding door, the same color as the wall. In fact, there are five doors, evenly spaced. Five doors, five competitors.

The director's hand hovers over the button without touching it as though she's waiting for our anticipation to grow.

"Skins are the greatest technological advancement since the invention of the computer," she says. "They have the potential to change everything about our lives. The way we work. The way we interact with others. And especially the way we play." She pauses, meeting all of our eyes in turn. "You're about to see the next stage of human evolution. The future is here, behind this door."

Evolution? It sounds ridiculous. But the fervor in her voice makes my stomach clench.

She turns her gaze to me. "Rayne, this is the first Skin we made. It's the simplest of the five Skins, but has a purity that makes it quite lovely."

She presses the button. The door slides open, revealing a small room.

There's an animal inside.

All five of us shrink backwards. It's a huge cat, bigger than a person. More beautiful—and frightening—than any cat I've ever seen on the Holo. Its fur is pure white with silver markings in a dappled pattern over its back, and its eyes are a startling ice blue. It's standing poised, ready to spring.

"It's moving," Cale breathes in a tone so stunned it echoes the way I feel.

But the animal isn't moving. At least, it's not leaping out or attacking. But I swear it's breathing.

Director Morelle walks to the animal and extends one manicured hand to touch its fur. The cat's as tall as she is, and maybe twice as long. Her hand rests well below its shoulder.

"Skins combine leading-edge materials science with advanced biotechnology. Each has a ceramic composite skeleton with fiber-optics that perfectly mimic the function of your own spinal cord. Your brain will send signals to the Skin's nerves and muscles, to operate its limbs as you would your own."

"It's a leopard, isn't it?" I ask. The beauty of those ice blue eyes draws me forward. My heart's beating fast, but the director's lack of fear gives me the confidence to approach.

"A clouded leopard," the director says. "Over the synthetic skeleton we've grown living flesh, with real muscles, tissue, and organs. Much of this clouded leopard is biologically identical to one you would have found in the wild. Before their extinction, of course." She strokes her hand over its fur. "However, we did make several enhancements. It's larger than the original animal, the surface of its skin has a ceramic plating, and its fur is impregnated with carbon fiber nanotubes as a form of armor."

Armor? So the leopard's been built to fight? Whatever I expected, it sure wasn't this.

"That's not all, Rayne. Its claws are titanium, sharp enough to be lethal. With practice, you'll be able to traverse walls that are almost vertical."

"Does it have its own consciousness?" asks Sentin, blinking behind his glasses. He speaks even slower than most floaters.

"Not as such. It doesn't have what we would normally refer to as a brain."

The director beckons me close enough to touch the animal's fur. It feels luxuriously thick and soft, not like armor at all. And the leopard's chest is moving in and out, so it's definitely alive. How can it be breathing if it doesn't have a brain?

"Susan, has Rayne had the nano transceivers injected?" asks the director.

Doctor Gregory checks her band. "Over two hours ago."

"Good. Then she's ready for the CTU."

Behind the leopard is a long bench and lots of screens displaying numbers and graphs. There's also a large chair that's covered with hundreds of short rubber tentacles, all sticking up. The doctor takes something off the bench, and my heart lurches when I see it's a weird-looking gun.

Director Morelle keeps talking. "The Skin's automatic functions, such as its heart beat, breathing, and so on, are controlled by its brain stem and central nervous system. And to eliminate the need for a digestive system, it's fueled by a high-density nutrient solution."

I'm listening, sure. But I'm also watching Doctor Gregory walk toward me with the gun. Every grunt who's ever spent time in a shelter probably has the same reaction to guns as I do. When a stomper pulls one out, the grunts who survive are the ones who run fastest.

"Thank you, Susan," says the director. To me she says, "This delivery device will inject a chip, implanting it into the top of your spinal column, at the base of your brain." She taps the back of her head. "But don't worry, it won't hurt a bit." She smiles as though she's cracked a joke. Someone titters. Aza, I think.

Doctor Gregory touches my arm and I jump.

"It's okay, Rayne," she murmurs. "Really."

My heart's pounding so loud she can probably hear it. She leaves her hand resting on my arm, the other one still holding the gun up as though she's about to fire it at the ceiling. I hope she does. Anywhere but into my brain.

"Sit down, Rayne." Doctor Gregory motions to the tentacle chair.

No way. I'm not getting onto those tentacles, and I'm sure as hell not getting a chip shot into my head. I'm not going to move. But she tugs on my arm and steps forward, and somehow I find myself following. What choice do I really have, anyway? I've got Rayne's band around my wrist. I'm wearing the clothes they gave me. I signed the forms.

Remember the money. Five million credits. What could I do with five million credits? Set my mother free. Get William and Tori back. Make us all safe.

I can do this.

Sitting in the chair is like climbing onto a giant sea anemone. The tentacles move underneath me, creeping me out. But once I'm in it, the chair tilts back so I'm lying flat and it feels incredibly comfortable, like floating.

Someone's behind my head. Director Morelle or Doctor Gregory? I'm too nervous to look.

Something presses against my scalp. Something hard. The muzzle of the gun.

I close my eyes.

Chapter Six

"Open your eyes, Rayne." It's Director Morelle's voice. "Keep your eyes open. Don't shut them until I tell you."

The gun doesn't make a sound, but there's a sudden pain and then a tingle in the back of my head. It feels like my brain is itchy.

In spite of the director's command, I screw my eyes shut. I get the weirdest sensation in my brain, as if my thoughts are pulling away from me. Like my mind's reaching out for something. No, like it's being tugged.

Then I'm falling sideways with the same dizzy feeling I had after the stomper punched my ear. I clutch the chair, only I can't feel my hands and I'm not sure if I've moved at all. Bright light floods my vision, though I didn't consciously open my eyes. My stomach lurches, but the feeling is gone and then back again in an instant, like a switch flicking on and off. Colors blur and spin. I'm going to throw up.

Then I find something to focus on, a light, faded blue that's an oasis of solidness in the center of the swirling sensation. Concentrating on the blue makes the spinning slow, until finally it stops.

Cale's T-shirt. That's what the blue is. And as soon as I make out its entire shape, the rest of the room comes into focus.

I can see.

But I'm looking at the room from a different angle than I was a few moments ago. And now that everything's in focus, it's almost too sharp. Shapes are so defined they leap out at me. Reality's been switched onto a higher setting.

When I take in the others, it's the tiny details that leap out. Small things I wouldn't have noticed a few moments ago. Brugan's mouth gapes open and saliva glistens on his teeth. A hint of darkness peeking from under Cale's sleeve is a bruise. On one arm of Sentin's glasses is a tiny switch. And the blue of Aza's eyes is now so bright it almost hurts my eyes.

Eyes.

How come I can blink two good eyes without any ache or flicker? There's no annoying black spot where one of the sensor arrays in my cybernetic eye has blown.

And I can see the tentacle chair. I can see myself lying on it. There I am, with Director Morelle and Doctor Gregory both standing behind me. I can smell everyone in the room. Distinctive smells, but all tangled up in each other.

Could I be dead? No, I feel alive. Really, really alive. Someone fiddled with the controls and turned everything up. But I'm not me anymore. I'm the leopard. Somehow I'm seeing through the leopard's eyes and my thoughts are inside its head.

"Open your eyes, Rayne." Director Morelle's talking into my ear. I hear her as though she's right next to me, but she's a few feet away, bending over my body. The sensation makes everything start to spin again.

"Open your eyes now."

My eyes must already be open because I'm looking around. But my body's lying in the tentacle chair with its eyes closed. Can I open them? How can I?

The room lurches, and I squeeze my leopard eyes shut. I'm flying sideways again, only this time it feels more like being sucked through a tube that gets narrower and narrower. There's nothing to hang onto, because I have no body to hang on with. But I must have a stomach, because I'm queasy, and I must have eyes, because I can open them. Now I can blink, and is that the ceiling above me? As it settles into place, I feel the familiar ache of my cybernetic eye.

"Are you okay, Rayne?" asks Doctor Gregory.

"No!" It comes out as a yelp.

Doctor Gregory chuckles and pats my shoulder.

The director says, "It's disorientating at first, but you'll learn to control it. As long as you're close enough, you'll be able to transfer your consciousness in and out of the Leopard Skin at will."

My fists clench as I will myself not to blink.

"Try again, Rayne. Transfer back inside the leopard. Go into your new Skin."

I take a breath and force my fists to uncurl. *Stop pounding so hard, heart. Stop churning, stomach.* I'm not going to throw up. Not in front of the others.

Five million credits. I can do this. I can be the leopard. *I'm the clouded leopard.*

The transfer's not as bad this time, although my brain still feels like it's being sucked through a grinder, and vomiting is still a strong possibility.

But when I look out of the leopard's eyes, everything's

in such sharp focus that I forget to feel sick. Things that are too close are hazy around the edges, but I can see the entire training room in perfect detail. In the far corner, a spider's spinning a web, its front legs working like knitting needles. Surely there's no way a regular person could see that?

The tangle of smells hits me again, each scent strong and distinctive. If it were pitch black in here, I'd probably still know who was in the room.

"Hello Rayne," says Doctor Morelle, looking at leopard-me. "Can you move your head?"

The others gape at the leopard. I try to ignore them, thinking instead about what the director's asked me to do. I've got a leopard's body. Four paws and a tail. But the best part is that I have no pain. In my own body, I'd become used to ignoring the aches, but without them I feel light and free.

I turn my head and Cale's scent sharpens. Not with fear, but something else. Excitement maybe? Fear smells bitter, with a tang of overripe fruit and sweat. I know that's how it smells because I'm still getting a faint whiff of it from my own body, although that's starting to change. My fear's disappearing.

"Very good," says Director Morelle.

I swing my leopard head to look at her, then lift a paw. Put it down. The other side. Can I walk? I'm not sure. I'll need to think about how that might work with four legs.

Tail. I can sense it there, sticking out behind me like an extra limb. It feels weird, but by concentrating, I manage to move that too. It's strange being able to twitch it from side to side. Will it sway as I walk? I want to walk. I want to feel how the leopard moves.

"Excellent!" exclaims Director Morelle. "Now transfer

back to your own body again, Rayne. Get used to the feeling."

I can hardly bear to look at the reclining chair where my body is lying. My eyelids have drifted up and my ugly cybernetic eye is peeking out. Instead of the glimpse of white with a green iris that's on my good side, my damaged eye socket contains a small, shiny black lens with visible circuitry behind it. My cheek is a ravaged hollow surrounded by scar tissue, twisted ridges that cut across my face. No, it's not a face, it's a dystopian landscape. My mouth's slack and slightly open, sagging on one side, and moisture glistens at the corner of my lips. I can't see the pain that's become a constant part of living in my body, but I know it's there.

What if I don't want to go back to that body?

"Think about being yourself again," says the director. "You can do it."

I want to object, to refuse. I'm only beginning to discover this new world, and the last thing I want is to cut it so short. But the expression on Director Morelle's face makes me hesitate. While the others have turned to my human body, waiting for it to come back to life, she's still staring at leopard-me. Her lips have twitched up, and her smug, knowing smile unnerves me. She looks like she knows exactly what I'm thinking. Like she's playing some sort of game, and I'm a chess piece that she's just moved into place.

Her look sends a cold shiver down my spine.

I think about being in my own body again, and after another sickening rush, I am. The first thing I do is shut my slack mouth and wipe it. The second thing is to lift my head and look at the leopard. It's huge and powerful. So beautiful, I have to fight the urge to transfer right back into it.

"How was it, Rayne?" asks Cale. The four of them stare at me with open curiosity as the back of the tentacle chair lifts up so I can climb out of it. The trace of envy in Aza's expression gives me a stab of triumph. Not so repulsive anymore, am I?

"Incredible." It was so much more than that, but how else can I describe it? Running my fingers over the back of my neck, I can't feel the chip.

The others all turn back to the director, except for Cale. Smiling, his gaze lingers on my face. For a moment, caught up in the elation I still feel from being the leopard, I smile back. Then I remember where I am—who I am—and jerk my gaze away.

Why would a floater, my competitor, want to be friendly? There's no possible reason. He's just trying to unnerve me. In the scale of people I'm ever likely to trust, floaters are way down the list, and men least of all.

"Who wants to go next?" asks Director Morelle.

"I do." It's Brugan who shouts loudest.

The director nods at him. "Come this way."

Doctor Gregory sticks close to me as I follow everyone else over to one of the other doors, I suppose so she's ready to grab me if I accidentally transfer back into the leopard. I want to be the leopard again, but I'm also curious to see what the others' Skins will be like.

Is the Skin Hunter contest a battle between Skins? It could even be a life-or-death fight. Perhaps if just our thoughts have been transferred into the Skins we can't actually get hurt.

All I know for sure is that I have a chance not to be *me* anymore. And that's the best thing I've ever felt.

Chapter Seven

I'm not expecting Brugan's Skin to be like mine, but I'm not ready for how different it is.

It's man-shaped, with a bear's head that's covered with shaggy black-and-grey fur. Its torso is hairless and human, with bulky muscles. A thick pelt starts again at its waist. It's standing upright, but its legs are more animal than human. Its hands are claws.

Is it a mix of man and bear? Its nose is sharper than a bear. More like a wolf.

"Brugan's Skin combines the DNA of several animals, with a skeleton that's basically humanoid in structure," says Director Morelle. "Most of the DNA is from a wolverine, an animal known for its strength and ferocity. It has another name: the devil bear."

"Devil bear," repeats Brugan, drawling the words in his floater accent. He scans our faces to check we're all impressed.

"Wolverines are excellent climbers. We also mixed in some characteristics from other members of the Canidae family to enhance its range of movement. You'll notice how wolfish its face is? And there's some grey fox in there too. Wolverines are fairly small animals, but we've manipulated the DNA to make yours the largest and strongest of the Skins, Brugan. It looks quite bear-like, don't you think? The name Devil Bear sums this Skin up nicely."

Brugan nods, smirking. He's as puffed-up as though he designed the Skin himself.

No wonder he's pleased. The animal in front of us is a savage beast. I bet it could tear me to pieces in the time it takes to blink.

There's a tentacle chair in this room too, and Brugan gets in it without hesitation. As soon as his chip is implanted, his eyes shut. It's weird watching the devil bear come to life. One minute its eyes are dull, then it's looking around. I wonder if he has a wolverine's vision and sense of smell, like I had the leopard's?

Like me, he gets to transfer in and out of the Skin a couple of times. He turns its head, blinks, and moves its hands. I can't tell whether he's as reluctant to go back to his human body as I was, but when he gets up from the chair, I notice he keeps staring at the devil bear. Just as I kept turning to look at my beautiful leopard.

At the next door, Director Morelle turns to Sentin.

"Sentin, your Skin is highly specialized, designed specifically for climbing. It uses both reptilian and human DNA."

Reptilian? Maybe this Skin will give me a hint of what the contest will be. I wonder if the different Skins will have to fight, or work together?

Director Morelle opens the door, and I gape at Sentin's Skin, which is the most bizarre yet. Its body is human-shaped, and covered head-to-toe with jewel-green scales.

It has enormous round eyes set deep into its face, a flat nose that's barely more than a slight bulge, and no ears that I can see. Who'd have thought a mix of lizard and man could look so regal? Whether it's the shape of the head, or the amazing eyes that shine silver and have a black pupil that's a vertical slit instead of round, it's definitely a proud face.

Sentin's Skin is as tall as Brugan's, but not as muscled. More wiry. Its arms are longer than human, and its hands are oversized. Its fingers are long and thin, but rounded at the ends, each one ending in a bulb.

Although it's standing on its back legs, its stance is crouched and I wonder if its knees won't fully straighten. Then I see its feet. They're just like its hands. Long lizard hands where its feet should be.

"We used a complex mix of reptile DNA for this Skin," says the director. "Its scales come from a chameleon, and its strength from a komodo dragon." She turns to Sentin. "I think you'll find your Skin's senses quite startling at first. You'll be able to see colors invisible to humans, right into the ultraviolet spectrum. Your Skin has no sense of smell. Instead it has sensors that can detect heat and cold with such accuracy, your heat-mapping ability may be of more value than your improved eyesight."

Sentin's eyes glint. Though his face doesn't show much, I can tell he's pleased. And why wouldn't he be? As amazing as my leopard is, I wish I could transfer into his Skin to find out what invisible colors look like.

When Sentin transfers into it, the reptile's head moves quizzically, as though questioning what's around it. His tongue flicks out, long and blue, then his scales shimmer and change color, becoming a deep turquoise flecked with gold. His silver eyes blink slowly, but the lid comes up from underneath instead of down from the top. The simple act of blinking makes his Skin seem so alien that I get a strong pang of anxiety. Brugan's Skin I can understand: it's a big, mean powerhouse. But Sentin's? I have no idea what his Skin is capable of.

"Aza, your Skin is next." Director Morelle leads us to the next door. "I think you'll be happy with it."

When it's revealed I can see why.

Aza's Skin is gorgeous. And nightmarish. A dazzling killing machine. Its body is stick-thin, even thinner than Aza herself, and covered with sleek black armor... or is it a shell? It looks organic rather than metal. Its layers cover the body in a complex pattern.

The only bit of the Skin that isn't covered with black shell is the bottom of its face, a normal female face with a long, thin nose and full red lips. Above the nose it's as though the woman's wearing a helmet. I can't see any eyes.

Then I realize what's on its back.

Wings.

Red wings that reach up above its head and are long enough to graze the floor. They're translucent, shimmering red. Now I really hope the contest isn't a race, because how would I be able to beat a Skin with wings?

"For this Skin we combined a woman's DNA with the DNA from two species of wasp. Specifically, an Indonesian warrior wasp and a rare species of hawk wasp. Neither have the traditional black-and-yellow coloring, rather a black body and red wings. They're known for their size and aggression. Both wasps attack prey much larger than themselves."

When Aza transfers into the Skin, the front of its helmet shimmers as though moving lights are shining from inside. The wasp's head turns as she scans the room. Instead of moving an arm or leg like the rest of us did, she stretches the wasp's wings out.

"As thin and light as it is, your Skin is too heavy to soar into the air," Director Morelle says. "But you'll be so light on your feet, you'll be able to leap long distances with little effort."

After Aza transfers back into her own body, Director Morelle looks at Cale. He's leaning against the wall, his body relaxed.

Is it my imagination, or does the director's mouth tighten as she looks at him? "Lucky last," she says without a trace of a smile. "Cale, your Skin is similar to Rayne's. Both your Skins almost solely consist of animal DNA. You have a human larynx, for speech. But you'll both have to learn to walk on four paws."

As the door slides back, I try to guess what Cale's Skin is going to be. But it's not an animal I recognize. It's some kind of cat, striped like a tiger and even bigger than my leopard. Its body is lanky, as if it's been stretched.

Although the animal is slim, its four limbs look powerful. Two long fangs hang from its mouth, curving below its muzzle. Its claws are thick blades. It could swipe my head off with those claws. Or rip it off with its fangs.

"For this Skin, we used the DNA of a prehistoric mammal, a recently-discovered species of saber-toothed tiger. It was the largest and most powerful feline to ever walk the earth. So strong, it hunted mammoth."

Cale grins. "Mammoth? Then I guess the others should be easy to beat."

If Brugan had said that, it would have sounded like a threat. But Cale says it like he's kidding. While the others all share a determined intensity, Cale has a relaxed air. Like he's a spectator, while everyone else is playing to win.

"We mixed the tiger DNA with an animal called a fossa, to give it incredible agility. A native of Madagascar, the fossa would literally run up and down trees."

Huh. So his Skin is both powerful and agile. And those fangs are impressive.

Cale runs his hand through his hair, a wide grin on his face. And when he transfers into the beast, its lips curl into a strange, almost-human smile that, though it shows off its fangs, still seems wrong. He seems too good-natured for such a fearsome Skin.

Do I see disapproval in Director Morelle's face? Maybe it's my imagination. But when she tells him to transfer back into his body, I catch an undercurrent in her voice.

Cale had better watch out. The director doesn't seem like someone who stands for second best.

It's good for me if Cale doesn't have a killer instinct, maybe he won't be so hard to beat. Shame about the other three.

Chapter Eight

Finally I get to transfer back into my Skin. Doctor Gregory stays with me, giving me advice. Other white-coated doctors help the others.

Doctor Gregory calls the tentacle chair a pod, and tells me it has sensors in it to monitor my vitals and make sure I'm okay. The rubbery fingers are meant to move my body around to keep my circulation going. She says the pod will keep me hydrated and inject me with nutrients if I need it. I don't like the sound of that. Like I trust a chair that can shoot me full of who-knows-what.

But by the time she tells me, I'm already the leopard again, and I'm taking my first steps. Four legs instead of two. It takes me a while to work out which ones should step when, but it feels good when I get it. I feel strong.

I keep looking over at the pod to check it's not doing anything to my body. I look way too vulnerable lying there, like I'm asleep in the shelter with nobody keeping guard. But there's no way I'm transferring back. Not while I'm getting the hang of smells like shapes that waver in the air, waiting for me to figure them out. Not when I can feel the incredible strength in my limbs and the promise of speed that already feels like freedom.

As absorbing as it is, I'm distracted by the others testing their Skins. And there's a faint smell that keeps bugging me. It's a scent that's strange and new, but at the same time weirdly familiar, like it's stirring up a memory buried deep in my brain. It smells good. What is it?

"Find your center of balance, Rayne." Doctor Gregory calls my attention back to what I'm doing, but still I'm distracted by that scent. It's coming from the far end of the big room, where Cale's taking his first steps as a saber-toothed tiger.

The scent of feline.

The realization makes me shudder.

Just because I'm wearing a big cat's Skin, better not mean I'm drawn to other cats. I don't want an animal's urges.

Cale's eyes catch mine, a flash of gold from the other side of the room. He can smell me too, I know it.

Leopards can't blush. Thank goodness. Still, I turn away so fast I almost get my four paws tangled up.

"Are you all right?" asks Doctor Gregory.

Maybe. Yes. Now I know what that scent is, I can ignore it. Except it chafes against my senses, as annoying as an itch. I turn my back on Cale and concentrate on how I'm moving, trying to make walking with four legs into something that comes naturally. I'm doing better now that I'm moving away from Cale. I'm even leaving Doctor Gregory behind.

When I reach the other end of the room, the stench of the devil bear gets stronger. Brugan's left his helper behind too, walking fast and easily, but of course he's only got two legs to worry about. He stops when I meet his eyes, then grabs an iron bar from the top of a rack of weights and grips it at both ends. His muscles bulge and he grunts with effort. He's trying to bend it. Typical. Only a floater would destroy a piece of equipment to show off.

Brugan makes a show of it, baring his long fangs as the metal groans and bows under his strength. The muscles in Brugan's hairless upper arms stand out like thick slabs of meat. Each arm looks bigger than my head. When he's bent the thick metal bar into a u-shape, Brugan holds it up so I get a good look, then tosses it aside.

He snarls. "Come here, little kitty. I'll bend you like that bar."

It's strange to hear a human voice coming out of his wolfish mouth. It hadn't occurred to me to try to talk, but now I reply, "You'd have to catch me first."

My voice sounds like my own, only huskier. There's definitely some feline growl in it. In spite of my big talk, I hope Brugan doesn't come after me, because I'm still in danger of getting my paws tangled.

Brugan lunges at me.

I leap back, avoiding his claws but stumbling when I land. Need to remember I have four paws now, and a tail I have to start using for balance. Still, I make it far enough out of Brugan's reach that he stops.

"Here, kitty, kitty." He lets his mouth hang open and his tongue roll out as he gives a rough laugh. Disgusting.

A soft voice comes from behind me, making me jump.

"May I offer one piece of advice?"

It's the shimmering Reptile Skin. It examines me as intently as its owner did when I was introduced to him. Sentin's scent was there all along, but I hadn't taken any notice. I'm not used to paying attention to my nose yet, but I'd better get used to it fast. I should use every advantage my leopard gives me.

The reptile's long arms are loose at his sides. He

doesn't look like he wants to attack, but Sentin's lizard's face is as difficult to read as his human one.

"What advice?" I'm tense, ready to leap away. Trying to watch both him and Brugan, who's still close enough to be dangerous.

Sentin is standing upright like a human. Even with his knees bent, he's tall enough that he needs to lower his head to murmur in my ear.

"The most important rule of war is that you should never let yourself get drawn into a battle you're not certain you'll win."

Without waiting for a reply, he straightens.

At the same moment, Brugan feints toward me. I leap back, away from both of them. Brugan laughs again. The look on his face is pure contempt, but what Sentin said makes sense. This is war, and I'm not ready for battle yet. And although I've got no idea why Sentin is giving me advice, I'm going to take it.

I head away from Brugan to practice. By the time Doctor Gregory calls a stop, I'm doing a slow lope, gradually building up speed. I'm dying to go faster, but I'm being careful not to trip over my paws.

"Come on, Rayne. It's getting late."

Can't be late, I've barely started. But when I look outside, it's dark. Where did the day go?

The others are just as reluctant to transfer out of their Skins. Brugan's left behind a pile of twisted bars, and he's making running look easy. Turns out the black rectangle in the floor is a giant treadmill, and Brugan's the only one who's tried it today.

Like me, Cale's still getting used to four paws.

Aza's fluttering at the base of the silver climbing wall. Her wings look incredible, but she's not getting that high off the ground. Judging by how hard she's trying, I'd say she's determined to use them for more than just to help her run and jump.

Director Morelle must have slipped out of the room at some stage, but I didn't notice her go. My leopard senses are so good, I should have smelled or heard her leaving. But my poor brain feels overloaded by all the smells and sounds, not to mention the sharpness of vision that makes everything look incredible. I can't pay attention to everything.

Doctor Gregory calls to everyone again, telling us to go back to our lab rooms and transfer back into our bodies. She and Sentin are standing between me and my lab. As I walk past, I'm conscious of the reptile's head turning to track me. I wonder what it's like looking through those silver eyes? I haven't noticed Sentin testing his strength or speed. He stands in a bent-legged crouch, so I'm not sure how easily he'll run. Maybe his Skin is designed to move faster on all fours?

In my lab, a big metal disc is set into the floor. Stepping onto it brings the screens around me to life, with 3D graphs and numbers flashing up too fast to read.

I hate transferring back into my human body. The ache in my side's going to drive me crazy. And as soon I open my bad eye and try to blink the graininess away, I'm wishing for my perfect leopard vision back.

Standing up, I feel heavy. And I'm so slow! Did the air get as thick as syrup while I was in my Skin?

The others head out of the training room. Sentin's first, still talking with Doctor Gregory. Cale is just behind, as though he's trying to listen in without being noticed. What is Sentin doing spending so much time with the doctor? Does he think he's going to get some sort of advantage? Maybe Doctor Gregory's giving him tips about how his Skin works.

Now I think about it, I should talk to her more, especially as I'm clueless about the contest. Tomorrow I'll stick close to her and try to dig out some details.

Ahead of me, Brugan speeds up to catch up with Aza. He glances back at me and speaks loudly enough to make sure I hear. "How'd you like having to spend the day with a sewer rat? I'm going to make her learn her place."

Aza looks back as well. Her top lip curls and her nostrils flare, but for once the scorn isn't aimed at me. "Don't try to drag me into anything, Brugan."

"Don't worry, I won't need help to send her back down the hole she crawled out of." Grinning, he cracks his knuckles. "I can handle it myself."

Aza sighs. "I was wondering if you were as stupid as you look, and now I know. I couldn't care less about her. She's no threat to me. None of you are."

Brugan stops dead. Aza keeps walking. I hesitate. If I keep going, I'll be level with Brugan. But if I stop to avoid him, we'll be the only ones left in the training room.

I speed up, hoping to get past and out the door ahead of him. I've only taken two steps when he spins around, blocking my path. His face is turning red. What Aza said obviously stung, but it's not her he's going to explode at, it's me. Great. Why is it such an insult to him that I'm here? Because I'm from Old Triton, or because I'm ugly?

The door closes behind Aza.

Brugan leans forward, fists raised. "They'll need to carry you out of here, sewer rat."

Shit. I don't want to fight him. Tori's voice rings in my head, her rules for survival. *"Fights aren't fair, Milla. The strongest fighter usually wins, and no matter how hard you train, men are just born stronger. First rule is to steer clear of trouble, but if you need to fight, hit fast, hard, and dirty. Use any trick you can to drop him, then run. Don't stick around to watch him get up."*

I bend my knees and shift my weight so I'm light on my feet, like Tori taught me. Dropping him and taking off is my only chance. If I let him get up again, he's sure to demolish me. Good thing he's big and heavy. I'm probably quicker, and thanks to Tori, I'm sneaky as hell.

Brugan lunges at me and his fist comes at me faster than I expected, flying at my face. I dodge, but his knuckles catch my cheek, snapping my head sideways. Like after any punch, I have a moment of disorientation, the shock and pain of being struck blanking out rational thought. But I've been hit enough times that my mind clears fast.

The triumphant gleam in his eyes tells me Brugan thinks he's got me. And when he swings again, he almost does. Desperately, I drop low, sliding under his fists, moving forward, not back. I lash out as fast as I can with one foot, going for his knee.

Just one chance, so hit hard.

I miss.

But when he jerks sideways, my leg snags his and we both go down. Because he's heavier than me, he hits the ground harder. I squirm away and leap up on my feet again in a second, the pain of the fall barely registering.

He's still dragging himself off the ground when I make it through the door.

Max is on the other side. He jerks around when I burst through and his expression is every bit as nasty as Brugan's.

"Sewer rat," he hisses.

I can't fight him, not with any number of sneaky tricks. Instead of running down the hall like I want to, I make myself walk. Back straight. Eyes straight ahead. I walk past Max like he's not there, like he doesn't exist. Doing my best to pretend my heart's not fighting to escape my chest. That I'm not terrified Brugan's going to burst out after me, and Max will help him take me down.

I walk on the edge of a blade, my entire body tensed to run. But the door doesn't open and Brugan doesn't chase me. And when I round the corner I let myself stop, put one hand on the wall and take a breath. I'm okay.

Except I'm not okay. Dammit, I'm angry. For a few short hours in the training room, I was a powerful creature with claws and teeth. For the first time in my life, I felt *strong*.

Brugan ruined that feeling.

I close my eyes a moment to make a silent promise. Soon Brugan and I will be competing against each other. And when the time comes, no matter what kind of contest it is, I swear I'll beat him.

Chapter Nine

T he rec room has a kitchen at one end, a dining table in the middle, and what Doctor Gregory calls a 'chill-out zone' at the other end. Couches are arranged around a holo, with five vReals lined up against the wall.

A delicious smell is wafting out of some covered serving bowls in the kitchen. I don't know if the chair was doing anything to my real body while I was in my Skin, but my stomach's rumbling, so I guess it didn't feed me.

Brugan slouches in a little after I do. An air of menace comes off him like the stink of his Skin. He glowers at me, but I doubt he'll try anything with Doctor Gregory here.

"Help yourselves to dinner," Doctor Gregory says. "Feel free to watch the holo, but don't use the vReals just yet." She puts on a motherly tone. "And make sure you head back to your rooms early because you'll have a busy day of training tomorrow." She heads toward the door. "If you need anything during the night, either call my band, or talk to the guard posted outside the training room."

Great. Only I can't do the first, and I'd rather not do the second. Hopefully I won't need anything.

After the doctor goes, I hold back, waiting to see what Brugan's going to do. Being good at reading people is an essential skill in the shelter, and I think I've got him pegged right: all bluster and no balls. As long as nobody knows I bested him in our scuffle, his pride shouldn't prickle hard enough for him to risk getting thrown out of the contest. I don't *think* he'll attack me where anyone can see, but caution is second nature. I'll stay wary until I know for sure.

With the doctor gone, the others scramble for the food. Aza gets there first. "Meatballs, of sorts." Disgust fills her voice. She checks another bowl, bending to sniff it. "The worst vegetables I've ever seen, and low-quality rice. Must be from one of the mass-production factories. Revolting."

Brugan lifts the lid of another bowl. "Bread rolls." He grabs one. "They're hot."

"They look cheap and they smell nasty." Aza picks one up with the tips of forefinger and thumb and drops it onto her plate, her delicate nose wrinkled.

I watch them dish out as much food as they want, and it's not until Brugan sits at the table and digs into a full plate that I head over to the serving bowls. Even mimicking the way the others all served themselves, I still feel self-conscious about heaping my plate up, as though some-body's going to catch me taking too much. I've never chosen how much I get to eat before, and this is my first meal in years that hasn't come out of a dispensing machine.

A bonus: there's a paring knife in the cutlery rack. Small but sharp. Perfect.

Once the others have all sat down, I pretend to drop something so I can bend over and slip the blade inside the leg of my jeans, tucking it into my sock. The cold metal against my ankle is comforting.

Brugan's fat lips twist as I sit at the table with the others. "We're going to be forced to look at that?" He nods at my face. "It'll make me sick." Even as he says it he's shoveling a piled fork into his mouth.

I've heard plenty worse, so it's not hard to ignore. But Cale snaps, "Don't be an asshole, Brugan." Like I need him to stick up for me.

Aza glances at me, then looks away. It's obvious she doesn't want to get involved. Her lips are pressed together but her eyes are straight from a fairy tale, and her face is as flawless as Rayne's was. Does she know how stunning she is? Looking at her makes me feel worse about my damaged face than any insult from Brugan ever could. What would it be like to have that beautiful face? To catch someone staring with admiration instead of disgust?

"It's a burn," says Sentin, his tone matter-of-fact. "It wasn't treated properly, because the skin puckered as it healed."

His plate holds a neat, even circle of rice with matching circles of vegetables on one side, and meatballs on the other. It looks like a math diagram. He uses both knife and fork to surgically remove a tidy mouthful, then chews slowly.

Brugan turns his snarl onto Sentin. "Who asked you, *Deiterran?*"

I just about choke on meatball. Sentin can't really be a Deiterran. Maybe it's a weird insult I've never heard of?

"Half Deiterran," says Sentin calmly.

Cale's gaping too, so he can't have known either. "You're really from there? What are you doing here? And what's it like over the wall?"

"I've lived in Triton for most of my life."

"But what was it like before you left?" Cale leans forward. "Do they really grow their food?"

"I'm afraid I can't talk about it."

"You can't tell us anything? Not even a hint? At least tell us why it's such a big secret."

Sentin just shakes his head, and Cale looks as disappointed as I feel. The Deiterran ambassador's always refused to talk about Deiterra as well. I've heard all kinds of theories why, and it's hard not to be curious.

Brugan points at Sentin's face with his fork. "What's with the spectacles, Einstein?"

I have no idea who or what Einstein is, but Sentin must get the joke because his lips twitch. "Einstein didn't wear glasses."

Cale frowns. "I wonder how I'd look in them," he says, putting his hand out. "Do you mind if I try them?"

Sentin hesitates. I'm expecting him to refuse, but after a moment he hands them over.

Cale puts them on and gives an exaggerated blink. "You guys mind if I dim the lights for a sec?" He touches his band and the lights die.

"Hey!" growls Brugan.

The sudden darkness makes my heart pound. My ears strain for the sound of movement. I'm bending to grab the blade from my sock when the lights flick back on. "Sorry," says Cale, sounding anything but. He hands the glasses back to Sentin. "But I bet your Skin's vision is even better?"

Sentin puts the glasses back on and makes another neat slice in his food without answering. I'd love to know what's so great about his glasses and why Cale wanted to test them in the dark, but the shock of Sentin being Deiterran is still filling my brain.

I've never seen anyone from the other side of the wall

before. He may as well be an alien for all I know about where he's from.

Funny how the others are well-matched to their Skins. Not just that Sentin's reptile is as mysterious as he is, but Brugan's devil bear is heavily muscled, while Aza's wasp is slender and lovely. Cale and I are the only ones who don't quite fit. But of course I don't, the real Rayne should have had the beautiful Leopard Skin.

I'm sorry she died, but glad I'm getting to experience it instead.

Can I transfer into my leopard from here? I close my eyes and reach out with my mind, trying to replicate the feeling I got when I transferred. Nothing happens. Maybe I have to be in the pod? I'll try again when I get to my room, just in case.

Aza pushes her still-full plate away. "I'm going to complain," she announces. "It's not good enough."

"Having to eat with her, you mean?" Brugan points his fork at me.

She gives him a look that could freeze off a body part. "I'm talking about the food."

"Yeah, it's not good enough," repeats Brugan, though he's almost finished everything on his plate already. "How are we supposed to stay fit eating this?"

Aza gets up, leaving her plate on the table, and sits on the floor in front of the holo. She extends her legs out in front, then bends forward so her torso touches her legs. Stretching her muscles, I guess.

Cale gets up too, but he goes to the counter and piles more food on his plate, making a show of it, not that either Aza or Brugan seem to notice. I catch myself gaping and turn my face away. Stupid to be surprised by such a simple thing, but it hadn't occurred to me I could go back to the serving bowls to get more food.

I've got to stop thinking like a sinker.

I wait until Cale sits back down, then fill my plate again too. Whatever Aza thinks, this food tastes delicious to me. A lot better than I'm used to.

Brugan pushes away his empty plate and saunters over to sit behind Aza on a couch in front of the holo. He flicks it on, but he's not looking at the picture, he's watching her stretch. Why can't he get the message and lay off her? Aza's convinced she's better than all of us, and though I'm bottom of the list, Brugan's obviously included. She's so generous with her disdain that, funnily enough, it almost makes me like her. At least she hasn't singled me out.

Cale looks at Sentin and drops his voice, though the holo's making enough noise that I don't think Brugan and Aza could hear him anyway. "Who'd you have to kill to get a pair of those glasses? And don't tell me you bought them on the net, because I know you can't."

Sentin lifts one eyebrow but doesn't reply. He arranges his knife and fork together on his clean plate, then slowly gets up, straightens his shirt, and walks to one of the couches.

Cale and I are the only two left at the table. He grimaces at Sentin's back, then shoots me a wry look. "Boy, can he talk! I thought he was never going to shut up."

I turn my face away, refusing to smile. Maybe Cale really is what he seems: a nice guy who thinks we can be friends. But I don't need a buddy in here. I can lock the door to my room at night to keep safe, and during the day I can watch my own back.

"So." Cale keeps trying. Got to give him marks for persistence. "What do you usually do for fun, Rayne? I mean, when you're not transferring your consciousness into a highly-advanced, bio-mechanical avatar, that is."

Fun? He's obviously not trying to be offensive, but he

may as well have asked whether I prefer wearing a crown or a tiara.

"Nothing." It's an honest answer, but a curt one. And when I hear myself say the word, I don't know why it makes me feel so sad.

"Nothing? You must do something."

My eyes drop to my hands. I have cuts on top of bruises on top of scars. The rough treatment from the stompers means they're even more battered than normal. Cale's fingers are as flawless as the rest of him. Not so much as a freckle.

No, the worst Mr. High Cheekbones has ever to had to worry about in his perfect life will have been which eager girl to date next. Can't he see we have nothing, not one single thing, in common?

"Oh-kay," Cale mutters eventually, after the silence has stretched out for too long. "Wonder what's on the holo?" He joins the others, putting his feet up on the couch and stretching his arms across its back. Watching him make himself comfortable, the strangeness of where I am hits me.

When was the last time I sat on a couch?

Can all this luxury possibly be real?

Maybe I was the one who died on the floor of the shelter with a blade in my gut, and this is some kind of weird afterlife with couches, private bedrooms, and Skins.

I snap out of it when Sentin tells the holo, "Morelle Corporation," and a familiar voice comes out of it. Director Morelle's being interviewed. I move closer, grabbing a chair to sit behind everyone else, and listen more than I watch.

"Interest in the transferal technology has been high," Director Morelle is saying. "Tickets to attend the Skin Hunter contest sold out in just a few minutes. The only part we're keeping secret is what the Skins will look like and how they perform. And when the public see what they can do, they'll want to experience them for themselves."

There's a scattering of applause. A man's voice cuts through it. "This technology is unproven. We don't yet know the risks, or if transferal is as safe as you claim."

I look, keeping my bad eye shut. The image is distorted with just one eye, but I can see the man arguing with Director Morelle is Vice President Burns.

His skin is very dark, and he's obviously had a lot of expensive tweaking because his face is almost ageless and impossibly handsome. He and the director are in a studio, sitting in armchairs that face each other. There must be an audience there watching them, but they're out of shot.

Doctor Gregory said the president was against the contest. The vice president sure is, that's plain.

"We must find a way to give people what they want," says Director Morelle.

"Fast track it?" Vice President Burns gives a contemptuous snort. "You mean, like Welcon Pharmaceuticals did?"

"The Welcon incident was seventeen years ago, and I'm utterly sick of politicians using it as an excuse to delay—"

"I'd hardly call millions of unplanned births an excuse!" The vice president's voice rises with indignation, and I'm not surprised. The Welcon disaster changed everything, and it sounds like the director's making light of it.

Director Morelle's expression stays icy cold, and her eyes are sharp as needles "The Morelle Corporation has a reputation for safety that should reassure —"

"Are you suggesting the Morelle Corporation should be above the law?"

"Of course not. All I'm saying is that—"

"Public safety is my primary concern. Is it yours, Director Morelle? Or are you only interested in making more money?"

"That's ridiculous! And downright offensive." For the first time, I hear anger creeping into the director's tone. I'd like to get a better look at her expression, but my good eye's aching and my vision is blurring.

There are a few mutters from the audience. Sounds like they're on Director Morelle's side, so they must be floaters.

New Triton was supposed to be the solution to the population explosion caused by the Welcon disaster, but it turned out to be just an excuse for the rich to raise themselves above the rest of us. Maybe for them, Welcon was an opportunity rather than a disaster.

The interviewer pipes up and the view pans back to include a woman in a formal suit. "But Director Morelle, don't you agree with the vice president that the public deserves some level of reassurance?"

Shutting my good eye to rest it, I hear the director draw in a sharp breath before she answers the question. "The Morelle Corporation has been delivering quality products since my grandfather started selling the earliest IV enhancers from his workshop. His nano-chip technology helped eliminate disease caused by blood-borne pathogens, can you deny that?"

"That's not—" The vice president tries to interrupt, but she keeps talking.

"The Morelle Corporation created the holo and the vReal. We brought you—"

"You don't—"

"Let me finish, please, Vice President. When we tried to release the vReal, it took almost three years to get approval. Three years! And for what? The vReal is about as dangerous as a washing machine or a gamenode."

Hoots and applause from the audience. They're definitely on Director Morelle's side.

"Yes, but—"

"Answer me this, Vice President," the director interrupts. "Exactly how much longer will it take President Trask to approve Skin technology?"

"That depends on many factors."

"You can't give me a straight answer?"

"You know we need to do a variety of tests..."

Boos and jeers interrupt him. I open my good eye in time to see Director Morelle sweep her hand in a wide gesture. "Speak to the audience, Vice President. Tell them how long they'll have to wait, while you and President Trask do your multitude of tests."

He snorts. "I don't need to answer to you, Director."

The interviewer leans forward, pressing the question. "But Vice President, could you not give us an indication here, tonight, on how much more testing you intend to do?"

The vice president jumps out of his chair. "Do I have to say it again? President Trask is only concerned with public safety. If that's inconvenient for the Morelle Corporation, I refuse to apologize."

The interviewer tries to stop Burns from storming off, but when he's gone, she turns back to the camera. "Once again it seems we're no closer to a release date for the Morelle Corporation to be able to sell their fascinating new technology. But thank you to both our guests for participating tonight."

Brugan brings up a panel with his band to take control of the holo, and switches the channel to scan. It's a dizzying sequence that scans through everything both currently playing and stored in memory.

Cale says, "If they're right and the Skins need more testing, the director needs to let them do it."

"President Trask is a dinosaur," Aza says in a bored voice. She's in a really complicated position now with her legs folded over each other and her torso twisted around. "He's afraid to release Skins because he's stuck in the past. Time we got rid of him and elected a new president who isn't scared of his own shadow."

"Sounds like the only reason the director's running the contest is to pressure the president into allowing the testing to be rushed," says Cale.

Sentin clears his throat. "To obtain approval for the first Skin prototypes, the Morelle Corporation had to prove a certain level of safety." He speaks as slowly as if he stops to examine every word before releasing it. "It's only the testing required for full public release that's still in progress."

Aza untwists her body and stands up. "If Skins aren't on sale by Christmas, President Trask will be voted out. And he knows it." She tosses her long hair back before striding out.

Brugan watches her leave, giving her back an up-and-down leer that makes me shudder. He leaves the holo on scan mode, jumps up and strides out after her.

Cale looks back at me. "What do you think, Rayne?"

Boy, he really doesn't give up.

I shrug, uncomfortable at the way both he and Sentin are looking at me. Sentin's examining me too closely from behind his glasses, and I've no idea what they help him to see.

I don't want either of them to be able to read my face, to know how clueless I feel. I'm the only one who'd never heard of the Skins, so it must have been all over the news feeds. Since I lost my eye, watching the feeds became too difficult to bother with. What else have I missed?

When I don't reply, Cale glances at Sentin. "You think the transferal technology's safe?"

"Until all testing is complete, that's impossible to answer."

Cale gives a little laugh. "I thought I was transferring into a saber-toothed tiger. Really, I was becoming a giant guinea pig."

"Both a guinea pig, and a social experiment," Sentin agrees.

Cale's mouth twists. "We're the bait dangled in front of millions of people to convince them to forget about Welcon. He looks at me again. "How does it feel to be part of a plan to fast-track another untested product?"

I swallow. The question is a blade in my gut. Seventeen years ago, Welcon Pharmaceuticals released the world's first anti-cancer vaccine and everyone went crazy for it. It wasn't until a giant wave of new pregnancies was reported that they realized that the vaccine reversed contraceptive tweaking, switching fertility back on with a vengeance, even for women who thought they'd turned it off for good. Clinics were overloaded, and most women had no choice but to give birth.

Welcon's baby boom couldn't have come at a worse time. The city was already crammed against its borders.

To add insult to injury, second-child taxes both paid for the building of New Triton—the raising of the rich— and made life all but impossible for the low-paid workers who lived below. My brother was one of the children born in the Welcon boom, and I'm pretty sure my father died from overwork and exhaustion from trying to pay taxes.

Everything miserable that's happened to my family can

be traced back to Welcon Pharmaceuticals fast-tracking a drug that hadn't been tested properly.

Though I should know better than to let my guard down with my competitors and risk being caught as an imposter, I can't keep silent.

"How does it feel?" My stomach churns as I admit the truth. "I should care that the Skins aren't tested. But I don't." I meet Cale's gaze, my caution overcome by the need to know whether he felt the same as I did when he transferred into his Skin. Being the leopard feels like peeling a useless body away and becoming something I'm *meant* to be. Is it like that for the others too?

"How much do you care?" I demand. "Would you give up your Skin?"

"No." Cale studies one of his hands, keeping his gaze low, like he's ashamed. "I did care, a lot. But that was before I felt what it was like to use one. Transferring into my Skin was like nothing I could have expected." He glances up at me for just a moment, and I can sense the conflict going on inside his head.

Maybe Cale's not just an over-privileged floater. There's more going on behind that too-handsome face than I gave him credit for.

Sentin clears his throat, and we both look at him. "I've been acutely aware of the risks. But because the experience was more pleasurable than I'd imagined, my reservations matter less." He tilts his head. "Interesting we all feel the same way."

"When I entered the draw, I never thought my name would come up," says Cale. "Over a million entries, and we were the lucky ones."

"A long shot that paid off." Sentin's words sound like he's agreeing, but there's a question in his tone. "The random draw is another interesting factor."

"Why do you say that?" asks Cale.

Instead of answering, Sentin turns to me. "Rayne, when you entered, were you aware of the odds?"

My cheeks warm. "Sure. Didn't everyone know?"

He can tell I'm lying. Perhaps it's those mysterious glasses, or maybe I'm just not very good at it. Either way, his eyes narrow.

"Anyway. Goodnight." Scrambling to my feet, I bolt for the door. As much as I've learned about why we're here and what's going on, I think Sentin might have learned things about me too. And that's the biggest danger yet.

I'm in over my head. Realizing that I'm helping a corporation fast-track new technology that hasn't been tested properly is a shock. Add that to the fact I'll end up in prison when they find out I'm here on false pretenses, and I should be searching for a way out.

But after just one day in my Skin, getting out isn't an option. No matter how dangerous it is to be here, or what terrible things I might help happen, there's only one thing I care about. Only one thing I *need* with an intensity that scares me.

I need to be the leopard.

For that, I'll risk everything.

Chapter Ten

I sleep with the blade tucked under my pillow. For the first time in years I don't have nightmares of desperately searching for William or fighting off evil, faceless men. Instead I dream about running in my Skin, my leopard's paws moving so fast underneath me that it feels like flying. When I wake, I want nothing more than to go back to my dream.

Then I remember. The leopard isn't just a dream.

A moment later I'm out of bed and showering. Man, I could get used to having my own bathroom. Not to mention my own bedroom. Do floaters really live like this? Do they know how lucky they are?

But the best part is knowing I'll get to transfer back into my Skin today. Thinking about it, I find myself singing in the shower.

My band vibrates. I mean, Rayne's band. Who could be calling? Maybe her mother?

Ma must be calling *my* band, desperate to get hold of me. Or maybe they've told her I'm dead? Just another stabbing in a shelter and in spite of the dead girl's tanned skin they wouldn't have bothered checking her DNA. After all, that's what the band does so well.

If I'm dead, then Ma only has William left. One child. No taxes.

I turn my face up to the shower jet and close my eyes. I don't know if I'm crying or if my good eye is stinging because of the force of the water.

Ma's free.

Why didn't I think of it before? As hard as it'll be for her, my death means she can finally live a real life again. Now she can afford to get William back.

It feels like I stand there a long time, letting the hot water pummel my face while my stomach twists into knots. I should be happy for her, so why is my heart pumping lead? Ma's going to be okay. I have to let her go.

Milla's dead. I'm Rayne. I have to focus on becoming her. On winning. With five million credits, I could get my family back. Whether I kept Rayne's name or became Milla again, we could afford to get a house and pay any amount of taxes.

But if I lose the competition, I'll have to stay dead—at least officially—so Ma can live safely with William. Both scenarios are a million times better than the life we were living.

The only way I can really lose is to get found out. Then I'll go to prison, and Ma will be worse off than before. Two living kids, and down to just one income. She'd have to work herself to death like Papa did.

I won't let that happen.

Dressing slowly, I think about taking the blade with me. But I can't afford to get caught with it. Better to hide it here. The room's pretty bare, just the bed, a desk and chair, and a closet that the clothes Doctor Gregory gave me don't come close to filling. The floor's made out of a smooth imitation wood, and the ceiling doesn't have any panels I can lift.

Finally, I carry the chair over to the closet, and stand on it to push the blade to the very back of the top shelf. Hopefully it should be safe enough.

When I get to the rec room it's empty, and cereal is waiting. The others aren't long in arriving, but by the time they do I've already gulped down three full bowls, with a lake of milk and plenty of honey.

Brugan doesn't so much as look at me when he comes in, so he's obviously decided to ignore me. Good. I'll ignore him too, and make sure I'm never alone with him.

Aza complains about the food again, and I roll my eyes when she's not looking. Cale catches me doing it and grins. I shouldn't encourage him, he's way too friendly, but I can't help smiling back. Maybe it's because I've realized Ma won't have to work so hard anymore. Or maybe it's the excitement fizzing inside me, the anticipation of transferring into my Skin. Today I'll get to be neither Rayne nor Milla, but something far better.

"Good morning." Doctor Gregory comes in carrying a bag. "How are you all today?"

"The food—" starts Aza.

"We've all eaten." Cale speaks over her. "We're ready to transfer into our Skins."

Doctor Gregory swipes at some wisps of hair that have escaped her bun. "Instead of going straight to the training room, we're going to have a session here, in the vReals."

So I'm not going to get to transfer into my leopard? I can't keep my face from falling.

"Don't worry, you'll be training in your Skins again this afternoon," says Doctor Gregory. "But this morning you'll run through a simulation of the contest."

It's what I wanted, to find out about the contest. But I feel sick to my stomach.

"Doctor, I can't use a vReal. My eye..."

"Oh. Of course." She looks stumped for a moment, then brightens. "We can wrap your eye to protect it. It won't be as good as being able to use two eyes, but you'll get an idea of what you'll be up against."

I'll have a disadvantage compared to the others, but it's better than nothing.

"The contest is designed to be like the Morelle Corporation's newest vReal game, *Skin Hunter*," she says. "The contest is the game come to life. It'll be released on the same day of the contest, so people will be able to watch you compete before they play the game themselves."

My heart sinks. Sounds like I'll need to learn how to play a vReal game to have any chance at this contest, but I have no idea how my bad eye will react to virtual reality. Will it be like the holo, which it doesn't cope with at all?

"The game's been kept secret," she continues. "Our security's been tighter than for any other new release. But I've got some special advance copies of the game here for you to play."

The other four whoop for joy. My silence must stand out, because the doctor shoots me a small frown before opening her bag. "Anyone need a suit?"

I'm the only one who puts my hand out for one of the cloth suits she pulls out of her bag. Great. The others all play so many vReal games, they have their own suits.

"Go and get changed, then we'll get started."

I finger the thin fabric of the suit and stay where I am.

"Are you all right, Rayne?"

"Um." I wait until the others have gone before I motion to the vReal units. "I haven't used one of those things before."

Doctor Gregory blinks. "Didn't you work in a factory that made them?"

"I guess someone forgot to install a rec room at the factory."

It's supposed to be a joke, but she reddens a little anyway. "Of course. Go and change, then I'll show you how to play."

I head back to my room and struggle into the vReal suit, hating the tight fit and the way it clings. I feel totally exposed. Do I really have to leave my room in this thing? Some pro players go naked instead of wearing a suit in the vReal because they think the fabric dulls the signal. Ha! Now I've got one on, I don't see how this suit could block anything.

I crack open the door and peer down the hall. There's nobody in sight. With any luck the others are already in their units.

I find myself tiptoeing instead of walking normally down the hall, resisting the urge to cover myself with my hands. Dammit, how can people be so casual about these stupid suits? I've seen people wear them in public, and not just around the entrance to a gaming room, but even walking down the street, as though they want to be ready to jump into a vReal unit at any second.

When I get to the rec room, three units are upright, and I can see hazy shapes through the semi-transparent outer shells. The vReals look like giant eggs with cables and wires snaking out of them. Cale's the only one not in his yet. He's still putting his helmet on.

He turns to look as I walk in and my face goes hot. And when his eyes flick down my body, my heart lurches and my palms go damp. An automatic reaction to danger. In the shelter, a look like that would mean I'd be extra cautious.

Not here, though. I need to calm down. Take a deep breath. Cale's not likely to be a threat. He's not the type. Anyway, what would Mr. High Cheekbones want with someone like me?

"Here you go, Rayne." Doctor Gregory holds up a piece of cloth. "It has an anti-magnetic surface that should block the force enough so your eye won't be damaged."

By the time she's finished winding the cloth around my eye, Cale's a shadow moving inside one of the vReals. I move to the last unit and press the button to slide it open. Inside it's empty, but once I'm in, it'll fill with gel. I used to like feeling the stuff at the factory, sticking my hand in as it oozed from the machine that made it. When it moved by itself, I flinched. Though it looked like it should be sticky, it pulled away from my skin as if I repelled it.

Picking up the helmet on the floor of the giant egg, I tug it on, making sure it doesn't pull the cloth off as it slides over my face. The helmet is connected to the top of the egg by a retracting cable that shortens as I step into the unit.

Once the door shuts, sealing me inside the unit, gel oozes in. This is the bit I've been dreading. Theoretically the gel can't get in my helmet, and I'll be able to breathe. But what if the cable gets blocked? What if the helmet seal leaks?

"Okay Rayne?" Doctor Gregory's voice comes through the speaker in my helmet, startling me. "Don't be afraid to talk normally. It's perfectly safe."

"Easy for you to say," I mutter. The egg's almost full now, and the gel is lifting me. Though I can see myself rising, I can't feel any pressure on my body.

I know exactly how a vReal shell is made. I could describe the shape of every mechanical part and how it fits. Plenty of times I've imagined how claustrophobic it must be inside the egg-shaped shell, but the feeling of floating surprises me. This must be what weightlessness feels like.

"When you're comfortable, say *Ready*. If you say *Stop*, it'll switch off and drain so you can get out. *Pause* by saying the word. It's simple."

"Okay." I take one more deep breath. "Ready."

My helmet goes dark for a moment, then floods with light. I'm outside and now I'm not wearing a helmet, or even a vReal suit. Instead, a heavy cloak weighs down my shoulders and flutters behind me as I stand on the precipice of a high cliff. A long way below, a wide, flat plain stretches away. The sky looks closer and bluer than I've ever seen it.

When I look down, I'm wearing boots. Snow crunches underfoot as I shift my weight. I've never seen snow before, and it's beautiful. The breeze lifts the edge of my cloak, flapping it around my legs. The air is cold against my face.

The wind increases, getting so strong that I need to lean into it.

It's too strong. It's going to push me off the cliff.

I twist around and try to grab onto something, but the wind lifts me off my feet. Pain burns through my eye as I fall. Clapping both hands to my face, they smack hard against the invisible helmet. The pain intensifies as the ground rushes toward me.

But I slow just in time and the searing pain eases as I land lightly on the snow-covered ground at the bottom of the cliff. My legs buckle, and I stagger.

What the hell was that? I know it's just magnetic pulses running through the gel that somehow made me feel like I was falling, but it sure wasn't my idea of fun. And my face is throbbing.

Now the ground is shaking, an earthquake breaking it

apart. Something's coming up out of the ground. Giant letters. Words. They rise out of the snow and settle like huge boulders. I read, *Skin Hunter*, before my eye burns with pain again.

The words are breaking apart. They reform themselves into a longer sentence: *A Morelle Corporation Multi-Format Event*.

"Rayne, are you okay?"

"Pause." The word comes out panicked.

Everything freezes. Another sharp pain sears through my bad eye and I realize it must be moving by itself. My cybernetic eye's trying to stare out the back of my head.

"Are you all right?" she demands.

"My eye keeps trying to turn in its socket."

The doctor lets out an audible sigh. "I was afraid it might. The magnetic field created by the gel is very strong. Even with the wrapping, it's pulling at the metal components in your eye. Don't worry, it won't be strong enough to tear any of your nerves or tendons that hold the eye in place."

"Are you sure?"

"Absolutely."

Dragging in a breath, I try to calm my racing heart. "I fell off a cliff."

She chuckles. "I should have warned you. It's like the opening credits of a movie. Very dramatic, I know. But soon you'll find yourself in the arena that'll look exactly like when you play the game for real. From then on, everything will obey the laws of physics, I promise."

I take another deep breath. Though I'm not a fan of the vReal, I need to keep playing. Still, when I think of another question for Doctor Gregory, I know I'm only asking to give myself a few more seconds before starting it back up. After all, I'm going to find out the answer for myself soon enough.

"This game is called *Skin Hunter*, right?" I ask.

"That's right."

"What are we going to be hunting?"

She hesitates. I hear nothing but silence for a long moment. Then she says, "I'm sorry Rayne, but you've asked the wrong question. It's not what you'll be hunting. The question is, what will be hunting you?"

Chapter Eleven

"Ready."

I'm back where I was, at the base of the cliff. For a moment the letters are still frozen, then they fly at me like shrapnel. I don't move, don't even flinch. Sure enough, they miss me by a hair's breath, so close I feel the wind against my cheeks as they fly past.

"Please choose your Skin," says a woman's voice in my ear. It's not Doctor Gregory's voice, so it must be part of the game.

Five Skins appear on the snowy plain in front of me. The virtual reality versions look just like they do in real life. My leopard's so beautiful, I can't believe anyone would want to choose any of the others.

Sentin's reptile steps forward. No, not that one. I lift my hand and make a swiping motion. It steps back and Brugan's Skin steps forward. I swipe again and my leopard steps forward, which must mean it's selected. But how do I choose it?

Feeling foolish, I walk toward it, first pointing, then

making random hand gestures. Something I do works, because my leopard comes to meet me. When it's close enough, it leaps as though it's going to land on me, but instead of hitting me it melts away and I feel myself change. Now I have four paws instead of two feet. I can even feel my tail.

But it's nothing like being inside my real Skin. I don't have that amazing feeling like I'm fast and strong, and all my senses are turned up to full power.

My bad eye's twisting in its socket, shooting pain though my head. Looking with just my good eye means I can't see anything on my left side, and it's hard to judge distance. Yeah, I'm still just me. No matter how much I wish I wasn't.

The woman's voice again: "Are you ready to play *Skin Hunter*?"

I don't need to reply. The ground's already shifting under my paws, changing from snow into stone paving. I thought Doctor Gregory said the game would obey the laws of physics?

It's not just the ground that's changing. Everything's fading and becoming something else. It's like I'm underwater for a moment, then when the world goes solid I find myself at the bottom of a circular arena that's so tall it seems to go up forever. The sides of the arena are lined with countless levels of seats, all the way to the top. All the seats are full of people. Thousands upon thousands of spectators.

I know where I am. I heard about this arena when the Morelle Corporation built it, but this is the first time I've been inside it. The floor of the stadium is in Old Triton, and it rises through New Triton and up into the sky, going up a hundred and sixty stories. It's an incredible sight. What did the ads say? *An arena symbolic of our vertical city. It brings old and new together in one structure, uniting both layers of Triton.*

Amazingly enough, the real thing lives up to the hype.

Inside the arena, the space is mostly filled with an enormous metal frame, as tall as a scraper. It's a single building that looks like it goes all the way to the top of the arena. The structure is tapered, so the top is narrow while the base is wide. It has no solid walls, only beams and platforms that crisscross in complicated patterns. It reminds me of the Eiffel Tower, the most famous of the buildings that are now rusting and crumbling in the dead zone.

Craning my head back to see the top of the tower, its height makes me dizzy. Are we supposed to climb it?

That must be why there's a climbing wall in our training room.

Is the contest a race to the top? Good thing I'm not afraid of heights. If this is a climbing race, Aza's wings will give her an advantage. Brugan's Skin looks heavy and his muscles might slow him down. I have no idea how well my leopard can climb, but I guess I'm about to find out.

As I pad closer to the tower, the crowd roars. I flinch, tilting my chin down to hide my scarred face from thousands of eyes.

Except I'm a leopard, and my face isn't scarred. Not to mention that this isn't even real.

Shaking my head at myself, I head for one of the tower's thick legs.

The structure has levels, like a normal building. But where each floor should be is just a framework of beams. The first level would be too high off the ground for a person to leap up to. But a leopard? Easy.

I spring up to the first beam and pace, claws clacking, along the length of metal. The tower looks even bigger once I'm inside it. I can barely see the far side, both because of the distance, and because my view is blocked by interspersed diagonal struts at steep angles that run up to the tower's next level. The horizontal beams on this level have such wide gaps between them that they'll be tricky to navigate. Basically, there's a lot of empty space for falling through.

Still, if this what the contest will be like, it's not as hard as I'd feared. Man, I really hope this is all I'll have to do. Racing up this tower should be easy once I'm in my actual Skin. I might even win a race to the top, even against Aza.

As I'm about to spring to a beam on the next level, I catch a movement to the side. I jerk my head around and another pain sears through my bad eye. My vision goes blurry. Shit! I blink furiously until my sight clears enough to see what was moving.

It's only an insect.

I must be more jittery than I realized. Startled by a bug.

But the bug doesn't look like anything I've seen before. Its body blends in with the metal beam so I only see it when it moves. I stretch my head forward for a closer look. The thing's body is made of nuts and bolts. Its legs are nails and wire, all different lengths. A little robot, thrown together from bits of scrap. Its uneven legs are jerking up and down to drag it forward.

Weird.

It's coming straight for me. Its hinged mouth drops open as though it means to take a bite out of me. Surely this metal bug can't hurt me?

Rather than sticking around to find out, I spring to the next ledge. Chains are dangling over the beam, short lengths that twist over and around it in loose loops, so I have to be careful where I set my paws.

Though I've only climbed two levels, when I look down, I'm amazed at how far below the ground is.

A clanking sound makes me jump. A length of chain slides toward me, scraping along the metal beam. It's moving by itself. What the hell? And now another chain is moving.

Suddenly, all the chains on the beam come to life. The links at my feet slither across the metal surface like clanking snakes. The closest chains lift their metal ends from the beam to strike at me. Heart thumping, I jump back to evade them.

Cold metal touches my back paw and loops around it. I leap sideways, yanking my leg free. The chains are moving faster. One flies at my eyes. I jerk my head just in time and it cuts into the side of my face. Ouch!

My breath comes short and hard, and blood runs hot over my face. I've got to get off this ledge. As the chain draws back for another strike, I barely have time to leap sideways, scrabbling for a narrow, sloping beam, the only one I can reach.

Pain sears through my bad eye as I jump. The beam I land on slopes on a steep angle, but I dig my claws into the metal, and though I'm teetering, I'm safe. The chains on the beam I came from have collapsed and lie completely still. Dead. As though I imagined the whole thing. But the side of my face is throbbing and sticky with blood, and my bad eye feels like it's on fire.

A scratching sound from above makes me look up.

Hundreds of mechanical bugs crawl over the beam above me. It's so thick with them, it's writhing. They're all different. Spiders, crickets, beetles and centipedes. A mass of moving bolts, screws, nails, wire, and shards of metal and glass, crawling over each other as they work their way down the beam toward me. Like one creature, their mouths gape open at once.

I've got to get out of here. There's another beam beside me, but the one I'm on is at such an angle that when I let go to jump, I slide backwards. Too late to stop, I leap anyway, trying desperately to reach the next beam in spite of the awkward angle and my lack of momentum.

My front claw touches metal, but the rest of me doesn't make it. I fall, twisting in the air so I'll land on all four paws. I have time to brace as the ground rushes at me.

I land hard. Pain explodes through my bad eye. I curl up and my hands fly to my face, hitting the helmet instead.

"Game Over," says the female voice in my ear. "You made it to level three of one hundred and sixty levels. Your time was twelve minutes and thirteen seconds. You scored 3 points." The voice pauses as though to let me take in the information. Then the woman asks, "Would you like to play again?"

"No." It comes out as a groan. Not being able to practice the game will give me a serious disadvantage in the competition, but the pain in my eye is so intense, I can't go on. I can barely unclench my teeth for long enough to tell the machine to turn itself off.

I can only pray the doctor was right about the vReal not doing any permanent damage to my cybernetics. If I break my eye, I can't afford another.

Chapter Twelve

The others had high scores. Even allowing for exaggeration and lies, they progressed much further through the game than I did. When they laugh about the little metal insects on the first few levels and compare notes about how much bigger and nastier they became further up the tower, I say nothing.

What's the point in complaining when there's nothing anyone can do about the way the vReal messes with my cybernetic eye? I'll just have to be train harder than any of them in my real Skin, that's all.

I can be better than them, I know I can. After all, I have a lot more to lose.

And when I finally get to transfer back into my clouded leopard for real, the euphoria makes up for the morning's disappointment. Being in my Skin is even better than I remembered. I've never been able to see this well, even before I lost my eye. And the smells around me create a 3-D map, with scents lingering where the others have been, leaving a trail that lets me track their movements.

One scent is stronger than the others.

Cale.

Watching the saber-toothed tiger walk from its lab room, I can't help but admire the beauty of it, the easy grace of its movements. But the Skin's scent disturbs me. It calls to me, stirring something so deeply imprinted in the leopard's body that it feels like pure instinct.

The tiger's beautiful head swings to look at me, his gaze finding me so quickly that I know he senses me as well as I do him. His eyes are golden. They hold mine for what seems a long time, sparking a heat that spreads through my belly into my limbs.

But a feline attraction based on scent is the last thing I need. Deliberately, I turn my back on Cale, then head to the other side of the big training room where his scent can't confuse me.

We're competitors. Enemies. Nothing will ever make me forget that.

It's easy enough to put him out of my mind as I lope across the floor, moving far more easily than I did yesterday. I hardly need to concentrate on moving four legs instead of two. Already it feels natural.

And I never imagined my vision could be this good. Looking through the leopard's eyes has brought the world into sharp focus. Until now, I may as well have been living inside a bubble, with everything around me murky and faded. This is waking up. This is being *alive.*

After finding out we'll need to hone our climbing skills for the contest, the others want to get straight onto the big silver climbing wall, so Doctor Gregory calls us all over to explain how it works.

"We call it the never-wall," she says with a smile. "Because it's never just a wall. In fact, it's made up of nano-particles which can instantly bond to form shapes, then break apart and reform. It's set to morph automatically as you climb, so its landscape is constantly changing." She pauses, looking around as though to check we're keeping up. No doubt the others are, but if she can read my leopard's expression it must be blank. "Aza, I had the morph feature switched off yesterday, but as you've already had a little climbing practice, would you help me demonstrate how it works?" When Aza nods, she says, "Please jump to the first platform."

The wasp leaps gracefully. Her wings beat hard, but she still has to clutch on and pull herself up. Her determination to fly hasn't got her there yet.

She clings to the wall, her black wasp face turned to Doctor Gregory. Then her head jerks back to stare upward.

Above her, some of the shapes that jut from the wall are changing. They melt away or transform into new platforms, ramps, or beams. The change ripples downwards, a waterfall of movement. Aza pushes off and leaps to a newly-formed beam as the one she's on gets sucked back into the silver wall. A ladder forms where she was clinging, growing out of the wall in place of the old platform.

"You can get down now," Doctor Gregory calls.

Aza's wings slow her fall so she lands lightly.

The wall's motionless now Aza's off it, the platforms frozen in their new positions. Doctor Gregory says, "The never-wall senses movement and will adjust itself accordingly. If you're not climbing quickly, it gives you more time before reshaping."

"But Aza wasn't moving," objects Cale. "It still morphed."

"Yes, but it did so slowly." She smiles. "It's not designed to let you rest."

Slowly? If that was slow then I can't imagine what fast must be like.

As soon as Doctor Gregory nods that he's free to get on, Brugan jumps onto the never-wall. It's not a smooth, gliding jump like Aza's but a heavy, clumsy leap. He hits the wall hard and only just grabs the first platform. Hauling himself onto a rail, he swings across it to catch hold of a ladder. Above him, the wall is changing. The changes travel down and across at a steady rate. He must see the ripple coming, but Brugan doesn't jump away. Instead he climbs faster, like he's running to meet it head on. The ladder he's on is sucked away one rung at a time, but still he scrambles up. At the last minute, he leaps for a ledge.

Too late.

He falls, crashing to the floor, then jumps straight to his feet, his devil bear eyes blazing, daring anyone to laugh. None of us do, though Aza gives a quiet, barely-there sigh. Maybe the others feel the same as I do. Why laugh when I'm likely to hit the floor just as hard and fast as the devil bear did?

Brugan launches himself back at the silver wall, leaping as though the platform he's aiming for is an enemy he's determined to destroy. Aza does a much more graceful leap, and Sentin follows, clinging so easily with his elongated fingers and toes that it's clear this is what his Skin was designed for.

Looks like Cale's going to try climbing as well, which is a good reason for me to do something else. Besides, the speed I managed yesterday was intoxicating. I want to find out how much faster I can run today.

I start out doing a circuit of the training room, then get brave and move to the treadmill. It automatically matches my speed so I can go as fast or slow as I want. I start with a slow lope and build to a run that's not quite flat out, a little pulled back from top speed, but still it feels so totally exhilarating that my tongue lolls out of my mouth and the corners of my mouth pull up in a feline grin.

The leopard's heart beats faster than my human one, and now it's speeding. But it feels good, not like I've over-done it, but as though I'm just getting started. My paws pound soundlessly over the black rubber as my limbs stretch out and back. Blood pulses hot through my veins... this is bliss! I wish I could run forever. I'm so fast that if I wasn't on a treadmill I'd be a blur. Nobody could ever catch me.

"That's it for today," calls Doctor Gregory. "Time to finish up."

I have to force myself to stop. Already? Time goes too fast in the training room.

The others are still climbing, and I sample their scents on the air.

Aza's doing the most incredible jumps, leaping from ramp to ramp, her wasp wings a red blur of motion. She lands lightly, clinging on with hands and feet for a split second before vaulting to the next ramp. Though the wall's constantly changing, her timing's perfect.

Sentin slithers up a vertical bar, ignoring the horizontal ones on either side. His limbs bend at just the right angle to hold his streamlined body against the smooth bar. He easily pulls himself to the platform above, barely glancing up to see which shapes are changing. His Reptile Skin is faster than I could have imagined.

Cale's quick too, jumping from ramp to ramp like I did when I was playing the game in the vReal. He totters on a ramp that's starting to morph, but instead of dropping he stretches out and stabs his claws into the next one, just managing to pull himself over.

He doesn't seem as good at anticipating the changes as the other two. But when he twists his body and leaps again,

I'm impressed by how agile his saber-toothed tiger is. His long tail's helping, acting as a counterbalance to keep him stable when he leaps. Can my leopard do that? I won't know until I try.

Brugan's lowest on the wall. His fur-covered legs power him up fast enough, but he keeps misjudging the morphing platforms, falling several levels before grabbing hold again. He climbs more like a person than an animal, gripping with his clawed front hands and pushing with his back legs. He's clumsier than the others, but the devil bear looks solid and tough.

Doctor Gregory calls again, and reluctantly the others jump down and head back to their lab rooms. I linger, watching them transfer back into their own bodies, making sure Brugan leaves before I do, and stretching out my time in the Leopard Skin for as long as I can.

I'm the last to leave the training room, and Max is outside, standing stiffly, hands by his sides, like he's practicing for stomper academy. As I go past he murmurs, "Sewer rat."

If my blood wasn't still pumping hot from being the leopard all day, I'd ignore him and walk past. After all, it's not like he hasn't insulted me before.

Instead I stop dead and meet his gaze.

"Careful, sewer rat," he says with a sneer. "Watch your back."

Being threatened by a shark like him should make me run, but the fearlessness from being the leopard is strong. Still, I can't quite believe my own nerve when I move my face closer, tilting it slightly sideways so he's staring into my black cybernetic eye and nightmare of scars. The mess the super-heated fluid made of my face is hard to look at, especially on the side that's angled toward him. I've seen enough disgust and turned-away faces to know most people can't handle it.

My bad eye shows no emotion. It's a hard lens on top of a mass of circuitry. A lens so dark it's like a black hole, sucking away light. It's bad enough on its own, but staring out of the mass of scar tissue that runs in a fleshy, hollowed-out waterfall from my eyebrow to jaw, splashing across to the cheekbone on the other side... yeah, it even gives me chills.

"What are you looking at, freak?"

I don't reply, just let the silence stretch on while I stare at him. Waiting... hoping... to see what I'm looking for.

There.

A slight shadow, a hint of uncertainty ghosts across his eyes.

"Crazy bitch," he mutters, and his feet shift back.

It's enough.

I turn and walk away. Steps slow. Pace measured. My heart's beating wildly, but it's not from fear. It's from jubilation. A vise I hardly knew was there has loosened from around my chest.

From my first day in the shelter all those years ago, I've spent every minute being afraid. Surrounded by grunts with blades, and stompers with guns, my fear has kept me alert. Kept me alive.

Until now.

Now for the first time, those ice-cold fingers have loosened from around my heart.

I'm not afraid.

Without fear, I hardly know who I am. I'm becoming someone new. *Something* new. And damn, does it feel good.

Chapter Thirteen

When we go to the rec room for dinner, the rest of us eat like we're starving, but Aza picks at a tiny bit of food, then moves over to the empty space by the holo. She starts stretching, standing with her legs straight and bending over so her head's against her knees. She's flexible, that's for sure. She's got to be a dancer or some kind of performer.

Brugan stares at her with his mouth open and his fork hovering in mid-air. A lump of food drops onto the table, but he's too busy gobbling her up with his eyes to notice. His expression makes my stomach clench. I've seen men look at women like that too many times in the shelter, and it always means trouble.

I force my gaze back to my food, but my appetite has faded. I can't believe how Aza can just ignore him. It's like she doesn't even notice his expression.

Aza's band goes off and it's a relief when she sits down on the couch to talk. A hologram of a guy's head appears, hovering in the space above her band. His tweaked face makes it obvious he's a floater. Her boyfriend? Her brother? His lips move, but no words come out. None I can hear, anyway. She must have an implant, which is why she can hear him and we can't.

Then Aza's lips start moving without her making any sounds either. A silent conversation. I've heard about sub-vocalization implants, but this is the first time I've seen them in action. Nobody in the shelter could afford implants like hers, but it'd make the place a lot less noisy if they could.

After a minute or two of soundless talking, she discon-nects and the guy's head shrinks back into her band. Then she stands up again, not looking in our direction although we're all watching her. Facing away from us, she sinks into the sideways splits, then shifts her torso so she's looking forward over her front leg. Her chest goes down and touches her knee. Her tight little T-shirt has tugged up, and her snug jeans have ridden down so her lacy underwear shows.

I don't want to look at Brugan, but my eyes move against my will.

He's drooling. No, it's a piece of rice stuck in the corner of his mouth, trembling between those fat lips. Still, he may as well be drooling. The look on his face makes my face feel hot. Man, I so want to let him have it right now. But I know exactly what Tori would say. *"Don't be so damn stupid, Milla. Keep your head down, unless you want it kicked off your shoulders."*

Aza straightens her torso and then twists so she's looking over the opposite leg. Again she bends forward. This time, her back is angled more toward us. Her jeans have ridden down so low, I can see the line of her butt crack under the skimpy lace.

My gaze goes back to Brugan and he must feel it,

because his head turns. "What are you looking at?" he growls.

Sorry Tori, I can't keep quiet.

"You're the one who's staring," I snap.

"I'm not." He puffs up his fat lips, glancing around at the others for support.

"Don't lie, Brugan. I've noticed how you watch me." Aza pushes herself gracefully to her feet and turns to face us, but she barely glances at him as she lifts her arms over her head and stretches.

Her tight T-shirt rides up further to show her tiny waist. Her stomach's decorated with a glittering butterfly tattoo, sparkling jewels set into its wings. As she stretches, the butterfly seems to lift off her skin, its wings fluttering. A hologram.

Her breasts also lift with her movements, her nipples extending out so far, they don't look natural. She must have had them tweaked.

How could I've been so stupid? Aza *wants* Brugan's eyes all over her.

She's not afraid of him, but Brugan is flushed. His discomfort is obvious, as is the way he's trying to keep his desire in check. Weirdly enough, Aza hasn't made herself into a target. Instead, Brugan's lust seems to be giving her power against him. How does that work?

In this world, the rules are clearly different from the ones I'm used to.

When Aza lowers her arms, she shoots Brugan a scornful look. "You can stare all you like, Brugan. I'd never be interested in someone like you."

Brugan goes even redder. Instead of answering her back, his eyes shift to me and narrow into a glare. "You foul bitch," he snarls. "You're so ugly, you make me sick."

I don't know why his insult stings when I've had plenty

that were a lot worse. Still, the words burrow into me, eating through my tough shell. Maybe he's getting to me because I'm clueless about how Aza's weaving a spell that makes him lash out at me instead of her. Or perhaps it's because Aza's butterfly's glinting at me from where her T-shirt's still pushed up. She's so damn shiny it makes me feel even more of a monster. Without thinking about it, my face jerks away to hide the worst of my scars.

Time to go.

But when I stand up, Brugan jumps to his feet as well. We've got the table between us but he's so tall that when he leans forward he's way too close.

"Why don't you learn to keep your ugly mouth shut?" he demands.

Yeah, good question, why the hell did I open my mouth? Aza sure didn't thank me. All I've done is stir up Brugan.

Cale scrapes his chair back. "Leave her alone, Brugan."

Great. Like I can't fight my own battles. Cale probably thinks he's doing me a favor, but he's just making me look weak.

"Aw, how sweet. The two pussycats are sticking together." Aza's lazy voice cuts in.

"Yeah," Brugan snarls. "But the devil bear *eats* kitties."

Aza rolls her eyes. "Shut up, Brugan. God. You're giving me a headache."

She tugs her T-shirt down, smoothing it with her hands in a way that makes her nipples push out harder against the fabric. Then she struts out of the room, hips swaying. As the door shuts behind her, the air relaxes as though everyone in the room has collectively let out their breath.

Brugan looks from me to Cale and back again. "This

isn't over," he says, but I can tell the fight's gone out of him.

"It is." Cale stares him down. "So back off."

Hell, what is *with* him? "I can take care of myself." It comes out angrier than I intend, and Cale's gaze jerks to me.

"What?" He sounds almost comically surprised. Like in his head he was a superhero rescuing a poor damsel from certain danger. A damsel who's just grown claws and ripped his arms off.

"Stop sticking up for me," I snap. "We're not buddies, okay?"

He blinks, and for a moment, his puzzled expression almost makes me feel bad.

Then he shakes his head, his mouth hardening. "Fine." He heads for the couches, flops angrily down in front of the holo, and turns it on.

When it starts up, a man on the screen is mid-sentence, saying something about defusing the tension with Deiterra. A woman interrupts to insist that war is closer than we think, and if the Morelle Corporation starts manufacturing the Skins, it'll be the trigger that forces our neighbors to breach the wall.

Brugan's laugh distracts me from the holo. It's an unpleasant sound. "Bad kitty," he tells me in a mocking tone. Then he swaggers out of the room after Aza.

The old me would have been afraid for her, sure he was going after her. Now I don't know what to think.

"Deiterra can hardly complain about the Skins when one of their own citizens is participating in the contest," says the man on the holo.

Sentin is watching the holo impassively, his expression, as usual, giving nothing away. Is that why he's part of the contest? Did the director arrange for him to be take part so the Deiterrans couldn't complain about the Skins?

Cale stares at him too. "Is it true?" he demands.

Sentin ignores the question. He keeps his gaze on the holo and doesn't so much at glance at Cale.

"Deiterra is making a fuss about nothing," says the man on the holo. "Skins aren't weapons, so they don't breach the treaty. It's ridiculous to limit our technology because of their paranoia."

"It's too dangerous to provoke them," argues the woman. "Why risk starting a war? Besides, the Skin technology hasn't been properly tested, and—"

Cale makes a sound of disgust. He switches off the holo and bounds up from the couch in the same movement. Then he strides to the door as though he can't stand to be in the room another moment.

"Night," he flings over his shoulder, addressing the air between me and Sentin. If it were possible to slam the door after him, he probably would. Unfortunately for him, it slides.

Sentin and I look at each other, the only two left in the room. He's still sitting on the other side of the table, his empty plate pushed to one side. He never says anything or gets involved. And he's always talking to Doctor Gregory.

What is up with him and those mysterious glasses?

As intently as I stare at him, he stares back, unblinking. His eyes are a smoky gray color, and they seem to reflect the light as much as his glasses do, hiding his emotions. Why can I never tell what he's thinking?

One of Sentin's eyebrows twitches up. He looks like he's waiting for me to ask a question. Well, okay, I can do that. It's not like I'm short of them.

"Your glasses," I say. "What do they do?"

He cocks his head, and I get the impression I didn't ask the question he expected. I'm expecting him not to answer, but he says, "The glasses enhance normal vision using thermal imaging and a movement magnification algorithm."

"In English?"

"They detect very small movements and changes in body temperature." He pauses, but must be able to see I still don't get it. "For example, when you become uncomfortable or say something that's not true, your temperature rises and your pulse spikes. It's subtle, but the glasses are highly sensitive."

Does that mean he can read my thoughts? My heart's started beating so fast his damn glasses must be glowing. "You can tell if I lie?"

"It's not you who interests me."

"Then who?"

He doesn't answer, just gives a cryptic half-smile. I swear he's being annoying on purpose.

"Who the hell are you?" I struggle to keep my voice from rising.

"Perhaps you should answer the same question."

"What does that mean?"

His gaze moves down to my band. Rayne's band. My blood stops pumping. His eyes are fixed on the stolen band, like he's making a point. Like he knows I'm an impostor. How much does he know about me?

I drop my hands under the table. But he's already bringing up something on his own band. A holographic image projects from it. A girl's head.

It's Rayne. The real Rayne. Her hair is shorter than when I saw her in the shelter, but it's unmistakably her.

I feel all the blood run out of my face.

Sentin nods as though I've just confirmed his suspicions, which of course I have. My expression must tell him everything.

"At first I thought you could have been her." His tone is conversational. "You're the same age, the same height, and your hair color is similar. If you had a fall from grace, you may have had to move to Old Triton and stop darkening your skin. And you could have been in an accident that scarred your face. It's rare for a New Tritoner to descend. An unlikely scenario, but not beyond the realm of possibility. If anyone else manages to find this image, they may assume you've had a run of terrible luck since it was taken."

"That's exactly what happened." I say, not dropping my gaze.

His mouth twitches as he switches off the display. "I'll keep your secret."

My heart is beating too fast. I can't bluff while he's wearing those damn glasses. "What do you want from me?" I demand.

"I told you, it's not you I'm interested in."

Sentin could have me removed from the contest and sent to prison. I can't believe he'd keep quiet without asking for something in return. The world doesn't work that way.

"I don't understand," I say.

"Not many do. But this is bigger than you or I, Rayne." He says the name deliberately. "The next few weeks have the potential to change our world forever. And I may need your help in the days to come."

Great. He means to hold my secret over me. Whatever cryptic cause he thinks he's part of, he intends to drag me into it.

I push my chair back from the table and stand up. "What kind of help?"

He unfolds his lanky body from the table too, pushing his glasses more securely onto his nose. "There are several variables in play. I can't tell yet what kind of help I may need, just that the possibility exists."

I stare after him as he walks for the door, my fists clenched in frustration. Once he's gone, I drag in several deep breaths, trying to calm my racing heart.

I should have known my secret wouldn't stay hidden for long. How many others already know the truth? The director? The doctor? Have they also figured out my scars hide a face that isn't Rayne's?

If only I didn't need any human name. I don't want to be Rayne, and I sure as hell don't want to be Milla. All I want is to forget about them both and be the leopard forever.

Man, how I wish.

Chapter Fourteen

Once back in my room, I stand on the chair to get my blade out of the closet. But that night, even with my fingers curled around its hilt for comfort, I lie awake in the darkness.

What is Sentin up to? Why would he keep my secret? Was today the last day I'll ever get to be the leopard? And if he doesn't spill the beans, what crazy plot is he planning to drag me into?

Sometime before dawn I doze off, and when I wake I feel calmer. Whether they find out I'm not Rayne isn't something I can control, and worrying won't help.

If Tori were here she'd tell me to forget about everything except what's important. Winning the contest. A new life for Ma and William. Learning how to use my Skin.

There are ten days until the contest, which means only ten days of practice. I have to work hard to be better than everybody else.

The thought tugs me out of my warm, comfortable bed. It's still so early that I have to turn on the light to find my clothes. I put my blade back in its hiding place, then head to the training room.

There's a guard posted at the door. Is it Max? No, it's a woman. Her red uniform still gives me the creeps.

Her lip curls as she watches me come close. Some floaters seem to take it as a personal insult that while they're tweaked to perfection, my face scares children.

"Can I use the training room?" I ask, stopping a good distance away.

"Not without Doctor Gregory, Director Morelle, or another authorized person present." She looks happy to be turning me down.

Dammit. What now?

The only other way to train for the contest is to use the vReal. As much as it hurts my eye, as afraid as I am of permanently damaging its cybernetics, what choice do I have? Having to twiddle my thumbs until Doctor Gregory turns up would drive me seriously insane.

I'm heading to the rec room when I run into Cale. He's slipping out of one the doors off the hall. Weird. I thought all those doors led to offices. He'd have to swipe his band to get in, and surely the security system wouldn't let him through?

"Oh. Hi, Rayne." He flushes, reaching up to push his fringe off his forehead, and I can tell I've caught him doing something he shouldn't.

"What's in there?" I ask.

"Nothing. Just, you know. Offices and stuff."

"Wasn't the door locked?"

He hesitates a moment, looking at me as though trying to decide whether he can trust me. Then he pulls a little metal stick from his pocket. "I used this. Ninety-nine credits from a dodgy electronics store down in Old Triton. You'd think the security in a place like this would be a little more up-to-date, wouldn't you?" He shoots me his disarming grin. "Amazing how a building used to create Skin technology can still be using band-readers they probably installed back in the forties."

"Doesn't sound right."

Surely the Morelle Corporation wouldn't let him get away with breaking into an office? They must be monitoring us. I glance up. Though I haven't spotted a camera yet, they've got to be hidden up there. And a cheap electronic gadget unlocking their doors? No way. Something strange is going on.

"Looking for cameras?" he asks. "There might be some. But do you know how huge this place is? They can't possibly watch everything all the time."

"You think?"

He shrugs. "Nobody came running to stop me."

I can't believe he's being so casual. Isn't he worried about getting kicked out of the competition?

"Anyway, what are you doing up so early?" he asks. "Heading to the rec room? Are you hungry, or are you planning to have another go at the game?"

"Hungry," I lie in a curt voice, hoping he'll get the hint and leave me alone.

"Good, I'm starving. I'll come with you."

Dammit, that screws up my plan to get some alone time in the vReal. I don't need an audience or want any of the others to know about the problem I had with it. Let alone letting anyone see me in that embarrassing skin-tight vReal suit. But what can I do to get rid of him?

Oblivious to my inner turmoil, the object of my frustration gets himself breakfast before sitting at the table. Watching him act like all this is totally normal, I get angrier and angrier with both him and myself. Why is it so hard to tell him to get lost? Is it that boyish grin? The way he talks to me as though I'm just like him?

Whatever it is, I can't afford to get suckered in by it.

"Everything okay?" he asks.

I slam myself into the chair opposite him. "Look, Cale, we aren't friends. I don't want to eat breakfast with you. And I don't want you to stick your nose in my business again, like you did last night. I can look after myself, all right?"

He stares at me, the cereal spoon half-way to his mouth. Instinctively I jerk my head away so my hair falls over the worst side of my face. I know it's stupid when he's already seen my scars, but I hate people staring at me. Especially someone with a face that's so perfect.

"You're not really here for breakfast, are you, Rayne? You were going to use the vReal." His tone is level. Unaffected by my anger.

"So?"

"Yesterday you started after everyone else, and you were out of your unit well before I was, which means you weren't playing very long. Is it your eye?"

"No."

"Want me to give you some pointers on how to play?"

"Why?"

"Why wouldn't I?"

I shake my head in disbelief. "Seriously, don't you ever give up? Do I need to wear a sign? We're not friends."

With a shrug, he sticks the spoonful of cereal in his mouth and chews it. His eyes are a rich, warm brown, and his long dark eyelashes make them striking. He's a total mystery. Rich and privileged, and so good-looking he must have girls falling at his feet. Why is he even *talking* to me? Does he pity me because of my scars?

"All I want is to beat you in the contest." My voice

softens against my will. "And you should be figuring out how to try to beat me. Not offering to help."

"You won't have a chance unless you let me give you a few tips, so why don't you just say yes?"

"Because I don't know what you think you're going to get out of it."

"I want to help you. Is that so hard to understand? Do you want Brugan to win?"

"Of course not."

He puts his spoon down and looks a little sheepish, like he's about to make an embarrassing confession. "Listen Rayne, I play professionally."

"What?"

"You're looking at last year's *Hellspawn* national champion. A hundred thousand credits in prize money."

My stomach sinks. I'm up against a pro gamer? And I'd thought Cale would be the easiest competitor to beat.

"A hundred grand?" I repeat. I had no idea the prizes were that high for gaming competitions.

"I know what you're thinking." He screws up his nose. "There are people starving and they give away all that money for playing a vReal game. It's not right."

That's not what I'm thinking. I don't care how much he's won, except it tells me I've underestimated him. "What's *Hellspawn*?" I ask.

"It's an RPG, first person shooter hybrid. You start as a dead soul and have to move up through the demon ranks by killing other demons..." I still look blank and his explanation trails off. "Anyway, I can help you in the vReal, and in return you can help me."

"Help you how?"

"You have skills I don't. Let's be allies, at least for now."

"What skills do I have?"

He hesitates, then picks up his spoon again. But instead of taking another mouthful of cereal, he jiggles the spoon between his finger and thumb. "It's obvious you're from Old Triton. The others are saying you were working in a factory. Is it true?"

I tense at the question. I shouldn't be surprised they've speculated about me. Rayne's not a sinker's name, but Sentin was right and occasionally floaters can fall, literally, to the bottom of the city. Some starve before they can find work. Others end up like Rayne. A few get lucky and find a place in a factory.

"I'm good in the vReal," Cale says when I don't answer. "But that game is virtual. The Skins are real, and reality never goes as well for me as games do." His gaze stays on me, direct and true. The spoon in his hand has stilled. "I'm not prepared for this competition. Compared to you, I've had it easy. I've never even been in a fight."

"So?"

"I think you can help me."

"Because I've had to fight?"

He finally scoops up another spoonful of cereal. "Exactly."

I shake my head. He was embarrassed to tell me he was a gaming champion, but all trace of shame disappeared when he admitted he wasn't ready for the competition. For anyone else in the world, it would have been the other way around, but weirdly, his take on things makes me like him a lot more than I want to.

Cale is a mystery, but he doesn't seem dangerous. Not like Sentin.

Heaven help me, I think I'm even starting to feel comfortable around him. Maybe it's because he doesn't have any problem meeting my eyes, and I've never seen him flinch when he looks at my face. He acts like my scars aren't there.

"I don't understand you, Cale," I say truthfully.

"There's time." He's about to put the heaped spoon in his mouth, but pauses. "You're not going to eat?"

"Not hungry," I admit.

"Then why don't you get into your vReal suit while I finish this?"

In spite of my misgivings, I do what he says. Doctor Gregory wrapped the anti-magnetic bandage once around my eye, but by stretching it, I can fit it twice around. I secure it a lot tighter than she had it, hoping that'll help.

And once I'm in my suit I also wrap a towel around myself so I don't look naked. Cale looks bemused when I walk back into the rec room wearing a towel over my suit, but doesn't mock me for it.

Dropping the towel at the last minute, I climb quickly into the vReal and manage to get it going. I'm bracing myself to get swept off the cliff and feel that searing pain through my cybernetic eye again, when I hear his voice in my helmet.

"You can skip the intro if you want, Rayne."

"I can? How?"

"Just say, 'Skip intro'."

"Why didn't Doctor Gregory tell me that?"

"She probably doesn't know the shortcuts. I mean, she's pretty old. I doubt she even plays." His voice sounds like he's fighting a laugh. "Anyway, I'm a much better person to give you pointers. National *Hellspawn* champion, remember?"

"Skip intro," I say. Sure enough, the wind vanishes, the cliff dissolves, and I find myself standing on the white snowy plain with five Skins in front of me. As soon as I've chosen my leopard, the arena appears.

Instead of climbing the tower right away, I pace around, gazing up at it. I keep catching glimpses of movement, shadows flickering across surfaces.

"Tell me about the metal tower," I say. "But just because I'm asking doesn't mean I'll agree to help you in return."

"Well, its AI is sophisticated." I swear I can hear the grin in his voice. "And most events are randomized to make them unpredictable."

"The tower *thinks*?"

"That's right. The structure is made up of thousands of components, all of which have a simple electronic brain. They're networked together so each piece can work as part of the collective. It's programmed to do a number of things, depending on where you are on the structure, but there's an element of randomness. If you jump on the same beam each time, you'll keep getting a different reaction."

I frown, trying to understand. "So the bugs are bits of the tower?"

"Exactly. Every nut, screw and bolt has its own basic electronic brain. The bugs form themselves spontaneously."

"They make themselves up? And the chains came alive because they saw me coming? I didn't see any eyes."

"The tower's covered with electronic sensors. And it's networked, remember? Every piece of it knows exactly where you are."

Great. Now I *really* don't want to jump onto it. The thought that a giant tower of steel parts is going to feel me walking on it and figure out how to throw me off is creepy.

But this is what I'll be facing on the day of the contest and I need to learn how to beat it. To win, I'll have to make it to the top. My eye is starting to hurt, but I ignore it. I can do this. I have to do this.

"What's the best way to get up the tower?" I ask.

"As fast as you can."

"So helpful," I mutter. Then, "Here goes."

I leap onto the structure. This time, instead of stopping to judge my next move, I keep going, leaping from beam to beam.

In spite of double-wrapping the bandage, pain stabs through my eye each time I jump. The pain is strong enough to throw me off my stride, and one of my leaps falls hopelessly short. I stretch out in mid-air and manage to catch hold of a beam with my front claws. They're sharp enough to dig into the metal, but my weight lands hard on my front legs and shoulders.

Clinging on with only my front claws, I hang from the beam, swinging in space. Should I even be doing this? What if I break my eye? I've already lost my band. If I lose both my eye and the contest, I'll be left with nothing.

More importantly, if my human body is blind in one eye, will my leopard still be able to see with both eyes? Maybe my attempt to get an edge in the competition will end up seriously disadvantaging me.

I shake my head at myself. No time to worry about it while I'm dangling from a beam. I'm in the vReal now. Nothing to do but get myself back on the metal and to the top of the tower.

Can I haul myself up? I claw at the air with my back legs like I'm dog-paddling through water and heave with all my strength.

My back paws are almost on the metal when the beam makes a loud groaning noise that's too loud to have been caused by my weight. The sound startles me and I miss my grip with my back claw. I drop back, dangling from the beam by my front legs again.

The groaning gets louder. A few inches from my paw, a rivet flies out of the metal like a bullet. It whistles past my head and hits the beam behind me with a sharp crack.

There are metal rivets spaced along the edge of the beam. I stare at them in horror. Will the structure fire the rest at me?

Another groan and the next closest rivet bursts free. I duck my head just in time for it to miss me.

The next one's underneath my paw.

Though I'm already scrambling away from it, the rivet flies out too quickly and my paw's still over it when it fires. Sharp pain sears through my right paw. Blood sprays out, hot and wet over my fur.

One paw isn't enough to hold my weight, and my claws scrape off the beam.

I drop five floors. The landing sends searing pain through my eye, making me groan with pain.

"Game over. You made it to level five of one hundred and sixty levels. Your time was three minutes and ten seconds. You scored 5 points. Would you like to play again?"

I already hate that voice.

"No," I say. Then "Shit."

"Are you all right?" asks Cale.

"I'm coming out."

As soon as I pull the helmet off, I flex my right hand, examining it. Of course there's nothing there, not a mark, let alone a hole where a rivet tore through it. I'm not hurt. And my eye has stopped hurting now too.

"That was quick," says Cale, holding out my towel. "What happened?"

I shake my head, wrapping the towel back around my

suit. Truth is, I'm disgusted with myself for doing so badly. I need to stop letting myself be distracted by pain and try again until I beat the damn thing.

But my hand... I don't know, it just felt so real.

"Was it the Kraken?" he asks.

"The what?"

"You know, the big creature with all the tentacles. Starts appearing about level fifty." He pauses for me to say something, and when I don't, his eyes widen. "Tell me you've seen the Kraken. You must have made it up that far?"

Instead of answering, I tear the bandage off my bad eye and squeeze it like it's to blame. My chest feels tight. Level fifty? How did he get that high so quickly?

"That's not a great sign." His voice softens. "How are you going to do it for real if you can't play when the game is fake?"

"When it's real, I'll get to the top."

He raises one eyebrow. "You sure?"

I grit my teeth. "Watch me."

Chapter Fifteen

S entin hasn't told anyone I'm an impostor. Not yet. But I'm determined to find out more about him, to figure out how much of a danger he might be.

After breakfast, when we're allowed in the training room, the others transfer into their Skins and go straight to the never-wall.

As usual, getting into my Leopard Skin fills me with energy. My disappointing session in the vReal fades away, replaced by a feeling of being invincible. I can't wait to see how well I can climb the never-wall, but instead I hang back and wait until the others are on the wall, leaping and clawing their way up with grim determination.

Now's my chance to talk to the doctor, while she's watching them climb.

"Hey, Doctor Gregory." I nod my leopard head toward the silver wall. "Happy with how it's all going? Everyone doing okay in the Skins?"

"Excellent, Rayne. But you haven't tried the never-wall yet?" She sounds distracted. Her gaze flicks down to the tablet she's holding and she makes some notes before looking back up at the wall, watching the others. Good. If she's distracted, hopefully she won't wonder why I'm asking questions.

I sit down to make myself seem smaller and less obtrusive, if that's possible. The doctor isn't short, but I feel enormous next to her. I could probably take off her head with a swipe of one paw—not that I ever would.

"I do want to try the never-wall. But I was wondering if you were worried about what the competitors would be like? I mean, before we turned up. The contest was a random draw, wasn't it? You could have been saddled with anyone."

"Not *completely* random, as you know." She shoots me a quick smile, flashing her dimples. "But yes, we've been lucky. All five of you have impressed me immensely."

My ears prick toward her. Good thing she's not paying full attention to me, or she'd catch my curiosity. If only I could ask what she means by the contest draw not being random.

"So we're all doing okay in the Skins?" I ask instead.

"Absolutely. You're exceptionally well suited for the contest."

"Our backgrounds, you mean?"

"That's part of it." She makes some more notes on her tablet.

With my leopard's heightened senses, I can't hear any suspicion in her voice.

"What is it about our backgrounds, do you think?" I ask.

"Well… an example would be that Brugan and Aza are both athletes, which means they're aware of their own physicality. That makes it easier for them to adapt to a Skin."

"Athletes?"

"Haven't they told you?" She hesitates, and now I have her full attention. I can detect faint changes in her scent. She *smells* wary. "I suppose they won't mind me talking about their achievements," she says slowly. "It's public knowledge."

I flick my ears forward, lowering my head to look as small as I can. "I'm sure they won't mind."

Her gaze goes back to the competitors scaling the wall. "Well, both are outstanding in their separate disciplines. Aza's a gold-medal gymnast, and Brugan plays professional loopball."

"And Sentin?"

"Sentin's not as physical, but I understand he's the youngest student ever to achieve a doctorate in military tactics. He went to university here in Triton."

"Military Tactics?" That's the last thing I'd have guessed. "Is he with the army?" A lot of soldiers were reassigned to stomper duty after the Welcon riots, but if we end up going to war with Deiterra, that'll change fast.

"Oh, no. He's *Deiterran*." She shoots me a sideways look as though it were a silly question. "But he moves well, don't you think?" She nods to where Sentin's scaling the wall. "His center of gravity is quite different from yours. He hugs the wall more, see?"

I grunt my agreement, too distracted to say more. The contest draw can't have been random at all. They just happened to get two sports stars, a military genius, and a pro vReal player? No way. It must have been rigged.

Wonder what Rayne's skill was? Whatever they expect from me, I can only hope it won't be too obvious when I fall short.

The doctor glances at me again. "It's only natural to be curious. But if you want to know more about the others' backgrounds, you should ask them directly."

Sentin jumps off the wall and turns to look at us. Perhaps he senses we've been talking about him. For all I know, his hearing could be so good he might even have heard us. And his reptile eyes are probably just as sharp as his glasses, helping him to see the secrets I want to keep hidden.

"Has anyone been asking about me?" I ask the doctor, pitching my voice low.

"Don't worry, I wouldn't say anything they couldn't easily find out on the net."

Wish I could do a search to see what the net says about Rayne, but without a band, I'm blind.

"Who's been asking about me?"

She shakes her head. "As I said, being curious is natural. Are you going to climb now, Rayne? Or did you want to try something new?"

"New? Like what?" I'm instantly wary. The climbing wall's sure to be a big enough challenge, and finding out who I'm really up against has shaken me.

"I can show you how to use the battle bot."

"The what?"

"Come on." She leads me to the large silver circle set into the floor. It's close to the wall and roped off with a rubber cord running around it. The circle looks like it's made from the same silver stuff as the never-wall.

Against the wall is a locker. The doctor opens it and takes out a silver metal skull.

it has cybernetic eyes, newer and more high-tech than mine. They look like real eyes with pale blue irises, and it's only my sharp leopard vision that lets me glimpse the circuits hidden underneath.

"The battle bot can take any form," says Doctor Gregory. "Watch."

She puts the skull down on the silver circle and it triggers movement on the floor of the boxing ring. The silver floor turns to liquid. It flows over and under the skull, covering it and building a body to support it. It's like silver water pouring itself upward to create a silver person.

The skull becomes a human head. Ice-blue eyes stare out of a featureless face. Its body is a plain metal mannequin, bigger than a regular human, about the same size as Sentin's Skin.

"This is the battle bot," says Doctor Gregory. "It's made out of the same nano-particles as the never-wall."

"It fights?"

She nods. "The nano-particles will give way under pressure, so you won't get hurt when it hits you. I can set the bot to automatic mode, and it'll be controlled by a sophisticated AI. Or, you can—"

She cuts off as I turn to the training room door. Over the noise of the others panting, grunting, thumping and clawing up the never-wall, I've caught the click and swish of the door opening.

It's Director Morelle.

What's she doing here? Has she discovered I'm an imposter?

My body is stiff, except for my tail twitching back and forth, a reflex action that feels so natural it'd be an effort to stop. I flare my nostrils for the director's scent, but all I get is a sharp floral perfume, the tang of a chemical that must have been used to clean or press her navy suit.

Underneath that is a hint of shoe polish and whatever hair products she uses to make her bobbed hairstyle so sleek and perfect. I can't catch any hint of her body excretions to detect what she's feeling, especially because Max is by her side, his stride arrogant, arms swinging and boots clomping. The closer he gets the more his smell overwhelms everything. His scent makes my nostrils burn. It screams hostility.

"I've asked Max to assist with the battle bot," says Director Morelle, stopping next to us.

The casual way her gaze moves over me lets me breathe again. I hadn't even realized I'd been gripping the floor with my claws until I feel them relax. She's not here to throw me out. But how can she not know the truth? Sentin discovered my secret easily enough. Even if he hasn't let it slip, it's hard to believe she doesn't know I'm not Rayne.

When she looks at me, I drop my gaze. Then I jerk my head back up. No, I'm not going to question whether she knows. I'm not even going to think about it, in case she can somehow read what I'm feeling. I'm not Rayne or Milla. I'm the leopard, that's all that matters. I belong in the Leopard Skin.

The other competitors jump off the wall and gather around as Director Morelle starts to talk.

"The battle bot has two modes," she tells us. "There's an automatic mode, with the computer controlling the robot. There's also a manual mode so you can fight another player, which Max will now demonstrate." She nods at Max. He turns to the same locker the doctor got the metal skull out of, takes out a helmet, and puts it on.

"The helmet enables Max to see through the bot's eyes. Sensors detect his movements and transmit them to the bot."

In the fighting ring, the battle bot changes. Its blank face transforms into Max's face, and now it has his body. It's a giant silver Max carved from metal, mimicking every detail of his features and clothing, but without any color except for those cybernetic blue eyes.

The real Max, his face covered by the black helmet,

bends his knees and lifts his arms, moving into some kind of martial arts stance. The silver copy in the ring mirrors him exactly, settling into the same stance.

On the wall above the fighting ring, a digital sign lights up.

BOT: 0 | CHALLENGER: 0

Director Morelle looks at me, and I know what she's about to say.

"Max needs an opponent. Rayne, would you...?"

Looking at Max's hate-filled eyes, I want to refuse. If he beats me in front of everyone, they'll see me as weak. If I beat him, he'll find a way to get revenge.

But those thoughts belong to the old me, the human me. The leopard is strong. *Fearless*. The leopard wants to fight. I flex my claws in anticipation of the battle, and my hair lifts along my spine. I have an overwhelming urge to growl.

Stepping over the low rubber barrier, I face the metal robot in the ring.

"Unfortunately, the battle bot doesn't have the unique characteristics provided by your Skins' augmented DNA," says the director. "The bot has enhanced strength, but in manual mode it's limited to the speed of the operator. Fortunately, Max's extensive training in multiple fighting disciplines should even up the fight."

Beside the ring, Max moves to a new stance. Inside the ring, the robot's motions are fluid as it moves with him. Its hands are raised and flat like blades.

Hemmed in by the small fighting ring, I shift my weight from paw to paw, waiting for the bot to attack. I flatten my ears back against my head, and bare my teeth. My vision narrows as I block out everything but the silver bot in front of me.

Just like Max, it wears heavy stomper's boots that lace

up the front. Boots for kicking and bullying. It wears a stomper's jacket. Its silver face could belong to one of the stompers who beat me. It could be any stomper who's ever cursed me, cuffed me, or drawn his gun on me. They've only ever caused me pain.

But now the tables have turned.

I've never been as strong as a stomper before. I've never stared one in the eyes and felt no fear. If he had a gun, I'd attack him before he could draw it. This time, no stomper's going to bully me.

I crouch back on my haunches as the stomper's weight goes on his toes. I'm snarling, nostrils flared and lips drawn back.

Can you see my fangs, stomper? My blood's on fire, my heartbeat deafening. You'd better be afraid, because I'm going to tear your evil throat out.

The stomper comes at me. I spring to meet him, launching myself at his neck. Got him! My jaws close on soft stomper flesh, ripping... but it melts away to nothing. My fangs snap together.

What the hell...? What happened? How'd he get away?

"Excellent, Rayne." The director's voice snaps me back to reality. I'm panting, my sides heaving, bile churning in my guts. Where'd that rage come from? Now it's fading, I feel shaky. The stomper... I mean, the bot's standing in front of me. It dissolved from between my jaws, then formed again once I let go.

BOT: 0 | CHALLENGER: 1

Max's enraged, hateful stink wafts over from where he stands next to the fighting ring. He reeks of fury.

From the others I sense shock. I don't blame them, my ferocity shocked me too. I'm not sure where it came from... well, I do know, but I didn't realize it ran that deep, that I could lose myself in it.

I still can't catch Director Morelle's scent, but her expression is like a proud pet owner whose dog has just learned a new trick.

"A new shape, Max?" the director asks. She reaches into the locker and does something to a control panel.

Though Max doesn't move, the silver battle bot falls forward, flat onto its face. Its arms press into the mat and its body lifts like it's doing a press up. Its silver bulk is morphing. Changing. It forms an animal. Not just any animal. A big cat, tail flicking from side to side even as it solidifies.

It's me, the clouded leopard.

The silver substance has copied my clouded leopard exactly, each hair carved in silver. The bot's blue eyes shine out of my leopard's face. Instead of being beautiful, it's hideous. It's taken my gorgeous leopard and twisted it into something monstrous and wrong.

Max is still wearing the helmet, so he must still be operating the bot. He's standing, but his hands have formed claws. When he crouches, the bot-leopard matches my stance, low to the ground.

Heart pounding, I stare into a silver mirror, into the bot's chilling eyes. A snarl rips from my throat.

The bot lunges, silver teeth snapping for me. I leap back, scrambling, off balance. Another leap and it's on me, claws cutting into my side, teeth closing on my shoulder. There's a sharp flash of pain as its teeth pierce my flesh, then nothing. The creature's mouth melts away with the force of the bite and I get a glimpse of the metal skull underneath.

My leopard can bleed. A few drops of blood mar my gorgeous fur. It smells surprisingly strong considering how little there is. Just a scratch I must have gotten from the metal skull. The rest of the bot's head dissolved before it could do any real damage, and I bet that's programmed in, not a choice Max would have made.

BOT: 1 | CHALLENGER: 1

"Well done, Max!" exclaims Director Morelle. "The next point will be the match decider. That's clearly a good shape for you, but let me change it a little."

She presses something on the control panel, sending a ripple across the bot's silver metal. Its form stays cat-like, but its mouth changes, growing long fangs from either side. Its body becomes longer and thinner, its legs stockier, its silver hair shorter and less thick.

Cale's saber-toothed tiger.

At least it's not a horrible copy of my leopard anymore. Beside the ring, Cale's scent changes. I shoot him a glance. His ears are flat, his tail low and swishing back and forth. He hates this false silver version of his Skin as much as I hated mine.

The bot's crouching. This time that morphing monster's not going to catch me out.

I feint left, but as the creature's paws leave the floor I spring right. It leaps at the place I was a moment before, its saber-teeth just missing me. My body twists and my outstretched claws stab into its chest.

Its chest melts away with the force of my thrust, then solidifies. But not into the cat's form. Instead the bot turns back into a featureless human-shaped statue. Max has ripped his helmet off. He glowers at me from beside the ring, his stench strong enough to turn my stomach.

BOT: 1 | CHALLENGER: 2

"A decisive victory, Rayne." Director Morelle gives me a smile that's plump with satisfaction. "You're living up to my hopes."

I stare at her, wishing she was easier to read. Am I being paranoid, or was that an odd thing to say if she doesn't know about my deception? Have I passed some sort of test?

"Me next," growls Brugan. As I step out of the ring, his mouth drops open and his nose extends toward me. He sniffs the drops of blood that have matted the fur on my shoulder.

His scent changes, and I flinch back. There's a strong tang of musk mixed in with his devil bear smell. *Arousal.* The smell of my blood excites him.

I back away, stomach churning, and suddenly Cale is beside me. With his hackles up he looks huge. His ears flatten and he snarls at Brugan.

The devil bear's stance changes. He crouches forward, evil teeth bared. His low, vicious growl makes my own fur stand up. A rush of adrenaline surges through me. It's the same feeling I got in the ring. I'm not just ready to fight, but eager for it.

Behind us, the director clears her throat. "Good," she says in a pleased voice. "But let's keep it contained for now, shall we?"

I don't move, don't take my eyes off Brugan. Neither does Cale. The three of us stare each other down for the space of several thudding heartbeats.

Brugan breaks first. His gaze goes to the director and the change in his scent makes my muscles relax. Cale's hackles flatten so he looks less threatening.

"I'm afraid I must leave you," says the director. "But Max will stay to assist with your training. With the never-wall, the treadmill, and the battle bot, you should have all the tools you need to ensure you're ready for the contest."

"I have a question," says Aza. "Are we allowed to train by ourselves? Ten hours a day isn't enough. I'd like to train later, or start earlier."

"Very well. I'll allow the training room to open at six

o'clock each morning and close at seven each night. But there'll be no training outside those hours." She pauses. "And tomorrow you'll have no training at all. You'll spend the day doing media interviews."

What? No! If my face gets broadcast, they're definitely going to find out I'm not Rayne.

Director Morelle turns to me. "Except you, Rayne. You won't be joining the others for tomorrow's interviews."

My heart flips. Does she know I'm an imposter after all?

"Doctor Gregory informs me you're having trouble in the vReal because of your eye. I must admit to being surprised when I saw it. It was one of the first my company ever made. A pioneering eye in its time, but it's been obsolete for many years."

I flick my ears backward and forward, confused by the change of subject.

"You shall have a new eye. Tomorrow you'll go to the hospital so they can get the growth process started. It'll be a few days before they can implant the eye, but it should be as good as new before the contest. You'll be able to compete to your full potential."

She stops, waiting for me to say something. My thoughts are fuzzy, like my head is full of vReal gel. I swallow hard.

"Really?" It comes out as a whisper.

She nods, but it's not enough. I have to know it wasn't some cruel joke. I need to hear her confirm it.

"You're really going to grow me a new eye? Honestly?"

"Yes, Rayne."

"Thank you." I can only just manage to croak the words out, but if I could I'd scream them at the top of my lungs. Thank you, thank you, thank you, thank you.

Chapter Sixteen

I float through the rest of the day in a bubble of pure joy. I'm going to get my eye back! That night, sleep is impossible, but that's okay. I'm happy staring at the ceiling.

I don't even mind when my cybernetic eye starts aching in the early hours of the morning, like it always does when I'm tired. Ache all you want, eye. You'll soon be gone. I won't miss you, not a bit.

On my shoulder, in the same spot where my leopard was injured in the ring, I have a red mark on my skin that's a little tender. Maybe the pod did something to me. I'll have to remember to ask Doctor Gregory about it.

But in the morning, I'm too excited to think about anything but getting a new eye. The smell of breakfast turns my stomach and I pace the halls until a cab arrives for me. I'm terrified when I get into it, in case it's going to demand payment and I'm going to be found out. But the director must have organized everything, because when I swipe my band against the control panel, it pulls away and drives me to the busy entrance of a hospital.

Inside the hospital, there are more scanners. As I touch my band to one of them, I'm convinced my luck's going to run out and it'll detect I'm wearing a stolen band. Then writing appears. *Rayne Walker. Ophthalmology Room 3877. 11:35am.*

A mechanical voice says, "Follow the green light" and a green marker lights in the floor at my feet. I follow it to a lift. It guides me to the right floor and leads me through a maze of corridors to a desk where a bored-looking woman hands me a tablet, and I have to swipe through pages of confusing small print and sign Rayne's name at least a dozen times. Apparently I'm having an Optic Sample Extraction, whatever that is.

A technician in a white coat takes me to a room filled with machines, and scans my face, looking through the damaged tissue to see the nerves and sinews behind my cybernetic eye. Then I sit fidgeting in a waiting area until a nurse comes in and gives me a capsule that dissolves into a sweet-tasting liquid on my tongue.

"To calm you," she says.

I sit in the waiting room for another couple of hours, but I don't mind. It feels like something that was tight in my brain has unwound and is floating away from my head.

Everyone else waits only a short time before getting called for whatever procedure they're having done, but still I sit, watching them come and go. One man must be here for a limb regrowth, because he has a bandaged stump where his finger used to be. Most don't have anything obviously wrong with them, so I imagine they're here for tweaking. It's so common in New Triton that every person I see looks perfect.

Finally, a nurse calls my name, leads me to a small room, and tells me to lie on a padded bench. Next to it is a tall contraption, but I'm feeling too relaxed to worry what it might be, or try to work out what it does. When I'm flat on my back, a metal clamp comes out of the bench and fits itself over my head, tightening until I can't move.

"Okay?" the nurse asks. "It has to be tight to keep your head perfectly still."

"Fine." It's so tight it hurts, but I'm not about to complain. Not when I'm going to get a new eye. And not while I'm still feeling so relaxed from that capsule.

She brings up a transparent holo display above her band, and taps a virtual button. A robotic arm extends from the contraption by the bench. It hovers over my face. There's a needle on the end of it.

A metal arm comes over the top of my head and fixes itself around my good eye, pulling my eyelid up and my lower lid down and clamping them tight. It doesn't really hurt, but even the drug they gave me isn't enough to stop my heart racing.

"Hold your breath, Rayne. Stare past the needle, at a spot on the ceiling. That's it. You must be completely still now."

Shit. Without that capsule, I'd be freaking out. I'm frozen in place, staring so hard at the dot on the ceiling my good eye is watering and my bad eye is glitching.

The needle stabs my good eye. It pierces my eyeball and there's a moment I want to scream. But then the needle retracts and the clamps release me. The mechanical arm pulls to one side where a vial's waiting for the sample. Both of my eyes hurt. The whole thing can't have taken longer than a minute or two, but I feel drained and the blissed-out feeling's gone.

The nurse holds up the vial. "That's it," she says. "Chemical soup. It's full of blank cells with all the nutrients and triggers needed to make a new eye." She fits the vial into a holder. "This'll go to the lab, and it'll take a few days for the cells to form your new eye. We'll call you when it's ready."

She points me to the door and a yellow light leads me back to the street. The cab is waiting. Getting in, I feel sick and shaky. The after-effects of the capsule? Or the shock of having a needle poked into my eye? I lean my head back and close my eyes. Then I hear Tori's voice. Her raspy laugh, making fun of me. What the hell am I feeling sick for? I'm going to get a new eye!

After a double shift, when I was so tired I'd retch up dinner, Tori would come out with something like, *"You think you have it tough? Once I worked fifty-six hours straight. Middle of summer, and the factory was so hot the paint ran off the walls."*

Or if the line for the bathroom was so long I had cramps from trying to hold on, Tori would say, *"This is nothing. One shelter I lived in, the food machines spat out nothing but protein paste for three weeks straight. Toilets stunk so badly, people were dropping dead from the stench. They had to close them, and too bad if you needed to go."*

It annoyed me at first. Then it made me laugh. After a while, it got so the only thing that would get me through some days was wondering what Tori was going to come up with that was so much worse than what I was going through.

I really hope she's okay.

If only I could let Tori know I made it out of the shelter, she'd be so happy for me. Now I have a chance to write my own future, and I'm not going to waste it.

When I arrive at the Morelle scraper, I head straight to the training room only to be turned away by the guard who's on duty. There's no training today and Doctor Gregory isn't available.

That's right. The others are having interviews today.

Disappointed, I head to the rec room. At least there's

food there, and thinking about Tori makes me extra grateful for the meal. Damn, but she'd love this place.

Taking my plate to the couch, I sit in front of the holo, adjusting a cushion behind my back and making myself comfortable. In the shelter I'd be allocated a single squirt of stew from the machine, and if I wanted to watch the holo, I'd have to stand or sit on the dirty floor, so this feels impossibly luxurious.

Without a band I need to turn the holo on manually, but then I just tell it, "Skin Hunter Contest," and it finds the right segment.

There they are, sitting in chairs lined up on a stage. It's a talk show. Brugan has a wide, cheesy grin plastered on for the cameras. Cale's smiling too, but only with one side of his mouth, like he's forcing it. When he looks down, his hair drops over his eyes and casts them into shadow. He's always so carefree, that look makes me wonder what could be troubling him.

Aza's wearing a deep red lipstick which accentuates the blue of her eyes and makes her even more striking. I've seen others as beautiful as her on the holo, but I'd always assumed it wasn't real, that nobody looked that polished in real life. I mean, not everyone in Old Triton is ugly, but what beauty there is needs to fight to be seen through a mask of exhaustion, work-stained layers of baggy clothes, and rough haircuts.

Aza's willowy legs are crossed at the ankle, but one delicate fingernail taps the arm of her chair as though she's fighting off boredom. Yeah, she's not fooling me. I'm figuring out that bored expression hides an iron determination that reminds me of Tori's, though I'd never have guessed it if I hadn't seen her battling her way up the never-wall. She looked as bloody-minded as Tori did when she'd fight through the dinner line to fill a plate for us before the machines ran out of food.

Aza seems delicate, but now I'm starting to know her, I can't see her that way. It's like she expands to fill all the space around her.

Sentin looks his normal serious self, glasses and all. If only I could figure out whether he's an enemy. In the shelter, I was good at spotting sharks. Here, not so much.

My good eye is streaming so I look down at my plate and concentrate on eating. The mashed potatoes have to be the best thing I've ever tasted. Rich and soft, and creamy.

Director Morelle is sitting beside the interviewer. She says, "Of course the contest draw was random, so it was pure chance Sentin was one of the competitors chosen."

"Sentin, how does your father feel about you competing?" asks the interviewer.

He's a handsome man with ebony skin, startling green eyes, and blonde hair that falls to his shoulders.

"I haven't discussed it with him." Sentin speaks as slowly as ever.

"Surely you must have spoken?"

I don't get it. Why is the interviewer making such a big deal about Sentin's dad?

"I've been completing my doctorate, and my father has been busy with his duties. I'm certain he supports me. Deiterra only wishes to ensure nothing threatens the peace we've enjoyed for almost five decades. And the Deiterran parliament hasn't yet come out with a formal statement about the Skins."

Could Sentin be the Deiterran Ambassador's son? That would explain what he's doing here. His mother's probably a Tritoner.

The director had to have chosen him for the contest to

reassure our neighbors they have nothing to fear. Either that, or she did it to provoke them.

"Let's move on." Director Morelle waves an impatient hand.

"Of course." The interviewer gives her a smile so white, it's blinding, then turns to the others. "How do the rest of you like the Skins?"

Brugan butts straight in. "Incredible! My Skin is the strongest. It could tear the others to pieces."

I expecting to see Aza give him a withering look, but she's obviously holding back in front of the camera. "My Skin is amazingly agile," she says, ignoring Brugan. "Its speed is what makes it so deadly."

The interviewer says, "Of course, when we use the word 'Skin', many of our viewers won't know what we're talking about. The net is full of speculation and rumor. You've released no official description of what they'll be like, have you Director Morelle?"

"I haven't," says the director.

"Will you tell us about them?"

Director Morelle smiles. She looks back to the camera, and I drop my eyes to my plate, both to rest them, and because her gaze makes me uncomfortable. Her stare cuts right though the holo, through the distance between us, as though she's staring straight into me, studying my thoughts.

"Most of your audience should already know about the transferal technology. As to what the Skins look like, I don't want to spoil the surprise. All I can say is that the contest will be a showcase for what they can do. It will be broadcast live across the country, so millions of people will witness their unveiling. I know you'll be impressed."

"You've been trying to obtain approval to release Skins for sale. Do you think President Trask is close to agreeing?"

By the smooth way the director starts her reply right after the interviewer has finished asking, I get the feeling this was a question she supplied him herself.

"Certainly. We expect to go into full production following the contest. The Skins you'll soon be able to buy will be smaller than the ones you'll see in the contest. They'll be strong and agile, but fit into your everyday life."

"And you're not concerned about condemnation from Deiterra?"

"When they watch the contest, the Deiterrans will see the Skins aren't weapons and don't violate our treaty."

"Is the Deiterran ambassor attending the event?"

"I've invited him. I hope he'll accept, and confirm for himself that the Skins will benefit all humanity."

I raise my eyes just in time to see the interviewer turn to the others. "Tell me, are you looking forward to the contest?"

"I sure am!" Brugan again. "I'm going to win."

Aza rolls her eyes.

The interviewer leaps on it. "You don't agree, Aza? You think you're going to win?"

"Yes, I do." She crosses her long, slim legs the other way.

"And you two?" He looks at Cale and Sentin. "You've both been quiet. Do you think you're going to win the contest?"

Cale hesitates a moment too long before he nods.

Sentin clears his throat and says, "Yes. I will win." It makes my own throat go tight, because the way he says it, I can't help but believe him. He says it with perfect certainty, like he's weighed the different options and arrived at an unshakable fact. I can't let him win. But if I were betting on the contest, I'd be putting my money on him right now.

I've lost my appetite, so I move my plate off my lap and

onto the floor. There's only crumbs left anyway, and over the last couple of days, I've figured out that people in New Triton don't lick their plates clean.

The camera zooms in on the interviewer. "It sounds like you'll have a battle on your hands. I'm certainly looking forward to watching." He seems to remember something. "...And to playing the vReal game, of course." He picks up a small plastic disc from a table next to him. "And here it is! The eagerly awaited game, *Skin Hunter*, which is out on the same day of the contest?"

He makes it a question and Director Morelle nods. "That's right."

"Security's been tight around this game. Nobody, but nobody, has been able to play or even see an advance copy. I can hardly believe I'm holding this one." He pretends to slip it into his pocket. "Perhaps I can...?"

"I'm afraid not."

He pulls a face, hamming it up for the camera. "Have you all played it?"

"I have." Brugan's grinning so wide I'm sure any minute his fat lips are going to split open.

"You've just made millions of viewers jealous, Brugan! Can you tell us anything about it?"

"I'm afraid they're all sworn to secrecy," Director Morelle cuts in. "But we're taking advance orders right now."

"That's right!" The interviewer holds the disk up to his face so the camera gets a good shot. "Don't forget to order the *Skin Hunter* game now, folks. And if you haven't yet bought your tickets for the contest, I'm afraid it sold out weeks ago. But as the director said, it's being broadcast live on b-Net."

"And watch out for our dedicated new Skin store opening soon in New Triton," adds the director.

The interviewer goggles at her. "A store? In New Triton? Can you give us a date, Director?"

"We'll be ready to open as soon as President Trask gives approval."

The interviewer widens his green eyes at the camera, and as I'm sure she's planned for him to do, he says, "I hope the president approves it soon, folks, and I bet everyone watching does too. Are you tuned in, President Trask?" He titters, and I can tell he's wondering if he's gone too far.

Director Morelle's smile grows wider. The way her lips draw back to show perfect white teeth reminds me of the wolfish grin of Brugan's Skin. It makes me shiver.

Chapter Seventeen

I wake with a jolt, my senses straining for any sound or movement. I'm glad I didn't obscure the window glass before I went to bed, because the moonlight glow coming through the window lets me scan the room.

What time is it? And what was it that woke me?

A soft rapping sound makes me jump. Someone at the door. I wait, heart pounding, and a moment later there's another knock. Whoever's there isn't going away.

"Rayne?" The voice is muffled, but unmistakably male.

"Who's there?"

"It's me. Cale."

"What do you want?"

"I need to talk to you. Open the door?"

"No."

"Come on, Rayne. I want to show you something."

"Show me what?" I get up and go to the door, but there's no way I'm opening it. Not in the middle of the night with nobody around. I'm not stupid.

"You need to see it for yourself."

"What time is it?" I ask, glancing at my dead band.

"Just after midnight. You have to come with me. It's not far."

"Why?"

He sighs so loudly I can hear it clearly. "Come on, Rayne. What do you think I'm going to do, attack you? I'm trying to help you, remember?"

"Then help me in the morning."

"It's something you'll thank me for, I swear."

If it were anyone but Cale, I wouldn't consider opening the door, not for a second. But Cale keeps insisting on trying to protect me, though it should be obvious I don't need help. It doesn't make sense he might suddenly want to hurt me.

"Wait a minute." I pull on a pair of jeans, then zip a light jacket over my T-shirt so I can tuck my blade into my pocket. The weight of it makes me feel ready for whatever might happen. But as I open the door I really hope I'm not going to regret breaking every rule Tori drummed into me.

The bright lights in the hallway hurt my bad eye. Cale's fully dressed, leaning on the wall like he has every right to be there. His cocky half-smile stops my breath in my throat. Does he have any idea how good-looking he is?

"That's better," he says. "Come with me." He starts off down the hall toward the rec room, motioning me to follow.

"Why?"

He turns to see I haven't moved and sighs again. "Just come on." When I still don't budge, he strides over and grabs my hand. "Trust me."

His touch sends a jolt of pure, animal awareness through me, a thrill of contact that goes deep into my core. I jerk my hand free, my face burning, and turn away to hide my confusion.

What's wrong with me? Men can't be trusted. Most women who live in shelters learn that lesson the hard way.

"You okay?" His voice is gentle.

I take a breath and nod.

"Will you trust me, Rayne?"

I don't *want* to trust him. But there's something in his voice that turns my insides soft, and I hear myself ask, "It's not a trick?" Officially the most idiotic question in the world, and I can practically hear Tori groan. *Like he'll admit it because you asked?*

"No trick. I wouldn't lead you anywhere bad, Rayne."

He seems sincere. And maybe I'm wrong, but I can't imagine Cale would be able to lie that well. I hesitate for a moment longer, then in spite of myself, I follow him down the hall. Are there cameras down here? There must be. I'm not sure we're supposed to be wandering around at night.

"Cale, where are you going? I don't want to—"

"Shhhh. Come on. It's in here."

He stops in front of the door I caught him coming out of yesterday morning and takes out his electronic stick.

"I'm not going in there. If we get caught they'll kick us out." I scan the ceiling, certain an alarm's going to go off. There must be security cameras so they can monitor the building. Somebody's got to be watching.

"I've snuck in here for the last couple of nights, and nobody's said a word." The door clicks and slides open, and he turns to me with a grin. "What's down here is well worth the risk. You'll see."

He slips inside and motions me in. Behind him it looks like a perfectly ordinary hallway with an office coming off one side. So what's so important?

"Rayne?"

I don't know what to do.

I've come this far, I guess. If I go back to my room, I'll

spend the rest of the night awake, wondering. So maybe just a quick look.

With one hand in my pocket, fingers curled around the handle of my blade, I step through the door, peering down the dark hall. There's nothing here. One more step, and the door clicks shut behind me. Suddenly it's so pitch black, I can't see a thing. My heart thuds, drumming a million beats per second. "What's going on?"

"Shhh, keep your voice down. This way."

He reaches out and fumbles for my free hand. I feel the jolt, the closeness of him, the heat of his skin. This time I don't pull away, but let him guide me through the darkness, though I pull my blade free and hold it ready in my other hand.

He walks confidently, like he knows exactly where he is and what's around him. There's some light coming in through some windows and my eyes are adjusting, but not enough to see more than vague shapes.

"Cale, stop."

"Okay. This'll do."

I yank my hand out of his and grip my blade tighter, ready to use it if I need to. I can hear my own ragged breathing. My chest is tight, every muscle tense.

"What are you talking about?" I demand.

"Lie down, Rayne."

"What?"

"Right here." He takes my arm and tries to tug me to the floor but I jerk away, fumbling for the wall behind me.

"I'm leaving. Don't try to stop me."

He's a dark shape on the floor. His tone becomes weary. "Can't you trust me, Rayne? Not even this much?"

"No." There's the wall. Edging along it, I keep the blade between him and me.

He sighs. "Okay, listen. This hallway runs right next to

the training room. There's only this wall between us and the lab rooms where they keep our Skins."

"So?"

"So, the transferal must work on proximity. If you're close enough to your Skin, you can transfer into it."

I freeze. Realization breaks over me like a wave. "Oh," I say, and my heart lifts, beating hard for an entirely different reason. "You're saying I can transfer into my Skin from here? I don't need to be in the pod?"

"Try it."

Keeping a wary distance between us, I stick my blade in my pocket and slide down the wall so I'm sitting on the floor with my back against it. The instant I close my eyes, my mind reaches out, searching for my Skin.

And finds it.

When I open my eyes I'm the leopard.

The lab room has no windows but I can see in the dark. My vision is every bit as sharp as during the day. When I take a step, I feel a flood of joy, the sense of euphoria that comes with being the leopard. It feels so good! I want to leap off the metal disc and run into the training room, but I don't dare. The computer screens around me have numbers falling down them in a constant stream. The Skin is being monitored. What if stepping off the disc sets off an alarm? Or the numbers change and somebody notices?

This is too risky. I need to stop. To transfer back.

But how can I bear to be human, when I can be the leopard?

"Come on, Rayne."

Cale's voice from the training room pulls me off the disc. As soon as I step off, the digital readouts stop. Shit. Well, I've done it now.

Padding into the training room, the moon through the

far windows is so beautiful it makes me feel giddy. It's drawing me toward it, pulling me into its light.

The room's alive. I smell Cale as much as I see him. He's stretching each leg as though waking from a long sleep, obviously loving the feel of being in his Skin as much as I am. His tiger stripes catch the moonlight.

He crouches on his haunches, then pounces forward as though hunting an imaginary mouse. His mouth opens, his tongue lolling out between his two long front teeth. He smells like pure happiness, such a wonderful scent that I laugh. Then I'm leaping too, springing forward over moonbeams for the pure fun of it. It's not a training room, it's a playground. And there's never been a more beautiful night or a better Skin to play in.

But why would Cale bring me here? We're competitors. If he kept it to himself, trained in secret, wouldn't he have an advantage?

"Cale, why did you—?"

"Let's talk later." Joy shines out of him like a visible glow. "Come on, Rayne. Race you!" He leaps forward, running toward the never-wall.

A surge of excitement forces my doubts away, and I take off after him. The ground soars under me. Ahead is the never-wall. I haven't climbed it yet, but I bet I can get to the top first time. My paws barely touch the ground. I leap onto the wall, loving the power in my muscles as I spring from ramp to ramp. The wall's changing around me, but I can see the changes rippling down and I know when to jump. My speed and strength are exhilarating.

Cale is climbing too. His claws scrape against the metal wall and I feel vibrations as he jumps and lands. He's behind me, but it sounds like he might be catching up. No way am I going to let him beat me to the top.

I push myself harder, searching for higher ledges,

taking risks. A platform suddenly morphs, surprising me. I slip and almost fall, but manage to catch myself. Then I discover my claws are sharp enough to pull me up vertical bars. I reach the ceiling, turn, and start leaping down even faster, using my tail to help me balance. I land triumphantly on the floor, sides heaving, panting with the effort.

Cale jumps down after me, breathing hard. He gives me one of his feline grins.

"Fun?" he asks between breaths.

"Hell, yeah!"

"You did well. Better than me."

I shake my head, but I know it's true. My leopard might be a little more agile than his tiger. So what if I suck at using the vReal? This is what counts, really being the leopard, not a stupid virtual reality game.

In my Skin, I'm fast and strong. If I'm faster than he is, maybe I could win the contest.

Cale cocks his head on one side, his tail twitching. "I could get drunk off your scent," he says. "I've never smelled anything so good."

It's no wonder I smell good when pure exhilaration is coursing through my veins. For the first time, I know I'm not trapped anymore. I can change my life, and I never have to be Milla again.

The director said the competition winner gets to keep their Skin.

I can be the leopard forever. This will be my permanent body. This strength and power will be fully mine, the last of my weakness gone for good.

The thought fills me with such hope I can barely stand it. Hope so strong it feels like pain.

Chapter Eighteen

I t's not for several hours, after we've worn ourselves out on the never-wall and the treadmill and we've stretched out to rest next to the fighting ring, that the doubts flood back.

"Cale, tell me the truth. Why'd you bring me here?"

He lifts his head for a moment to look at me, then drops it back onto his paws. Our bodies are close enough to be almost touching. If we were lying with our human bodies this close, I'd be nervous as hell. But when I'm the leopard, I'm too powerful for anyone to hurt me, and I like feeling his warmth. I like inhaling his scent.

The smell of feline stirs something deep inside me, but I'm not afraid of it anymore. I'm not afraid of anything.

"The truth." He considers for a moment, then lets out a long breath that's almost a sigh. "The truth is that I think you should win the contest."

"What?" I blink, my ears flattening with surprise. "Why?"

"Because I came here on false pretenses. When I

entered my name in the contest, I never thought I'd get in. And when I did, I swore I'd derail the whole thing." His tail gives an embarrassed twitch and he stretches his head forward to rub his whiskered snout against one paw. "I only came here because I thought I could be a saboteur. I was going to do everything I could to stop the contest."

"You don't want to win?"

"I'm against everything the Morelle Corporation stands for. And after Welcon, there's no way they should be allowed to release anything that hasn't been fully tested." His snout wrinkles. "But all my crazy ideas about sabotaging the contest changed when I transferred into my Skin."

"How?"

"You felt it, didn't you? The way everything was suddenly so much better, like you'd been half asleep and someone jerked you awake. I've played vReal games for as long as I can remember, but I'd never imagined anything like it. And I stopped thinking about ways to derail the contest. I can't bear to..." His tail rises, then thumps back to the floor. "I don't know, Rayne. I want to keep being able to wear my Skin, but winning would be like supporting them. It would go against everything I believe." He lowers his gaze, his eyes troubled. They're a warm gold, ringed with black. They're mesmerizing. Cale's tiger form is even better looking than his human body.

"I want to win," he says finally. "But I can't, not when I'm conflicted. You should win instead."

"Why me?"

"You've lived in Old Triton." He says it in an 'of course' tone, like it's a silly question.

"So?"

"Do you agree it's not fair how the city is divided?

Grunts are too busy scratching out a living to ever see the sun. Above them are the consumers who demand more and more products they don't need. Skins are the perfect example. Where will the factories be? In Old Triton. And the stores will be in New Triton. Will any sinker ever be able to afford one? Of course not."

The passion in his voice takes me by surprise. So does the way he said grunts instead of factory workers, and sinker instead of Old Tritoner. Hearing Old Triton slang from him is the last thing I expected.

"Deiterra has the right idea," he says. "Over there, I've heard everyone's the same. There are no giant cities, and nobody lives over the top of anyone else."

"Maybe," I say. "For all we know, it could be more crowded than Triton by now." Still, the idea makes my heart ache. If Triton was like that, my family might still be together. Do they have second child taxes in Deiterra?

But wishing things were different won't make them that way.

"Why do you care so much about Old Triton?" I ask. "You're a floater. You live in the sun."

His beautiful golden eyes look so hurt that I have to turn my face away.

"We've talked enough about me." His voice is surprisingly gentle. "What about you? Tell me your story."

"I want to know if you're serious about wanting me to win." I can't understand how he could bear to lose. To deliberately throw away his chance to be the tiger.

He cocks his big tiger head and blinks so slowly that I find myself blinking with him, as though his movements are controlling mine.

"Can you tell what I'm thinking, Rayne?"

My nostrils flare. His scent's pure. There's no hint of

anything hidden, nothing but a musky, intoxicating smell of feline, and beneath it, what I'm coming to think of as Cale's smell. It's a deep calming scent, so fresh I want to bathe in it.

It reminds me of when I was a kid, before the factory and the shelter, when Papa was still alive and New Triton was still being built. We lived in a tiny apartment on the eighteenth floor, and the roadway above us hadn't yet been finished. I'd stick my head out of the window after a rainstorm and I couldn't smell the homeless people in the streets below. I couldn't smell Old Triton at all. The air was so crisp I'd look up and imagine it was flowing down from our brand new city.

But even if I couldn't catch Cale's scent, I'm sure I'd be able to tell if he was lying or hiding something by reading the tiny movements of his ears and the flick of his tail. There's nothing secretive about him.

And when I look in his eyes, I know what he's thinking. He's admiring my leopard. Although my close-up vision isn't as sharp as my far-away vision, somehow I can see my own black pupils reflected back in his.

His whiskers twitch. He's waiting for me to answer.

"I can't read minds," I say, glancing away.

He stretches his nose toward me. His warm breath ruffles my fur. "We can be allies, Rayne. Will you let me help you?"

It's tempting to trust him, but not being wary can get you hurt. I've had that lesson beaten into me so hard, I'm never likely to forget it.

Instead of answering, I shift so his breath doesn't reach me. "What makes you think I won't report you and get you kicked out of the competition? One less competitor to worry about."

"You won't."

"So confident?"

His tiger's lips twitch in a feline smile, and his scent changes a little, becoming so warm I can't help but move my face closer to inhale it.

"You're a good person, Rayne. I trust you."

The simple words take my breath away. Where I come from, nothing is that easy. But the way he says it somehow makes it seem possible for two strangers to trust each other. And sitting next to him makes me ache for what he's offering. Trust. Friendship. An alliance. What if it were possible for me to believe him?

"Will you tell me about the vReal game, Cale?" I ask.

"What do you want to know?"

"Let's start with everything and go from there."

"The best way to get better is to play a lot. Playing's fun anyway, isn't it? It's not exactly a chore."

Yeah, it's easy for him. He earned thousands playing vReal games while I was busy burning half my face off and losing an eye.

I turn away, and notice moonlight isn't streaming in any more. In fact, the moon's disappeared and a golden light is filtering in. "We should go," I say. "It's dawn."

"I can give you some tips—"

There's a noise from outside the training room door. Cale and I scramble to our feet. The door opens. I freeze. It's Aza. Shit, she's seen us! No, it's too dark for human eyes. She's peering at her band. She makes an irritated sound and turns to the wall, her hand fumbling over the surface, searching for the light switch. That's right, her band won't work in here. Looking for the switch to turn the light on manually gives us a few precious seconds.

Cale and I race for our lab rooms, our paws powering

us silently across the floor. I reach my metal pad and skid onto it as the lights flicker on.

Transfer.

A second later, I'm back in my human body, in the dark hallway on the other side of the training room, slumped against the wall. Cale comes to life as I sit up.

"She didn't see you?" he asks.

"Don't think so." I scramble to my feet, my body stiff. "What's she doing there so early anyway?"

He checks his band. "It's six o'clock. She's right on time."

"We've got to get out of here."

We're both already heading for the door. Cale cracks it open and peers down the hall. "I think it's safe," he whispers. "Come on."

We slip out. My heart's thumping as I scuttle toward my room. Even when I get there safely, I'm so jittery it seems to take forever for my door to recognize my band and open.

"Rayne," calls Cale.

I turn, holding my door ajar.

"That was worth it, wasn't it?" he asks.

"I think so." But I've got a sick feeling in my stomach. A place like this has to be filled with sensors and cameras and hidden alarms. How could we not get caught? It won't have been worth it if I get kicked out.

"See you at training," he says.

I can't turn back time, so there's no point telling myself I shouldn't have gone. Trying not to think about it, I put my blade back in its hiding place, shower and change. I stop for a quick breakfast, then head to the training room.

When I get on the treadmill, my leopard's limbs still have as much strength and energy as ever, but my brain is so fuzzy with exhaustion, I can only move at half speed. It's not so much fun with everyone else there, anyway. Keeping tabs on where they are and what they're doing is tiring, especially when I see how good they are and all my hope from last night drains out like somebody pulled the plug.

Aza's wasp wings propel her up the never-wall faster than I can believe, Sentin close behind her. Brugan tears into the battle-bot, scoring point after point. Cale and I are sluggish and weak in comparison. Doctor Gregory frowns at both of us more than once, but I can't pick my speed up.

The whole time we're training, I keep expecting Director Morelle to come storming in and demand to know what the hell Cale and I were doing last night. But we don't see her, and nobody says anything.

When the day finally ends, I barely have the energy to eat before collapsing into bed. My head's aching, pain shooting into my eye. I'm so tired my body is weak with it. My veins are filled with sand.

Sleep. Awesome sleep. Beautiful, wonderful sleep.

Then I'm awake again. Confused. What was that? A knock from the door. That must have been what woke me. Another knock. The room's dark, the moon high in the sky. What time is it? Not morning. Not time to get up.

"Who's there?" My voice is croaky.

"Rayne?" It's Cale's voice. "You want to train again?"

I groan. But I drag myself up. "Give me a minute."

Into the bathroom to splash water on my face. Cold water. I gasp with the shock of it. Yeah, I'm awake now. But I keep looking at my soft, warm bed and thinking how great it would feel to lie back down, how easy to drift back to sleep. Instead I open the door.

Cale's got dark circles under his eyes, but he's grinning. "Want to be the leopard now?"

I shouldn't. Dammit, what am I thinking? But nobody said anything about last night, did they? And at the thought of getting back into my Skin, my bed doesn't look inviting anymore.

"I'm coming." I shut the door and leave sleep behind.

Chapter Nineteen

I spend the next three days fighting the battle-bot and running on the treadmill. I spend my nights racing Cale up and down the never-wall.

It's too dangerous to break the rules like this, but I can't bring myself to stay away. Each time Cale comes to my door, I convince myself we'll get away with it one more night. Exhaustion doesn't matter. Training is all I think about, all I want to do. At night, when it's just Cale and me, it's even better than during the day.

My beautiful leopard is all I ever want to be. Four paws are natural. Two feet are clumsy and slow.

I get into the habit of being first in the rec room after the day's training so I can bolt down my dinner while the rest are still getting organized. Then I head straight to bed to snatch a few hours sleep before night training starts.

Cale handles the long hours by taking a nap in the morning after stumbling back to his room. He turns up to training later and later each day.

On the third day he doesn't show up at all.

I watch the door for him, and by late afternoon,

I'm frantic with worry, convinced that something terrible must have happened. Did he get caught? Has he been kicked out? If so, why hasn't anyone come for me yet?

I'm so distracted, my performance suffers. I miss my step near the top of the never-wall, tumbling all the way down and hitting the ground so hard I see stars.

The hours I spend in the training room usually fly by, but now I'm all too conscious that every hour could be my last.

Will the director come for me? Will Max? What will I do if they throw me out?

When training finally ends for the day, everyone else transfers back into their human form. But I can't do it. I can't make myself become Rayne, I can't stand to go back to my hated human form.

What if I never get to be the leopard again?

Staring at the training room window, I imagine crashing through it, leaping head-first for freedom and landing four stories down on the ground far below. I could do it. I could steal my leopard. But then what?

My human body would be left behind. There's probably a way they could force my mind back into it. They could do whatever they wanted with my body while they hunted down my Skin. If my human body died, would my consciousness live on inside my leopard? Or would it die too?

"Rayne." Doctor Gregory interrupts my thoughts. "May I speak with you once you've transferred?"

My body stiffens, my tail dropping and my hair rising along my spine. Is this it? She's going to order me to leave? But there's no trace of anger or disapproval in her scent. She heads to one of the labs and starts punching numbers into a machine.

I have no choice. I can't be the leopard for good. Not yet.

With a huge, gut-wrenching effort, I force myself to transfer back into my body. Then I make my slow human legs walk over to her. My dull human nose has no chance of detecting how she feels. Although, now I'm thinking about it, I notice the flowery scent of her perfume long before I reach her. Is it stronger than usual?

"You wanted to talk to me, Doctor Gregory?"

She turns from the machine, smiling. "You're scheduled to get your new eye tomorrow, Rayne. You'll miss one day of training, that's all. And you'll have two real eyes again."

My heart lifts and I smile back, hardly able to believe it. No more black, dead cybernetics staring out from one side of my face. No more pain and glitching.

"Thank you, Doctor. I mean, that's amazing. Thank you so much."

Thanking her isn't nearly enough. I want to hug her, to swing her around. If only I could tell her how much this means, but I can't find the words.

"It's a shame they won't have time to do anything about your scarring. I wish we could have—"

"I don't care about my scars. I can't wait to have two good eyes."

I float down the hallway, heading for Cale's room. I need to make sure nothing bad has happened to him. If somebody discovered our night-time training sessions now, before my operation, I'd lose everything. I've been foolish to risk so much.

For the first time, it's me who knocks on Cale's door. And typical Cale, he opens his door without even asking who's there. He wouldn't last a day in Old Triton.

"Hey, Rayne."

"You're okay?"

He instantly knows what I mean. "I was exhausted, that's all." He steps aside and motions me in. "I don't know how you do it, staying awake all day and most of the night."

"They're going to give me an eye tomorrow," I blurt.

"Really? That's great."

It's lucky I'm too excited to sit because his bed's a mess with the sheets twisted and half on the floor. Clothes are scattered everywhere, giving off his distinctive Cale scent.

"Hey," he says. "You'll be able to use the vReal properly now."

"Oh. Yeah." I should be glad, but every minute spent in the vReal is one I don't get to spend in my Skin.

"Did I say the wrong thing?" He drags his hand through his already-messy hair.

"No. You're right, and it's a good thing. I have a lot of work to do in the vReal."

He hesitates, and when I see him looking at the bad side of my face, I turn away.

"They're not going to do your scars, are they?" he asks.

"Doctor Gregory said they weren't."

He moves toward me, his hand lifted, reaching for my face. I flinch away and his hand pauses. When he reaches out again, I keep still and let his gentle touch brush my scarred cheek. He traces his fingers ever so lightly over the ridges of my ruined skin.

My breath freezes in my lungs.

"Tell me how you got your scars?" His voice is as soft as his fingers on my skin.

I shake my head, the tiniest movement. I can't breathe, let alone talk. My stomach's getting jittery. He's too close. Part of me wants to take off, run away. The other part... I don't know.

He frowns as though he can hear the clamor in my head. His eyes are a deep soft brown but I'm sure I can see a glint of gold in them, a hint of tiger. He must see how confused I am, because after a moment he sighs and drops his hand away.

"I know you don't trust me yet, Rayne. And that's okay." He smiles, but his eyes look sad. "I hate whatever it is that hurt you. I wish our world were different."

Without his touch, my lungs unfreeze and I can draw a shuddering breath. "Your world *is* different."

"You're right." He sighs and sits down on the edge of his bed. "Did I tell you about the night I spent in an Old Triton jail?"

"What?" I should probably sit next to him, but instead I lean my shoulder against the wall and link my fingers in front of me.

He puts his hands behind him and leans back, angling his head up at me. "At a big gamer's tournament, I started hanging out with a couple of floaters who'd done some work for the Fist. They did small stuff, like digi-bombing on b-Net and virtual tagging, but they knew some sinkers who were real Fist members. They introduced me, and long story short, I went out with them one night to paint Fist slogans on the sides of buildings." He gives a tight, lopsided smile. "I thought it'd be fun."

"No way." I can't imagine Cale sneaking around Old Triton after dark. He's lucky he made it out alive.

"Yeah, well." He puts on an Old Triton accent. "I went spraying with two sinkers. Only some stompers snatched us."

I'm not sure I'll ever get used to hearing him use Old Triton slang. "What happened?"

"I spent the night in a holding cell." The accent disappears. "On a freezing concrete floor without so much as a blanket. But in the morning, they growled at me not to do it again, then let me out safe and sound." His tone's light, but his back's gone stiff and he's looking down at his knees, not meeting my eyes. "It wasn't until later that I found out what happened to the two guys who were caught with me. When they got out, they were covered with bruises. Both had their hands broken." His gaze comes up to mine, his expression dark. "You know what happens in Old Triton when an injury stops you from being able to work?"

"Better than you do." No work means no food, and they won't let you sleep in a shelter. A stinking mattress on a dirty floor is a privilege only working grunts get. Beggars have to survive any way they can.

"I told everyone what happened. The Fist even broadcast it on Sub Zero, but like all their broadcasts, it was ignored. Old Tritoners are used to it, and New Tritoners don't care."

"Did you really think they would?" Of course there are different rules for floaters and sinkers. Does he think any sinker doesn't know that?

At this time of day I'd usually be finishing shift. Right now, I should be walking out of the hot factory into the cold outside air, starting a weary trudge to the shelter. My sweaty clothes would go clammy and my joints always ached like I was a hundred years old.

I shiver.

Old Triton's the last thing I want to think about. Ma is still trapped there, and I can't do a damn thing to help her, or any other sinker. And if I'm forced to go back, I won't be able to get into a shelter. Definitely not something I want to dwell on.

"I want to *do* something about it. That's the reason I came here. But…" He breaks off and I can tell he's thinking about his saber-toothed tiger. Instead of finishing his sentence, he stands up. "Sorry, Rayne, I don't mean to drag you down. It's being tired that makes me gloomy." He shakes his head. "We should be celebrating your good news."

"I'm going to have two eyes again." My smile comes back at the thought. "Can you believe it? No more ugly cybernetics."

"Just don't get anything else done." His mouth twists. "I'm sick of everybody looking perfect. Everyone in New Triton wants to be the same. I hate it."

"But you're tweaked, aren't you?"

"I wish I wasn't." He only stood up a minute ago, but he sits again, his body heavy, as though he can't find a comfortable place to exist in. "For my sixteenth birthday my parents gave me the works. I don't mind the nano-bots they injected to keep all my insides working like they should. That actually makes sense. But at the same time, my nose was straightened and shaped." He runs one finger down its length. "My jaw line was adjusted. Eyebrows, of course, and cheeks. They even lifted one ear because it wasn't quite even with the other side, can you believe it?" He snorts. "I'm just glad they didn't decide to give me any stupid fashion things, like Aza's eyes."

If he's looking for sympathy, he won't get it from me. I'd change places with him in a heartbeat. "I'd love to look like everyone else."

He frowns at me, his expression puzzled. "That's the last thing I'd want. You're beautiful."

My stomach twists. Nobody would call me beautiful unless they were really saying the opposite. Normally when I hear something nasty about my face, I can brush it off. But this backhanded insult disguised as a compliment?

I hadn't expected to hear anything like it from Cale. That makes it hurt even more.

"Yeah?" My voice is bitter as I turn away and fumble for the pad to open the door. "I know what I look like. I don't need reminding."

"What? Rayne, you really are beautiful."

"Shut the hell up, Cale." The door finally opens.

"Rayne, wait!"

I tear down the hall. My human body doesn't move so slowly after all.

"Rayne!"

"Leave me alone, Cale." I fling the words over my shoulder. Then I'm in my room, my chest heaving like I've run a huge distance instead of just down the hall.

Damn him! I felt so good a second ago and now he's ruined it.

My hand goes to my face, to the scarred hollow where my cheek should be. I wish they were tweaking my scars, so I'd never have to hear anyone taunt me again. But hell, it's no good wishing. I'm having my eye replaced and that's enough. More than enough. It's wonderful.

Falling onto my bed, I bury my face in the sheets.

I don't care how I look. Sharks go for the pretty ones first. It's better for a sinker like me to be ugly.

When I look up a long time later, it's dark outside. Cale has usually knocked on my door by now, collecting me for training.

Will he leave me behind tonight? I can't get into the hallway next to the training room without his electronic stick. If he does come, will I go with him? Can I face him?

Yeah, no question. Once I'm the leopard I can face anything.

I hear slow footsteps. I lie rigid, listening as they stop outside my door. There's a long silence. Too long. I jump up and tear the door open before I hear a knock.

Cale is biting his lip, looking worried. "Rayne, I hope you don't—"

"Stop." I hold up my hand. "Let's not talk about it, okay?"

"But, I—"

"Let's just train."

I push past him and lead the way. Thankfully he doesn't try to talk again. When I transfer into my Skin, it's a such a relief that my throat closes up and my claws tighten into the floor like nobody's ever going to drag me out of my Skin again. Everything's so much simpler now. I'm not afraid of anything when I'm the leopard.

When I look at tiger Cale, I can feel his concern for me like a warmth coming off him. It's in the way his ears twitch toward me when I move, the smoky undercurrent through his fresh scent, the way his tail flicks to tell me how worried he is that he's upset me. There's no malice in Cale the tiger. If only I was so sure of it when he's Cale the man.

He lopes over and brings his face close. I let him gently touch my nose with his. His scent fills me up, like he's part of me. His soft heartbeat is in my ears, his breath is in my lungs.

"Rayne," he murmurs.

"It's okay," I answer. And it really is. We don't need words when we're in our Skins. I'm beautiful when I'm the leopard. That must be what he meant, I just didn't get it. A misunderstanding, that's all.

"Come on, I'll race you to the top of the never-wall." I wheel away and then I'm running so fast in my magnificent, wonderful Skin that my laughter's whipped away behind me.

When it's almost dawn and time to transfer back into our human bodies, Cale turns to me. "Good luck for the operation, Rayne," he says. "I'm going to miss training with you tomorrow night."

My heart twists as I realize what he means. "Oh yeah, I won't be able to train. I hadn't thought about that. I'll have to go a whole day and night in my human body."

His whiskers droop. "You're not going to miss me? I guess you'll be far too busy missing your Skin."

"Oh." I can tell he's disappointed by the way his eyes drop and the subtle change in his scent. "I'm sorry."

"That's okay. I know how you feel. I've fallen in love with being a tiger, and it's easy to see that being the leopard means even more to you." He tilts his head and his golden eyes catch the moonlight. "It's a little worrying how quickly our Skins have become so important to us."

"Scary," I agree.

Maybe he knows I'm lying.

Later, back in my room, I stand at the window to watch the pink and red warmth of dawn grow across the sky.

Needing my leopard isn't what scares me. What's scary is how I lived before I came here, every day barely managing to survive. I hated it so much I was willing to risk everything to escape it, but I had no idea how incredible life could be until I became the leopard. I lift Rayne's band and press it against my forehead, closing my eyes as I silently thank her. Her death gave me life. A life I never dreamed existed.

I look around at the bedroom I don't have to share with anyone. My soft, comfortable bed, my clean sheets and my private bathroom.

Outside, the sun's appearing above the scrapers, so bright and close up here in New Triton. The pink dawn reflects in a thousand windows and floods my room with light. It's stunning. Even so, it seems hazy and diluted compared to how I'd see it with leopard eyes. In my Skin

I'd be able to smell the dawn like fresh cooked breakfast, like clean, crisp sheets or the taste of joy on my tongue.

As great as it is, I'd trade this room in a heartbeat for my Skin. I'd do anything, work all day and night, never see another dawn. There's not 1 thing I wouldn't give if it meant I got to be the leopard forever.

Chapter Twenty

A couple of hours later, I'm in a cab on my way to the hospital. Strange that on the last day I have to put up with my glitchy cybernetic eye, everything looks sharper than normal. Smells seem stronger too. And the smallest noise makes me jump.

Must be because I'm hyped up, both excited and nervous about the operation. In spite of my nerves, my stomach's grumbling. I wasn't allowed breakfast before the surgery, so I'm starving, especially after spending all night training.

This time, I get directed straight to an exam room to see a doctor. "Do you know what's going to happen today, Rayne?" he asks.

"You're going to take out my cybernetic eye and put in the one you've grown?"

"That's right. Because the eye is cultivated from your own cells, we can knit its receptors to the ones in your damaged eye socket. We're going to use the latest accelerated growth techniques to do this, inserting blank cells between them, then stimulating those cells so they form a bridge between the eye and what's already there." He cocks his head to the side, looking at me doubtfully. "Do you understand?"

With his tone telling me he's sure I have no clue what's he's talking about, there's only one answer I can give him. "Every word," I say.

"Well. You'll find your new eye is a vast improvement on your cybernetic one."

"Thanks, Doc."

A nurse gives me a gown to change into, then puts me on a gurney to wheel me into the operating theatre. At least I'll get some sleep today. When they stick a mask over my face and I start to drift off, I realize I should have taken a look in the mirror this morning to drink in the ugliness of my old eye. After this, it'll be gone forever. The thought sends me to sleep even faster.

I wake in a recovery room, dry-mouthed, feeling woozy and sick. I don't feel like I've been asleep, but like a slice of my life is missing, as though while I was knocked out I didn't exist. I've no idea how long I was out for. A nurse angles up the top of my bed, then puts a drop of liquid on my tongue that clears my head and makes the sickness go away. When my hand goes up to my face, it hits a thick bandage.

"Does it hurt?" asks the nurse.

"No."

"Good. Don't touch it."

I doze until a meal arrives. When I've eaten I get up to use the bathroom, and stare into the mirror at the dressing that covers half my face. What's underneath? Fingering the white adhesive pad, I tug at the bottom edge where it's stuck onto my scarred cheek. I'm dying to see my new eye, but I don't dare pull off the bandage.

Night's falling and the ward's getting dark. When I get

back in bed I find I'm sleepy again. Each time I close my good eye, my brain automatically searches for my leopard, trying to transfer into it. Its absence is a hole in my mind, an aching emptiness I long to dive into. At least when I next wake up it'll be morning and time to go back to the Morelle scraper. I'll get to go back to being the leopard. I can't wait.

The surgeon comes back the next morning. I'm hoping he'll take off the bandage so I can see what's underneath. Instead he runs a scanner over my face and says, "Any pain?" in an absent voice, as though he's forgotten who I am.

"No."

"It's important to keep the eye still and dark, to allow maximum healing in the early stages. Come back in two days and we'll remove the dressing."

"Okay."

"We repaired the nerves around the eye to ensure a full range of movement." He stares at the scanner with a puzzled frown, as though he's never seen it before. Then he shakes his head. "The nurse will check you out. No physical exercise for the next twenty-four hours. Avoid jolting it or bending forward."

As soon as I get back to the Morelle scraper, I head straight to my room and into the bathroom. I turn off the light and leave the door open a crack, so it's gloomy inside but not completely dark. I know I'm not supposed to, but I need to see it.

In front of the mirror, I stop and stare. My face looks different. Below the white bandage, my scars are still there, but my mouth is straight. It doesn't droop on that side.

The doctor said they fixed the nerves around my eye. Did they fix the nerves in my cheek so they hold up my mouth? No more drool? No more ugly sagging?

I drag in a breath. No. I can't afford to hope.

If I let myself believe it, I won't be able to bear it if my mouth droops again once all their medication has worn off. I'll check again tomorrow. If my mouth still looks straight then, maybe I'll allow myself to celebrate.

I use my fingernail to get under the sticky edge of the dressing that finishes below the hollow in my cheek, then pull upward. The dressing tugs at my scarred skin, not wanting to come away. Working the dressing up, I drag it off my closed eyelid. My cheek doesn't look any different, my scars as ugly as ever. But beneath that closed lid...

No, I can't look underneath. Opening my eye might damage it.

But my closed eyelid looks the same as before. Could there really be a new eye under there? What if I open it and my cold black cybernetic eye is staring back at me?

I have to check. I need to know.

Slowly I ease my eyelid open just enough to see a sliver of white. There really is an eye under there. A real eye. No more black metal, no glitching circuits.

My vision blurs with tears as I gently press the dressing back down, but I furiously wipe them away. *Don't cry*. If my new eye has tear ducts, crying so soon might damage them.

Heading to the training room, I walk above the ground, not on it. My whole body's singing and there's a big stupid grin on my face.

I can't wait to get into my Skin, but Doctor Gregory shakes her head.

"You're not to train today, Rayne."

"What?" I look over to my leopard waiting for me. So close! "But when I'm the leopard, my real body's lying in the chair, resting."

"Not today. You can train again tomorrow."

"The contest's only a few days away. I need all the training I can get."

"Sorry, Rayne. Go and have something to eat, then lie down for a while. Take it easy."

Maybe now's the time to ask Doctor Gregory to go over the details of the contest? I've been training so much, I haven't come up with a plan yet. I'm not even sure what I'm supposed to do when I get to the top of the tower. Does just beating the others up there mean I win?

But the doctor's distracted, watching the others. She's got a mind-pad in her hand, and numbers are flashing across its screen.

Cale pads over, his ears cocked forward. He murmurs, "Come on, Rayne. I'll take a break with you."

"Why?"

"We should talk."

He refuses to say anything more until after he's transferred back into his human body and we're in the rec room, helping ourselves to the food that's been left for us. Sandwiches, and they smell delicious. The aroma of fresh bread is like heaven.

"What do you need to talk to me about that's worth giving up training time?" I ask when we sit at the table with full plates.

"About winning the contest. It's not just going to take speed or strength. We'll have to out-think the others. We need to talk strategy."

It's like he's read my mind. "You're serious about helping me?" I ask, taking a mouthful of sandwich.

"If we work together, I know you can do it."

"You'd really give up your Skin?"

"Actually, I've been thinking about that. If I help you win, will you buy a Skin for me?"

"What if the director won't sell it?"

"She's opening a store, remember? I know I won't be able to buy my Tiger Skin. The ones she's going to sell commercially won't be as good. But whatever I can get will be better than nothing."

"How do you know they won't be as good?"

He lets out a short laugh. "Can you imagine giant leopards and tigers bounding around New Triton? The president would never let her sell Skins like ours."

"I hadn't thought about it," I admit, taking another bite of my sandwich. "What do you think they'll be like?" I ask around the mouthful I'm chewing. "Normal sized? No claws? Will they still be animals, or look like people?"

"She can't make ones that look human. Didn't you see all the news coverage when she was arguing with President Trask about how much human DNA she'd be allowed to include? He set it at twenty five percent, maximum."

"Why didn't the president want her to make human-looking Skins?"

"Same reason he banned humanoid robots. They were used for creepy, violent sex, and all kinds of freaky stuff. The police kept getting callouts. People thinking their neighbors were doing nasty things to a real person." He wrinkles his nose, putting his half-eaten sandwich down.

"I've never seen a domestic robot, except on the holo. They're expensive, aren't they? Do many people have them up here?" The only robots in Old Triton are metallic arms on the factory lines.

He shrugs. "They're expensive. But yeah. Most people would rather buy a robot to do their housework than employ someone…" He trails off.

"Employ someone from Old Triton," I finish for him. "Don't worry, I know what your kind thinks of us. We're all thieves, right?"

He winces at the words 'your kind', and I immediately feel bad. That wasn't fair.

"What if I don't win the contest?" I ask to change the subject. "You won't get a Skin."

"With my help, you can't lose."

I take a big bite of my sandwich. Chewing gives me a chance to think. If I win, giving up some of the prize money won't matter. It'll be worth it to improve my chances. And if Cale hopes to get a Skin out of the deal, well, that's easier to believe than trusting him to help me because of some weird moral code he has.

I swallow and ask, "How much do you think a Skin's going to cost?"

"Probably a lot. A few hundred thousand credits, I guess. But you'd have lots of prize money left."

"And you'd trust me to buy it for you?"

"I trust you." His brown eyes lighten when he smiles. "But you can put it in writing if you want to. Write up an agreement on your band and transfer it to me."

I stuff the last of my sandwich in my mouth so I don't have to meet his eyes. He says he trusts me, but what if he finds out I'm not Rayne?

"You ready to talk strategy?" he says when I've swallowed. He brings up his band's holo display, and selects an option that replaces the display with a mist of blue light. Inside the mist he uses one finger to draw a circle, then makes a tower in the middle of it with his thumb and forefinger, pulling a solid shape out of nothing. "This is the arena." He puts in five dots, evenly spaced inside the circle. "That's us. We'll be starting at the edge, and we could be on opposite sides. If so, we should work our way toward the middle of the tower to find each other."

He moves two of the dots into the tower. With a flick

of one hand, he makes it transparent, so I can see the two dots in the middle.

I frown. "That'll waste time."

"Being together should give us enough of an advantage to make up for it."

I nod slowly. Eight sets of claws instead of four. Someone to watch my back. It could give me the edge I need to win.

"Besides," he says. "First up the tower gets to deal with the Kraken."

"Tell me about the Kraken. What is it?"

"You still haven't made it as far as—?"

Even with one eye bandaged, I can still give him a glare that cuts him off. "Just tell me."

"A Kraken is a giant sea monster with tentacles."

"You're kidding?"

He touches his band and says, "Kraken, image." The tower disappears and a picture's projected, a creature like an octopus. "The one in the game is metal. It's part of the tower, so it's hard to see until it starts attacking you."

"And it's big?"

"You could say that."

"How are we going to beat it?"

"We could fight it with teeth and claws. But I think we should wait until it's attacking someone else, then slip past."

"Aza'll get there first," I say. "She's got the fastest Skin."

"She might hold back."

I snort. "Can you imagine Aza the center of attention in a race with millions of people watching? She's got an amazing, super-fast Skin that can speed off and make the rest of us look like slow-pokes... and instead she decides to hold back?"

He grins. "So, that's the plan. We let Aza fight it for us."

He sounds way too confident for my liking.

"You don't think her Skin's fast enough to get by it? What if it's not quick enough to catch her?"

His mouth twists. "You haven't seen the Kraken."

"And the others? What'll they be doing?"

"Brugan might go after you. This may come as a shock, but I get the feeling you're not his favorite person."

"No kidding."

"Together we can overpower him."

"And Sentin?"

Cale shakes his head, leaning back in his chair. His mostly uneaten sandwich is still pushed to one side, and even though mine was big enough to fill me up, I can't help glancing at it. I'm not used to seeing food ignored.

"I don't know what Sentin will do," he says. "He's hard to predict. But the good thing is, you're even harder to predict."

"What do you mean?"

"You keep surprising me. Like the first time we had dinner and you stole a knife. Nobody but you would do something like that."

"You saw me?"

He laughs at my shock. "Don't worry, I'm the only one who did. And that's why you're going to win. Not even Sentin would steal a knife and keep it in his sock."

I shift uncomfortably, my face warm. I don't know why I'm so embarrassed he caught me, but I want to turn the conversation back to Sentin.

"I still can't believe he's Deiterran," I say.

"Me too." Cale shakes his head. "I think I would have been less surprised if he'd wandered out of the dead zone."

"Especially because there's all this talk of war."

"I keep asking him about Deiterra, but he won't say a word. Not really surprising, the way Brugan treats him."

"Brugan's been picking on him?"

"Making fun of him for being Deiterran. You haven't noticed? Sentin shrugs it off like he's used to it."

"He probably is."

Cale nods. "And those glasses of his aren't supposed to exist."

"What do you mean?"

"Gamers are always the first to hear about any new tech in the pipeline, and there was some underground buzz about them. Mostly speculation about how they might be used in secret, you know, to win gambling tournaments." He gives me a sideways look from under his dark lashes. "But the glasses were squashed. President Trask wouldn't approve them, so they were never made."

"How'd Sentin get a pair?"

"Good question."

"You think he could be in the Deiterran army? A spy? Doctor Gregory said he studied military tactics."

Cale snorts. "I studied business for a year and it didn't make me a desk monkey." I must look surprised because he rolls his eyes. "My parents insisted. For some reason they don't think playing *Hell Spawn III* is a 'real job'." He uses his fingers to make air quotes.

I can't help but smile. Then I glance at his sandwich again. The fact it's still sitting there is bugging me. "Aren't you going to eat that?"

He pushes the plate in front of me, motioning at me to help myself. Well, why not? Eating when I'm full is better than seeing perfectly good food go to waste.

"What else do you know about Sentin?" I ask around a mouthful of his sandwich.

"From what I can gather, he's lived in Triton most of his life. But you know how he hardly talks? I was listening to him with Doctor Gregory the other day, and he was asking her a lot of suspicious questions."

"Like what?"

"How long she's been working here, what exactly she does, how many others work on the Skins. Lots of things he doesn't need to know."

"With his glasses on, he could tell if she lied about anything."

"Perhaps he doesn't like the Morelle Corporation any more than I do. I wonder if...?" He trails off.

"What?" I put what's left of the sandwich back down and lean forward, not wanting to miss a word.

"It's probably nothing. But the Fist members I met said they were getting better organized now."

I nod. The Fist is a protest group that has a broadcast channel on Sub Zero, the indie web. They've been trying to get factories upgraded and shelters made safer, and they show footage of stompers beating up sinkers. Occasionally they vandalize a building, or disrupt a public event. Pretty much everyone in Old Triton knows someone who belongs to the Fist, and Tori used to go to meetings.

"They're stockpiling weapons," he adds.

"What kind of weapons?"

He shrugs. "Probably explosives. Unless they manage to print their own guns."

I raise my eyebrows. Only stompers are allowed guns. The penalty for anyone else is death.

"You think they're going to target the President?" I ask. Between the rumblings of war with Deiterra, and the Fist getting more militant, it feels like real trouble's brewing.

"Wish I knew. Anyway, the other thing I heard was that

they were trying to get their hands on a secret new technology."

"What technology?"

"The guys I know could only repeat the rumors. But it made me think of Sentin's glasses. Not that I think Sentin's the type to join the Fist. He's Deiterran, so why would he? And he doesn't strike me as much of a joiner." He gives me another sideways look. "Maybe you should ask him. I think he might have a soft spot for you."

"What do you mean?"

"I've caught him staring at you a couple of times. When you weren't looking."

Shit. If Sentin's been staring at me, it's because he's making plans to drag me into whatever crazy scheme he's hatched up.

"You okay, Rayne?"

Time for a change of subject. I motion to Cale's band. "Back to the plan?"

He fiddles with it, then shakes his head. "The holo app on this thing sucks. Let's go to my room. I've got a mind-pad."

Cale's scent hits me as soon as I walk in, that fresh, clean smell that's uniquely his. And is there a hint of feline too? It's musky and so heady I want to open my lungs to it and drag it in. But no, the tiger scent can't be in Cale's room. I must be imagining it.

Funny how I've been noticing smells and sounds more lately. Maybe my brain's getting used to having sharp leopard senses, so it's more tuned into everything.

Stepping over a pile of Cale's clothes, I need to search for enough clear space to put my feet. How can one person have so many *things*? If I put everything I've ever owned on the floor of my room, it would barely fill one corner.

His bed isn't made, but he pulls the cover over the messy bedclothes, making a lumpy surface. "Here, sit."

As I do, I'm very conscious of being shut in his room, and of the way he moves, so confident in his own body. He's taller than me, and strong, with wide shoulders and muscled arms, and he seems to take up far more space in here than he should. Running damp palms down the front of my trousers, I tell myself not to worry. This is *Cale*. The one man I can trust.

When he shoots me a smile, my muscles relax a little. The way his lips quirk, that cute indent in his cheek—his strong, honest character shows in every angle of his face. And maybe it's all artificial, but every time I look at him, I'm struck again by how good-looking he is. Instead of getting used to his handsome face, it only seems to get more perfect.

"Hey, have you noticed any difference with your sight or smell?" I ask him. "Like they're getting better?"

He considers it, tilting his head and looking around the room like he's testing himself. "Don't think so. Why, have you?"

"Probably imagining things. Forget it."

I perch on the end of his bed while he pulls his mind-pad out from under a pile of clothes, then sits next to me. Too close. I shift so there's no chance our knees will touch. As the leopard, I love spending my nights alone with him, but in my human body his closeness makes me jittery.

"How does that thing work?" I ask to cover my nerves.

"I have a chip implanted that transmits my thoughts."

"Like the one for your Skin?"

"Sort of. Okay, here's the tower." It shoots out of the mind-pad fully formed, and so realistic I swallow a gasp. It's a perfect miniature, exactly as I remember from the vReal game.

"How'd you do that?"

"This? Not hard. The tower's in my memory and the mind-pad accessed it."

"You remember all this?" I point to the tiny, intricate detail of the beams.

"Yeah well, it's obviously stored in my brain. The level of detail always surprises me too."

Tentacles extend from the middle of the tower, waving around. A metal monster, far bigger than I could have imagined.

"That's the Kraken. And here's Aza." A tiny version of her Wasp Skin appears in the tower near the Kraken's outstretched tentacles. "We'll look for the farthest point from its head to climb past." He puts our two feline Skins in, both poised in the act of leaping from the same beam. "Hopefully its tentacles won't reach that far."

I stare at the tiny version of my leopard. It's just as breathtaking in miniature. "What if they can reach that far?" I ask.

"We can fight it if we work together. It's not impossible to defeat."

"How many times have you—?"

"I almost did once."

"Oh."

Our two Skins look tiny and fragile next to the tentacled monster spilling out of the tower. It looks like it could wipe us both out with one swipe.

"It's vulnerable," he says in a determined tone. "Director Morelle wants this to be a spectacle. She won't want us all to be beaten by the Kraken."

"Okay. So, say we get by it. What then?"

He shrugs. "More creatures, I guess. Harder ones. Basically a race to survive and get to the top."

"A race... or a battle?"

"Both."

"And when we get to the top?"

"You know how I said the tower's intelligent? Its job is to slow down whoever gets there first. They'll have to fight metal monsters until whoever's left catches up. Then there'll be a Skin-on-Skin battle to the death, at the top of a narrow tower that's one hundred and sixty stories high. The kind of finale that sells vReal games and new technology, don't you think?"

"So it doesn't matter who's fastest? Only who's strongest?"

He shakes his head. "There's a lot to make it through before that final battle. If you're fast, you'll have a better chance of getting to the top without being injured on the way. And it's the first two to reach the top who'll get to fight."

"How exactly do you win?"

"You don't know?" He shakes his head, teasing. "This is my chance to teach you a special dance you need to do. Or, no wait. It's opera. Yeah, when you get to the top, you'll need to sing at least three verses of... OW!" It was the lightest punch — I barely touched him — but he flops onto his back and makes a big deal of grimacing and rubbing his arm.

"Shut up!" I can't help but laugh.

When Cale sits up, grinning, he's too close. I shift away, trying to make it seem casual. Dammit, why is my stomach clenching? I'm fine, it's only Cale. Nothing bad will happen.

He can tell I'm uncomfortable. His grin drops away and he makes a fuss of fiddling with the mind-pad. "Um. At the top of the tower, a light will shine upward." He looks back at me and swallows. I can tell he wants to ask me something personal, but I don't give him the chance.

I get to my feet and lean against the wall. That's better. The distance between us is calming my jitters. But his expression gets me in the chest. He's only wearing a slight frown, but I know him well enough now to be able to tell what's going on underneath.

"Sorry," I blurt.

"Rayne, are you afraid of me?"

"Of course not. So, what happens with the light?" My throat's too tight to talk about anything other than the contest.

He studies me a moment longer, then sighs. "Once the light appears, the first to stand in it wins the contest."

"That's it?" I drag in a breath, imagining that moment. When I step in the light, I'll never have to worry about anything again.

"It'll project your image into the sky. You'll have won, and you'll be rich."

"And I'll get to be the leopard from then on. I'll never have to transfer back."

He looks startled. "You'd really want to be the leopard all the time?"

"Of course, why wouldn't I?"

He shakes his head. "I love being the tiger, but I still want to be human sometimes."

"That's why I'm going to win, and you're willing to let me."

"That's the idea," he agrees. But I can see the doubt in his eyes as clearly as if he'd admitted it out loud. Underneath everything, I bet he does want to win. And just like me, the more he wears his Skin, the stronger the wanting gets.

Chapter Twenty-One

L ying in my room that night, staring into the darkness as I wait for Cale, I go over what happened when I was alone with him. He wasn't doing anything to make me uncomfortable. He's definitely no shark. But when he got too close, I was afraid of him.

I *hate* being afraid.

And it makes no sense to be scared of Cale. I'd be a lot weaker here without him. I love training with him and I've grown to trust him. So what's broken inside me? Why can't I let him get close?

Thinking about it is making me edgy. I keep imagining I hear noises outside my door and my stomach knots up each time. Cale has collected me from my room every night for the past week. Why is it suddenly turning into a big deal in my head?

He's later than usual. When I finally hear him, I jump up and fling open the door. His smile fades when he sees my expression.

"Sorry I'm late," he motions to my bandaged eye. "I

wasn't sure if it'd be safe for you to train while your eye's still healing."

"It'll be fine." For some reason, it comes out peevish. I don't even know why I'm angry, and it's not because of anything he's done. I'm mad with myself.

"Are you okay, Rayne?"

"Why wouldn't I be?" I push past him, into the hall.

He throws a frowning glance at me again when he uses his gadget to open the door, but doesn't say anything.

Once we're in the darkness of the hallway, Cale lies down first. I hesitate, staring at his dark outline, waiting for his breathing to slow.

This is crazy. I'm facing the most important day of my life, and instead of concentrating on how I'm going to win the contest, I'm getting myself worked up about Cale.

I wish I knew how he feels about me. It's much easier when we're in our Skins, I know Cale the tiger is attracted to leopard me. And when I'm the leopard I'm not afraid to like him back.

When I'm the leopard I feel strong, sure, but it's more than that. Leopard me is different from human me, a million times removed from a weak girl struggling on the filthy floor of a shelter. And a tiger's not a man. The tiger doesn't have a man's rough hands, or a man's eager, rancid breath.

But does Cale's tiger look at my leopard that way only because that's what felines do? Or is it more than that?

When I'm in my Skin the why doesn't matter so much. It's when we're not in our Skins that I get confused.

I lie down beside him, but don't close my eyes right away. For some reason I'm picturing my mother and father lying next to each other in their bed, before Papa died.

Funny that the memory's not as painful as it used to be. In the shelter I'd do anything not to have to remember that time. I didn't want to think about how easy it used to be to live and laugh and go to school and have a mother and father, and a baby brother. The memory used to stab like a blade in my chest, but now there's no pain.

Maybe it doesn't hurt because in spite of the pressure of the upcoming contest, life here is so good. Instead of sweating on my feet all day and spending dangerous nights in the shelter, I get to be the leopard instead. How blissful is that?

I close my human eye. Open leopard eyes. It's a rush. Far from the thrill wearing off, the more I'm the leopard, the better it gets. My human body feels so *wrong* compared to this one.

Cale is prowling in the big training room, waiting for me. As always, I can sense his joy at being the tiger. It mixes with my own and makes it even stronger.

Cale's head turns toward me. He's admiring how gracefully I move. My feet don't make a sound as I pad softly across the floor. Right now I could take on Aza, Brugan and Sentin at once. I *want* to fight them. I want to stretch my leopard to its limit, to find out if it even has a limit.

To win the contest I'll have to fight at least one of them. Am I ready? I feel invincible, but they're just as strong as I am. Cale's strong too, but I'm faster. Could I beat him?

"Let's fight," I say.

"In the battle-bot?"

"The battle-bot's too safe. Let's really fight."

He gets my meaning straight away because his tail swishes with eagerness and the fur along his spine lifts. He wants to test his skill as much as I do. But after a moment, his tail lowers and he shakes his head. "I don't want to hurt you, Rayne."

I snort. "Worry about yourself."

"I've got saber-teeth as well as claws."

"Afraid of me?" I taunt. "You've never been in a fight, have you?"

"Rayne, I—"

I cut him off with a snarl. I'm facing him, ears back against my skull, crouched low against the ground. He must be able to feel my excitement. From the tang of his scent and the way his weight's shifting between his front paws, his is just as strong.

"How're you going to fight in the arena, if you can't fight me now?" I mimic Brugan's voice. "Scared, little kitty cat?"

He growls, low in his throat. His ears flatten and his mouth drops open, his long front fangs glistening. He stretches his body into a long sleek shape. I can feel anticipation fizzing through him, matching my own.

We circle each other, slinking low to the ground, tails twitching. Both alert to the other's slightest movement. He won't attack first. He's holding back, waiting to see what I'll do. If I rush him he'll have the advantage.

I pace lightly, whiskers quivering, resisting the growl that's threatening to rise out of me, the instinct that's telling me to throw myself at him with claws and teeth. Think! When I fought Max, I feinted one way then lunged the other, but that's too clumsy a trick to use against the tiger. Is there another way to use my speed to get the advantage?

I crouch on my haunches and he mirrors me, anticipating my leap, poised to meet my spring in mid-air with his powerful front claws. Suddenly he's not kind, sensitive Cale anymore, but a savage animal.

I gather my strength and leap as high as I can, soaring over his head.

He isn't expecting it and doesn't react quickly enough. His claws rake my belly, but my thick fur protects me and I barely feel it. I hit the ground and don't slow down, racing toward the climbing frame. By the time he's turned to follow I've got a few lengths on him. Perfect. I launch myself at a low platform while I'm still a few strides away, then use it as a spring board to rebound from. I twist in the air, turning my body into a missile. My strength and weight is aimed at Cale's head.

I smash into him with claws extended. We tumble, skidding along the ground in a tangle of fur, teeth and claws. Pain sears through my side. We skid to a stop and when he tries to struggle to his paws I cry out.

"Rayne!"

"Just. Don't. Move."

I count three deep breaths, then gasp as I ease one of his big front teeth out of my body. I push myself away from him and stand, winded and unsteady.

"God, Rayne, are you okay?"

"Yeah." Pain turns the word into a growl. At least I can stand, but my side's on fire and the sweet, hot scent of blood fills my senses.

Shit, what have I done? They're going to wonder how my leopard got injured in the middle of the night when we're supposed to be asleep in bed. And the contest's only a few days away.

"I'm sorry, Rayne." He doesn't look good either. I must have torn a chunk of fur out of his head because tufts of hair are floating around him.

I manage to lift my tail enough to twitch it back and forth. Almost as good as a shaky smile. "Good move, huh?"

He grimaces. "I hurt all over." He steps close to me, nuzzling his nose against my neck. "But you're the one I'm worried about."

His face moves to my injured side. I feel something warm and wet against my fur. For a second my human brain makes me flinch away. Then the leopard takes over, and I move toward him, letting him clean my wound with long strokes of his tongue.

He's still breathing deeply. Both of us are. His tiger body is against me, closer than I could ever let anyone get to my human body. But I'm the leopard now, not a weak girl. I can let my human mind, my human fears drift away. His tongue moves over me, licking my shoulders, down my sides. A noise forces from my throat, an animal sound, halfway between a snarl and a purr.

He pushes against me, his tongue insistent. He's not just cleaning my wound any more. His scent turns to musk. His head moves above mine, his body pushing me to the ground. His teeth bite into my neck. I stretch out, not fighting, letting him pin me to the floor.

He's strong, but so am I. I could throw him off if I needed to, and the knowledge is enough to both soothe and excite me. It lets me press my body against his while he runs his tongue over my fur.

He growls and nips me as he licks. His tongue is first tender, then rough. As he covers my body with rasping strokes, I feel his need swell, his heartbeat speed up.

My pulse joins his, racing alongside it. His longing fills me. It's our longing, our hunger joined. It grows with every growling, urgent stroke of his tongue. It consumes me. He tastes of tiger musk. Dangerous. Beautiful. I suck him in like oxygen.

"Rayne," he breathes. "So fierce. So brave."

I let out a hoarse laugh, stretching my wound to test it. "It doesn't hurt that much."

He stops licking my side to nuzzle my neck. "I'm not

talking about that. You know what I feel whenever I see you?"

"Human or leopard?"

"Both."

Possibilities flit through my mind. Shock. Pity. Revulsion. But those words belong to my human body only, not my leopard.

"What?" I ask.

"Awe," he whispers.

I pull back to ask what he means. But then I see the heat in his beautiful golden gaze, and the question vanishes.

A shivery thrill runs over me, and I push my nose under his neck, biting him with playful nips. Wanting him with a fierceness that takes me totally by surprise. I've never felt anything like this. Though I wriggle against him, we're not close enough. I need his mouth on me, his body pressing hard on mine.

His front paws urge me to roll over. He nuzzles the fur on my chest and belly. When his head comes close enough, I take one of his ears into my mouth and worry it with my teeth. A sound of pleasure rumbles deep in his throat. As his body covers me, I answer with my own. His weight feels so good my growl becomes a cry.

Then I feel him hesitate. As if his thoughts were in my mind, I know he's worried about my injury. But I won't let him stop. Instead I bite his neck, pulling him down on me, pressing harder against him. My need for him is stronger than any pain.

"Rayne." He groans my name. "Oh God, Rayne."

Then he wrenches away.

There's a noise outside the door.

"It's Aza." I surge up to standing.

"Quick, Rayne, go!"

We race for our lab rooms. At first he runs beside me, supporting me across the training room floor, then we split to run for our own rooms. Aza's inside the door, in the training room, feeling for the light.

Cale reaches his room. But pain stabs through my side and I stumble.

The light goes on.

"Rayne?" Aza gasps.

I don't stop. One more leap and I make it into the lab room, onto the metal disk. I close my eyes and transfer.

As soon as my eyes flick open, Cale pulls me to my feet. "Quick, let's go."

I take off down the hall ahead of him before remembering I'm not supposed to jolt my eye. With an effort, I force myself to slow down.

Cale slows too. Worry is etched into every line of his expression. "Are you all right?"

"Aza saw me." My fists clench, and I want to beat my stupid head against the wall. "She'll go straight to Director Morelle and I'll get kicked out. Why did I risk breaking the rules?"

"We'll both go and confess. I'll say I talked you into training at night, that you didn't want to. If anyone gets thrown out, it should be me."

"Cale, I can't confess. I can't take the chance."

"But—"

"You don't understand. This means everything to me." I swallow hard. Have I just ruined everything?

"Then it's better if you tell Director Morelle your side, before she hears it from Aza."

I shake my head. "I'm going to keep my mouth shut and hope like hell they let it drop. There are only four days before the contest. They're not going to want to replace me now."

"Are you sure?"

"If I admit I've been breaking the rules, they won't be able to ignore it. Better to pretend nothing's happened and hope they do they same." We reach the door and I crack it open to check the coast is clear. "Get back to your room, Cale. Best if they don't catch us together, just in case."

He bends toward me like he's going to kiss me. Instinctively I jump back, pulling my arm from his grip.

His hurt expression makes me want to kick myself. If we had more time, I'd be able to explain how it's not his fault, and he hasn't done anything wrong. It's easy to be together when I'm the leopard, but in my human body I just can't.

"See you in the training room." It comes out colder than I intend. I don't want to be so distant, but years of fear and hurt and bad memories have clogged my throat. My human tongue feels thick and clumsy.

It's only the leopard that isn't afraid. Only in my Skin can I be free.

It's not until I'm safely back in my room, and my heart has slowed down from racing a million beats a second, that I realize my body's sore and blood is soaking through my T-shirt. Lifting my shirt in front of the mirror, I ease it away from a jagged gash that runs up my side.

I stare at it for a long time, because I don't want to believe what I'm seeing.

Sliced into my human body is a wound in the same place as the cut on my leopard. A wound that looks like it was made by a tiger's tooth.

Chapter Twenty-Two

I clean my wound as best I can with a wet towel, pressing hard on it until the bleeding eventually stops. But what can I use for a bandage? A strip of towel? I could use my blade to cut the cloth.

Even taking my time as I gingerly carry the chair to the closet reopens the wound so I have to stop and press on it again. But finally I'm on the chair, stretching up to feel the back of the shelf.

My blade has gone.

I last got it out a couple of days ago, and definitely put it back. Someone must have taken it. But how did they know it was there?

I'm being watched.

A cold shiver runs down my backbone.

I'm so stupid. Of course they've been watching me. All this time I've been kidding myself that security's slack, that I've been getting away with training at night, because I wanted to believe it. Because I hate not being the leopard and can't bear to stop. But Director Morelle must know what's been going on. The only question is, why has she let me carry on?

I can't think, my side's throbbing. First things first, I've got to take care of my wound. The towel's too thick to tear without the blade, so I rip one of my lovely new T-shirts into strips to tie around my middle. Wincing, I pull a couple of layers of clothes on over the top, choosing dark colors in case blood spots manage to soak through.

Could someone have cut my body while my mind was in my Skin? No, I can't believe that, the cut matches the one on my leopard too closely. Somehow my body must have conjured up a wound.

No time to worry about it now. I'm late for training as it is.

When I walk into the training room the others are already in their Skins. Cale's at the base of the never-wall, watching Aza and Sentin climb, and Brugan's fighting the battle-bot. I stride toward my lab room, my aching need to be the leopard making me walk as fast as I can while praying my wound doesn't start bleeding again.

But Doctor Gregory intercepts me. Her kind face looks concerned. "Rayne, Aza told me…" She hesitates, glancing across the training room.

I follow her gaze. Aza has soared off the never-wall and is flying at me, her wings propelling her across the hall in long, purposeful leaps. Cale lopes after her, his tail low and his ears flattened against his skull.

My stomach flips over. So much for my faint hope Aza won't say anything. I leave the doctor and step forward to meet her.

Aza rushes at me so fast, I brace for impact. She stops just before she ploughs into me, and towers over me, thin and beautiful. The top half of her wasp face doesn't show any expression, but her fury's so strong it makes even my dull human senses flinch. Her black helmet shimmers with light and her wings quiver, lifting and falling like red gossamer lungs.

"You've been cheating," she hisses.

Cale growls. His hackles are lifted, his teeth bared. I wave him back. Though I'm only in my weak human body, this is my problem to handle.

A stinger shoots out from Aza's right palm. She sweeps it in front of me, threatening me. It's a graceful move, like a dance. She reminds me so much of Tori, warning off a shark with her blade, that my heart twists. Tori has the same unconscious grace, and a fearlessness that kept both of us safe.

"I took some extra training time," I say, my thoughts of Tori making me more honest than I'd intended.

Aza curls her top lip as her hand sweeps back, completing the curve. "You admit it?"

Instinctively I lift my weak, human hand and extend my own soft palm toward her. The comparison is absurd. "I'm sorry. I won't do it again."

Aza's wings go still as she stares down at my pale, work-battered hand. I'm no threat, not like this. She may as well rage at a bug. Her stinger retracts back into her palm leaving it smooth. Her full red lips press together, then release as she lets out a sharp breath.

"Cheating won't help you. I'm faster than you and I'm going to beat you."

I incline my head. An acknowledgement, neither agreeing nor disagreeing. "We'll see."

She spins gracefully, dismissing me. The human me isn't worth bothering with. We both agree on that.

Cale pads beside me as I head to the training room, his tiger's tail switching anxiously from side to side. "Sure you're okay, Rayne? I can smell blood."

"It's okay." I touch his shoulder, running my hand across the softness of his fur, down the big muscle that's flexing as he walks. He blinks his golden eyes and when I offer him a smile, he nuzzles my cheek. His nose is cold, and his breath warm. His fresh scent is like soft rain falling around me.

Just one touch and he's forgiven me for stepping away from him last night. If only it were that easy to reach out to him when he's human.

A low, harsh snarl makes me turn my head. Brugan's in the fighting ring, his devil bear mouth twisted in a snarl, and his human-looking torso covered with sweat. He must really have been laying into the battle-bot. But now his eyes are fixed on me and filled with a rage blacker than Aza's. The strength of his fury chills me.

I need to be the leopard.

When I transfer, I find my leopard's wound doesn't hurt as much as my human one. But the stench of devil bear's getting stronger. Brugan's strides across the room toward me, and I walk out to meet him, Cale by my side.

"You slimy sewer rat. Who let you in here to train last night? Was it Doctor Gregory?" His eyes are blazing. "You're friendly with the doctor, aren't you, rat? Is she the one helping you cheat?"

His nostrils flare. He's scenting my blood from last night's wound and his tongue flicks out to lick his lips. A gesture that makes me shudder.

"Back off, Brugan." I put as much force in the words as I can.

"Leave her alone." Cale crouches, ears flat and tail swishing.

"Stay out of it, Cale." My voice is a warning growl. Brugan's anger could be just the cover-up I need to disguise how I really got the big gash in my side. All I need is to goad him into a fight. And for Cale to stop trying to protect me.

Nudging Cale with my shoulder, I push my weight into his flank, then move up so I'm shoulder-to-shoulder with him, staring up at Brugan. Hopefully Cale will get the message.

"You don't seriously think you can win, do you Brugan?" My voice is scornful. "You'll be the last to the top of the tower, if you make it up at all. And after watching you lumber up the never-wall, I doubt you'll get far."

His mouth drops open, showing glistening fangs. He snarls so loud it hurts my ears.

"Brugan!" Doctor Gregory's yell makes his eyes flicker sideways.

I can't let her distract him now. Growling, I spring forward as though attacking. He swipes at me, but I'm already leaping back out of range.

I'm faster than you, Brugan. Catch me if you can.

Slinking close to the floor, I'm careful to keep my injured side to the wall so he can't see it. Cale's circling to the side, head and tail low. He knows I don't want him interfering, but he can't help himself.

"Keep away, Cale." I don't take my eyes off Brugan. "This isn't your fight."

Brugan's teeth are bared, his eyes red. He ignores Cale, focusing his hatred on me.

"Rayne! Brugan!" Doctor Gregory sounds desperate. "Stop—"

I feint forward. Brugan's claws are already swinging. This time I make sure to angle my wounded side toward him and jump back in time so his claws rake through my thick fur and barely scratch my skin. Perfect. Except the movement reopens my wound and fresh blood seeps hot and sticky into my fur. The sweet, cloying smell makes my heart race. The scent's so strong, it fills the room and makes the air thick. Like breathing sweet, hot fire.

"Keep away from her!" Cales rushes forward, putting his body between us.

"Dammit, Cale!" Butting my shoulder into his flank, I catch him by surprise. He stumbles and Brugan's on him at once, stabbing his giant claws at Cale's face.

Cale jerks away and Brugan claw grazes the top of his head, catching one ear and ripping it. Cale howls, swiping at his torn ear with one paw.

Catching the scent of his blood sends a hot flush of anger through me. Hurting me after I goaded him is one thing, but all Cale's guilty of is trying to protect me. Brugan's going to pay for that.

I back up, trying to draw Brugan away and give Cale time to recover. Brugan's nostrils flare again as he drinks in the warm scent of Cale's blood. The tiger blinks and shakes his head as blood matts his fur and gums up his eyes. He's an easy target.

"You're the slowest, Brugan. You don't stand a chance." I angle my wound toward him to give him my scent. Enticing him to me and away from Cale. "And after all the extra training I've been doing, you may as well give up now."

His eyes narrow. They're so red, it's like the blood smell has filled them. I can sense how fast his heart is racing. The sweet scent of blood is a drug that makes him less human, more animal. I know because I taste it in my throat, feel it pounding in my veins. I want to throw myself at him, tear at him with teeth and claws, show him just how strong I am. I crouch, tail whisking back and forth, sweeping the floor.

"Stop it, Rayne! Brugan!" Doctor Gregory's shout

makes me jump, because now she's just behind me. What's she doing getting so close? We're twice her size. One swipe from a paw could kill her.

As my head swings toward her, Brugan's weight hits me. My legs buckle. I hit the floor hard, grunting as the breath whooshes out of me. He holds me down, impossibly heavy, crushing my body against the floor.

The stench of devil bear overpowers the scent of blood. He's panting, his body shaking, his coarse hair puffed out. When he roars, it's like the room's being blown apart.

Cale snarls. With my head pushed against the floor, I can just make out Cale crouching, ready to spring. Blood runs down his snout and his long fangs glisten red.

I struggle, desperate to get free, but Brugan pushes into me with his whole weight. Doctor Gregory's still yelling, but it sounds distant and muffled. Cale lunges at Brugan. The weight on top of me shifts so I can't see what's happening. Brugan gets even heavier and I yelp as my shoulder grinds into the floor.

The weight eases. There's a thud, and a grunt of pain. It's Cale, he's on the ground. He must be injured. Brugan reaches down and grabs my head, wrenching it around, forcing me to look at him. Pain lances through my neck and shoulders. It feels like he's going to twist my head right off.

He brings his face close to mine, panting. His hot, foul breath gusts over me. The stench of devil bear makes me want to throw up. His eyes bore into me, his pupils bulging, bloated with power. He's crazy with it. Drunk with his own strength.

I know that look. I've seen it before, in the shelter. A cruel glee that glinted in the eyes of the man whose big hand pressed against my mouth to hold in my screams.

I can't move.

Brugan's mouth sinks so close it feels like he's about to kiss me. "Too good for you." He's as much snarling as talking, so it's hard to understand the words. "This Skin's not ugly enough, sewer rat." He brings one hand up, running one sharp claw up my muzzle.

My eye squeezes shut as his claw runs over it, and my heart freezes when I realize what he intends to do.

I won't let him rip out my eye.

My body jerks and spasms. I fight with everything I've got.

He curses, and stabs. His claw misses its mark. It sinks into the lower edge of my eye and tears downwards.

Pain sears through me. My face is on fire. I'm screaming. The weight comes off and suddenly I can roll over. I paw at my muzzle, at the searing pain.

"Rayne!" Human hands grab me. "Rayne, it's all right. It's Doctor Gregory." The hands grip my face, steadying me. "Sentin, get my medical bag from the lab. Over there. Quickly! Cale, move back and let me take care of this. Brugan, transfer out of your Skin. NOW. In fact, all of you transfer." Then quieter, to me. "It's okay, Rayne. The cut's deep, but you'll be fine. As soon as you go back into your own body it'll stop hurting."

Go into my human body? I can't think how to do that. The pain's too strong.

There's a thump and Doctor Gregory says, "That's it. Thank you." Her steadying hands lift off me, and I hear the sounds of a case being opened. A moment later, a needle slides into my side. Right away, the pain's easier to take.

"Better, Rayne?" Her hands stroke my fur and her voice is soothing. "Can you make it back to your lab room before you transfer? If not, transfer here and I'll have your Skin moved and taken care of."

I blink away the blood in my eyes, trying to peer through the red mist. Cale's shifting from paw to paw behind Doctor Gregory, his head down and nose reaching toward me. He's got cuts on his front legs, and blood all over his face.

"I'm okay," I manage. But am I?

I'm not sure I can transfer back into my body. Even in pain, my leopard feels like my natural body. To transfer is to wrench free of it. It gets harder each time.

If I go to my lab room, maybe the technicians will be able to fix my Skin more quickly. With an effort, I push myself up onto my paws. Whatever the doctor gave me has all but taken away the pain.

"Wait!" Aza's cry is shocked. "Look."

Doctor Gregory turns. "Rayne..." The word chokes off.

I turn to look, blinking away the red haze that's clouding my vision.

My human body is in its pod. Blood covers my face. What's happened to my cheek? It's a mess of welling blood that's dripping into my hair and soaking through the bandage over my eye.

Shit, my eye. My new eye. Is it okay? Please let it be okay. I need to know my eye's not damaged.

"Rayne, wait. Let me attend to your body." Doctor Gregory runs toward the pod, calling as she goes. "Max, get help! Hurry!"

I rip my mind out of the leopard and into my human body, like pulling my thoughts out of glue.

My human face hurts as much as the leopard's did. Doctor Gregory grabs my shoulder, but I struggle away from her, launching myself out of the pod. My fingers slip through the blood on my cheek, searching for the edge of the bandage that covers my eye.

"Don't remove the dressing!" Doctor Gregory shouts.

Too late. I've yanked it off. Keeping my eye closed, I stumble over to stare into one of the blank, dark computer screens. Not much of a mirror, but good enough. My scarred cheek's a mess. Through the gore I can make out four deep slashes cutting through my scars. Claw marks. I press the bandage against my cheek to try to stop the bleeding. The cuts have ripped through the flesh right under my eye, and with all the blood it's hard to tell, but I think my closed eyelid might be unharmed.

I have to check my eye. I need to be sure.

The blood's sticky, so it's an effort to open my eyelid. When it comes unstuck, it's coated in red gunk. I blink madly, then stare into the screen.

My heart stops.

Two eyes.

I have two beautiful eyes.

Even with the gore covering my face, and my hideous scars, I almost look like a normal person.

My eye's okay. Better than okay. It's perfect. Beautiful. Look at me, I'm not a freak.

The screen blurs and I blink hard to drive tears away. I'm afraid to lose sight of my new eye in case it's not there when I look back.

Someone touches my arm. Doctor Gregory. I hadn't noticed she was standing next to me. Her arm goes around my shoulders and she hugs me tight. The movement hurts the wound on my side, but the pain is easy to ignore.

"Rayne?" Cale's voice comes from just behind me. It's about the only thing that could drag me from my own reflection.

Doctor Gregory lets me go and I turn to face him. I

meet his golden tiger eyes. They're wide open, as bright as though they're reflecting the sun. His muzzle stretches toward me as his scent wraps around me, warm and welcoming. His face comes close enough for his tiger nose to brush against my human one. He's smiling, not just with his mouth, but with his whole body.

"You're lovely," he whispers. "Even more so, I mean. You were lovely before, but... Hell, Rayne. I'm making a fool of myself, aren't I?" He gives a throaty, entirely unembarrassed chuckle and I feel my own smile come surging up. My joy is so fierce it feels like something too big to be inside me. Like an animal released from a cage.

Doctor Gregory clears her throat. "Rayne, we must get that cheek cleaned up. I don't know what could have happened to it, but I must say, I'm worried."

I lower the bandage from my cheek. It's soaked red and dripping. And my T-shirt is sticking to me, the blood soaking through my makeshift bandage. Thankfully nobody's noticed I have a wound on my side as well.

"They're deep cuts." The doctor peers at my face. "They'll need to be cleaned and sealed."

Cale steps back to give her some room, and I see the others. They're in their human bodies now, staring curiously. I meet their stares, lifting my chin.

Go ahead and look. For the first time, I want them to look.

Aza cocks her head as she studies me. She's judging me fresh, I guess, not looking away this time. Perhaps now I'm worthy of her notice. Sentin gives me a nod, though his expression is unreadable.

It's only Brugan who sneers. "Still ugly, sewer rat," he mutters.

Cale's anger comes flooding back, his scent so strong I

flinch. It's as though I'm still in my leopard, able to read his feelings as easily as my own.

He growls, low and dangerous. "I'm warning you, Brugan. One more word..."

Brugan turns on him. Though his human body is a lot smaller than the tiger, his fists are raised. "What you going to do, little kitty?"

"Cale," snaps Doctor Gregory. "Didn't I tell you to get out of your Skin?"

"Ignore him," I say, touching the soft fur on Cale's flank.

Cale's sleek body is close to the ground, his shoulders jutting up. His tail whisks back and forth. He's fighting his anger. I feel his rage warring against his control.

Brugan unclenches one fist and holds it up with his fingers stiff and splayed, as though it's a devil bear claw. With a horrible smile he stabs the air in front of him. "Meant to aim a little higher, carve out that eye," he snarls. "Next time, I won't miss."

"No, Cale, don't!"

Too late.

Cale's lunges faster than any human could. His claws flash and Brugan staggers back, clutching his chest. Brugan's shirt is slashed and hanging open. Blood wells through his fingers.

Cale crouches back on his haunches. He puts his head down, his ears plastered back against his skull. The stink of blood has made him stop, made him realize what he's done.

My heart is hammering, my stomach churning.

"Cale, get away!" yells Doctor Gregory.

I didn't notice the door opening, but suddenly Director Morelle's in the room. "What's going on here?" Her voice makes everyone freeze. Nobody answers, but she glares at

Cale. Her finger extends to point at him. "Get out of that Skin."

"Rayne's cheek—," starts Doctor Gregory, but the director cuts her off.

"It appears both Rayne and Brugan need medical attention. Please take them to be cleaned up."

"But you must know what—"

"Thank you, Susan. We'll talk about it later."

The doctor leads me to the door. She waves me through, but I hesitate. First I need to see if Cale's okay, make sure his human body wasn't hurt when his Skin was cut. He gets out of his pod slowly, but I can't see any wounds.

Director Morelle motions at me impatiently. "Go," she says. Then she turns to Cale, her face cold and set. "Cale, by attacking a weaker human opponent while in your Skin, you've broken the rules. You're disqualified. Go and pack your things. You'll be leaving today."

Chapter Twenty-Three

The surgeon pulls the scanner away from my eye and frowns.

My heart contracts. "What's wrong?"

"Your new eye is functioning exceptionally well." His frown deepens. "If I hadn't implanted it myself, I'd have thought you'd had the operation weeks or months ago. And it's not just the fast pace of your healing that's surprising. The scores from your vision tests show 20/10 or better."

"That's bad?"

"It's well above the normal range."

I don't get why he's frowning. Shouldn't he be happy he made me such a good eye?

"I need to run more tests, but I'm due in surgery. Could you book another appointment on your way out?"

I nod, but I'm lying. I don't have time to make more appointments, I need to get out of here. They wouldn't let me see Cale, and I have to make it back to the Morelle Corporation before they force him to leave.

Doctor Gregory's waiting for me outside. The

surgeon let me leave the bandage off my new eye so I'm struck speechless as I gaze around at the New Triton street. My vision's so sharp I can pick out tiny details of people and buildings. I can see every detail of the leaves on a plant in the window of an apartment building down the street. There are no black spots or blurring, and no pain at all.

Is this how everything looked before I lost my eye? I don't remember being so transfixed by the world, so absorbed by every detail.

I follow Doctor Gregory into a cab, and once inside, I start to ask about Cale, but she holds up one hand to stop me.

"I'm sorry, Rayne. If I could do something I would, but letting him go is the director's decision."

I press my lips together. Good thing Brugan wasn't hurt badly enough to need a hospital visit. If I'd had to ride in the cab with him, he might not have survived the trip.

The doctor's expression softens. "Please, let's talk about what happened to your face. I'm convinced your cuts were caused by a severe somatoform disorder."

"A what?"

"It's when physical symptoms manifest from an entirely emotional cause." In answer to my puzzled look she says, "Injuries inflicted on your Skin appear on your real body."

"How can that happen?" I shift a little, conscious of the ache in my side. A nurse bandaged the wound without asking how I got it, and I'm thankful Doctor Gregory still hasn't found out about it. She's worried enough about the cuts in my face.

"I wish I could be certain." Her frown's deeper than the surgeon's was, and worry lines have dug in around her eyes. Wisps of hair are escaping from her messy bun, and when she scratches the side of her head, more strands are released. "Cale and Brugan's Skins both had wounds, yet their human bodies were unhurt."

"So it's just me? Great." That means the others have a huge advantage. For them the contest will be a game. For me it could be deadly.

"I suspect it's to do with the intense level of attachment you have to your Skin. Your mind is unable to separate the two bodies. You're injured in one body, therefore a corresponding wound appears in the other." She reaches over and takes my hand. "It's obvious how much you love your Skin. More than any of the others, you're absorbed by it. I think you *need* it, Rayne. Your mind is escaping into the Skin, using it to flee bad memories."

I never thought of it like that. Does being the leopard feel so incredible because being Milla felt so awful?

I stare down at her brown hand wrapped around mine, and my throat closes up. I'm not used to being touched like this. Not since I had to move to a new shelter and leave Ma behind.

"You think I'm right?" she asks, her voice gentle.

I swallow. "But I don't get how my cheek could tear by itself."

"The mind is very powerful, Rayne. Studies have shown that your thoughts and beliefs can make you sick, or make you well again." She squeezes my hand. "One thing I'm sure of, you can't transfer back into your Skin. The more you use it, the stronger the effect will be."

"What?" I yank my hand from her grip. "No. I'm not quitting the contest."

"I don't think there'll be a contest. After what happened today, it's obvious more clinical trials are necessary and the Skin technology isn't ready for release. Not yet. Director Morelle will have to cancel it."

"Cancel? No, she can't!"

"I believe she must."

"But the others weren't hurt, you said so yourself. I'm the only one, and I'll take the risk. I *need* to compete, Doctor. I know you can't understand, but—"

"Believe me, if I can accept the need to cancel, you should be able to." She rubs her forehead as though trying to soothe away a migraine. "I've been working on this project for decades. Not just working on it, it's absorbed every waking moment. I'm the one who developed the technique for neural stimulation that makes transferal possible. I've given a significant part of my life to this project, and I'm disturbed enough by what happened to you to call a halt to the whole thing."

She glances at her band, then touches it, so somebody must be calling her. She doesn't activate a visual but listens for a moment, then says, "Yes, of course. We're on our way now."

She looks at me. "Director Morelle wants to see us both when we get back. She probably wants to make sure you're not seriously injured. And she and I have much to discuss."

I stare out the window, my mind spinning. What am I going to do now?

I need to be the leopard. I can't let her take that away.

When we arrive at the Morelle scraper, guards in red uniforms escort us into the elevator and up to a higher floor than I've been to before. Director Morelle's waiting for us in a big office, sitting behind an old-fashioned wooden desk. Behind her, through the large window, there's an incredible view over Triton. But I don't have time for more than a glance before I focus on the director. Why is it always so hard to tell what she's thinking? I'm getting even better at reading people lately, but she's still closed to me. Her face gives nothing away.

"Director, I'm glad you asked to see us." Doctor Gregory crosses to a chair in front of the desk and sits down, motioning me to sit in the other chair. "I'm very concerned. Damage done to the Skin has caused corresponding injuries to Rayne's body, with gashes spontaneously appearing in her face."

The director doesn't so much as glance at me. "The surgeon assured me that the damage to Rayne's face was caused by incorrectly implanted cells rupturing. A very rare problem, unrelated to the injury to her Skin. The timing of the burst was purely coincidental."

"Coincidental?"

"That's right." Director Morelle steeples her fingers on the desk. "And Rayne will be in no further danger anyway, as I'll replace her. She won't compete."

My stomach drops away, leaving an empty black pit inside me. "Don't kick me out," I say. "Please. I'll do anything."

Leaning forward, Doctor Gregory puts both hands on the director's desk. "You must call off the contest. It's too dangerous to go on."

"I can't do that, Susan. And there's simply no reason to consider—"

"What if the other competitors start exhibiting these symptoms? If their real bodies suffer somatoform injuries, they could be seriously hurt. Even killed."

"Ridiculous. You're making too much of this."

"Director, it wasn't a coincidence, and it certainly wasn't caused by ruptured cells."

The director stands and moves around the desk to rest her hand on the doctor's shoulder. Her expression softens. At least, it seems to. But her eyes stay as hard as ever. "You've been working too hard, Susan. It's my fault. I've put you under a lot of pressure."

"No." Doctor Gregory stands too, so she's eye-to-eye with the director. "You can't let the contest go ahead. Please, listen to me."

"You're upset. You should go home and get some rest. I'll ask one of the guards to take you, to make sure you get home safely." The director touches her band.

"I don't need to rest." But Doctor Gregory's voice has lost its conviction and her eyes flick to the door. She's not stupid, she can see what's happening.

I hate what the director's doing to her, but what can I do? Objecting isn't going to help. And if the director's going ahead with the contest there might still be hope for me.

"Please, Susan, go home and relax. Put your feet up and don't worry about anything. That's an order."

The door opens and a guard comes in. The director nods at him. "Escort Doctor Gregory home."

"But you—." The doctor bites back whatever she was going to say. She looks old, suddenly, her face haggard and grey. Her shoulders sag. "When may I come back?"

"Let's give it a few days and see how you feel, shall we?"

The guard steps forward to take the doctor's arm, but she pulls back. "Give me a moment." To my surprise, she bends and hugs me awkwardly. "Goodbye, Rayne." Then, in a whisper against my ear so low I strain to hear it, she adds, "Find me if you need someone. 133 Birchel."

She lets me go, gives the director a stiff nod, then turns and walks out.

When the door closes behind the doctor, Director Morelle shifts her attention to me.

This is my only chance. Before she can say anything, I start talking as fast as I can. "Please don't kick me out of the contest, Director. You won't find anyone who wants to be the leopard more than I do. I don't care what happens to my human body. All I care about is getting a chance to compete. I'll sign anything you want, do anything you ask. Nothing matters to me but the contest."

She raises one eyebrow. "This is your own fault. I doubt it would have happened if you hadn't spent both day and night in your Skin."

I swallow. "You know about that?"

"Did you think you weren't being monitored?"

"But. Why...?"

"Because you're unpredictable. After choosing New Tritoners for the contest, I started noticing uniformity in the way they think. You're different. I've found it interesting to watch you train, Milla."

My heart stops.

Did she just call me Milla?

I dig my fingernails into the arms of my chair. She's leaning casually against the desk, her arms crossed and her head slightly tilted. For all the emotion she shows, she could be carved from ice.

"You know who I am?" I can barely get the question out.

"I've known from the moment you arrived. This contest is the culmination of years of work. Each of the five prototype Skins is valuable beyond price. Don't you think I'd be careful who I let wear them?"

"Then why didn't you...?" My voice chokes off. What's going to happen to me now? I'm out of the contest, that's certain. Will the director call in the stompers and tell them I've stolen a band? If she does, they won't go easy on me.

"I'll admit, you've been a nuisance. My staff has fielded several calls from Rayne's parents, asking why their daughter won't answer her band. I've had to lie for you, Milla."

I gape, my mind racing. Nothing makes sense. "Why would you lie?"

"When you turned up wearing Rayne's band, I was curious. I needed a replacement for Rayne, after all, and it must have taken some daring for someone like you to take her place. When I checked your background, I was even more intrigued. Before your injury, you volunteered for the most dangerous job in the factory. Why? Because the pay for that job was a few credits more."

She frowns at me, like I'm some unusual bug and she's considering pulling my legs off to see how they join. "You don't keep any of your wages though, do you, Milla? You give it all to your mother, though you never see her. If you kept what you earned, you could afford to move out of the shelter. Why do you do that, Milla? Why do you give it all away?"

"Ma has to pay—"

"Second child taxes," she interrupts impatiently. "Yes, I know. Your brother is studying in one of my academies."

My heart leaps. "You know where William is? Is he okay?"

She makes a dismissive gesture. "Rayne worked for my company too, did you know that? She concepted some of our new game designs. Quite the up-and-coming star of her department. But apparently no match for you."

"Rayne came into the shelter. She was watching the contest draw." I want to tell her about the sharks and what happened, but my brain's tying itself in knots. What does she mean Rayne was no match for me?

"She was on a field trip, visiting some of my factories. Then after her tour..." The director shrugs. "Maybe she wanted to continue her tour by looking through a shelter. Or perhaps that foolish motorcycle she liked to ride broke down. She was a thrill-seeker." Her eyes sharpen. "What happened in the shelter, Milla? Did you kill her? Did you kill Rayne?"

The blood rushes from my face. What the hell? I open my mouth but nothing comes out.

She nods as if I've answered the question. Her mouth twitches. I get the feeling she's already convinced I did it, and she's not shocked.

Too late I find my voice. "No, I didn't." It sounds like a lie, even to me. Taking Rayne's place made me look guilty. How can I prove I didn't hurt her?

Director Morelle moves her gaze from me to the window and it's as though a physical weight has fallen away. Her tone changes, so it sounds like she's talking to herself. "You've taken to the leopard well, and you're certainly determined. The contest needs a wild card, and I think you'd put on an impressive show."

I suck in a breath. This entire conversation feels like a bad dream. Was she just asking me if I was a murderer? And now she sounds like she's still considering letting me compete. I can't take it in. All I know is this strange, cold woman has total power over me. She could send me to jail, or she could let me be the leopard. Right now, that's the only thing I can hold on to. It's the only thing that makes any sense.

I lean forward, shifting to the edge of my seat so I can reach out and grab her arm. "If you let me try, I know I can win."

She looks down at my hand, both eyebrows shooting up. Maybe nobody ever dares to touch her?

"Very well," she says slowly. "I'll allow you to compete. And I'll continue to call you Rayne."

I catch my breath. "And if I win? Do I get to keep my Skin?"

"Of course. I'll even give you a new band."

"Thank you." I'm so relieved, the word comes out as a whisper.

I don't care that the contest could be suicide mission, or that the director could betray me any time she likes. She's clearly the worst kind of shark and I don't trust her one bit. But as long as I still have a chance to win my Skin, that's all that matters. Do or die. If I can't be the leopard I may as well be dead anyway.

"That's all. You may go back to your room." She shoots me a cold look. "I don't think I need to spell out what will happen if this little chat doesn't stay private, do I?"

"No. Thank you, Director. I won't let you down." I'm already on my feet, ready to make my escape before she changes her mind. But as I reach the door, I can't help but hesitate. As foolish as it might be to push my luck with her, I have to ask. "And Cale? Will you reconsider and let him compete too?"

She's already sitting at her desk, activating her holo screen, and doesn't bother to glance up. "Cale's chip has already been wiped."

Chapter Twenty-Four

The door to Cale's room is open. A guard is waiting outside, but he doesn't stop me going in.

Cale is standing next to the bed, staring blankly at the floor like he hasn't heard me enter. He's packed all his things into a suitcase and the room looks weirdly empty without his piles of stuff lying around.

His eyes are bloodshot, his expression so desolate that my heart twists.

My feet scuff the ground and his face slowly lifts. I can feel what it takes for him to give me a weak smile. His pain soaks through the air between us. I ache for him. He's trying to pretend he's okay, but I can feel his loss. I can read his emotions in every movement he makes, just as clearly as if we were still leopard and tiger.

"Hey Rayne. Is your eye okay?" Typical Cale. His chip's been wiped and he's worried about me.

"Cale, don't worry. I'm going to buy a Skin for you."

His expression lightens a little, a flicker of hope ghosting across his eyes. Then he gives his head a little shake. "Do you know what happened when Brugan clawed you? How your face got the same cuts?"

"The doctor said there was a rupture because of my new eye, nothing to do with my leopard's wounds. The timing was a coincidence." I just about choke on the words as I repeat the director's lie. But I don't want him to worry about me.

"That's insane. I don't believe it was a coincidence and neither do you." He frowns. "You're not seriously thinking of staying in the contest?"

"Cale, I have to."

He takes me by the upper arms so I have to look at him. "It's too risky, Rayne. You need to pull out."

"I'll win, then I'll buy you a Skin."

"Losing my tiger feels like..." His voice breaks and he has to stop for a moment to get himself under control. "It feels like there's a hole inside me. An important part has been carved out and all that's left is a big gaping wound. I'm never going to feel fully alive again. The only reason I can walk around instead of curling up on the floor, is by pretending it hasn't happened." His fingers tighten around my arms. "But it's nothing to how I'd feel if anything happened to you."

My heart's beating too fast and my breath is stuck in my throat. As I stare into his beautiful, dark-lashed eyes, part of me wants him to put his arms around me, and another part's starting to freak out because I can't move away.

This is Cale, dammit, he'd never hurt me. But he's holding me so tightly, my palms feel clammy and my muscles are tight.

I put my hands against his chest, trying to silently tell him I need some space. He makes a low, quiet sound that's half sigh, half groan. He draws me toward him.

No! My chest tightens with panic and I twist out of his grip.

He steps back, his expression stricken. "You can't stand me touching you, can you?"

"It's not you. It's me."

He sits down heavily on the bed and folds his hands together in front of him, as though he's telling me not to worry, that he won't try to touch me again. I hate that I've hurt him. As difficult as it is, I owe it to him to try to explain.

"I'm sorry, Cale. This body is so weak, I can't help being afraid."

"You're not weak."

I drag in a breath, trying to figure out how to make him understand. "After I was burned, they moved me to a new shelter where I was on my own." Dammit voice, don't tremble. "I was easy pickings for the sharks."

I turn away so as not to see his expression, but it's a relief to say it out loud. Like letting the words go allows some of the pain out with them. "Then I met Tori. She wasn't much older than I was, but she wasn't scared of anything. The sharks respected her and when she was with me, they mostly left me alone. But I was always afraid. I was the weak one and she was strong. That's just how it was."

I stop, biting my lip, wanting to blurt out the whole story about stealing Rayne's band. What would he think of me if he knew? There shouldn't be any secrets between us. But there's a guard outside. Now's not the time.

He jumps up and touches my forearm so I turn toward him. His voice is gentle. "Being afraid doesn't make you weak."

"It does in the shelter. Especially if you let it show. Sharks go after anyone who can't fight back."

"I've never known anyone as brave as you."

The way he says it—gaze steady and so sincere—makes me want to cry. If only I were half as tough as he thinks. "I'm not brave. And the only time I'm strong is when I'm the leopard. My Skin has given me that. It's given me the strength to be able to win."

He draws in a breath and blows it out hard. "I couldn't bear it if you got hurt."

"I won't get hurt. I'm going to win the contest."

"Yeah. You'll win." He looks down and murmurs it in a low voice, almost to himself. A chill runs over me. He doesn't believe it. He thinks I'm going to lose. I know it with a cold certainty. Tiger Cale would never be able to lie to me, and I can see through this Cale just as easily.

"I can win. I will, Cale."

He looks up at me. "If there were no Skins and you were yourself for the contest, I'd have no doubt. You're the best of us, Rayne. Easily the toughest, even if you can't see it."

I can't believe what he's saying. Compared to my leopard, my human body is pathetic.

"Remember when you walked into the training room for the first time?" he asks. "We were staring but you never faltered. You charged in full of attitude and defiance, like you wanted to take us all on at once." He smiles and the shadows leave his face for just for a moment. "I could see it then. I thought, she's going to win the contest. It was the first thing I thought when I met you."

"But now you don't think I can." I don't need to ask, I know he doesn't. I can feel the doubt pulsing through him, as strong as his heartbeat.

"Your leopard's incredible, I know."

"But...?"

He touches my upper arms again, but instead of

holding me, he runs his hands gently down until my hands are cradled in his. "But with your human body at risk, you have to be cautious, and the others don't. The devil bear's stronger, the reptile's a better climber, and the wasp is faster. All three are ruthless. If they need to hurt you to win, they won't hesitate."

I stare at his long fingers, warm against mine. I was ashamed of my hands when I arrived, but they've healed a lot since then. They're still scarred and battered if you look closely enough. I still have callouses on my palms. But apart from being paler, they don't seem so different from his anymore.

I can't let him shake me. He's wrong. I'm going to beat the others because I have to. I don't have a choice.

"Please, Rayne," he whispers. "Won't you pull out of the contest?"

His face is so close, his breath lifts a strand of my hair. He lifts one hand to smooth it, and carefully tucks it behind my ear. The tip of his finger runs softly down the side of my neck. The way he looks at me, it's as though I'm not scarred at all.

"Please," he murmurs.

I can't answer. I can't move, or even breathe. He leans toward me, his eyes closing. His lips brush gently against mine, warm and soft. I feel them everywhere. It's as though my whole body is connected to my lips, aching into his touch.

He kisses me again, but this time his lips press longer against mine and I feel his longing for me, as plain as though he'd shouted it.

His arms snake around me, trapping me. He's bigger than me. Stronger. I can't break away.

I yank myself free, and stumble across the room. My head's spinning, and I hate myself. Cale didn't do anything wrong. He barely touched me. What's wrong with me?

"I'm sorry, Rayne, I shouldn't have…Are you all right?"

I swallow, trying to calm my racing heart. "It wasn't you. I mean, it was—" I don't know how to finish the sentence. How can I explain how broken I am? "I can't do this. Not in this body."

"Because I'm not the tiger?"

"Yes." I don't realize how it sounds until I've said it.

His jaw tightens. "It was the tiger you liked, not me. It was never me, was it?"

"That's not what I meant. It's just easier when you're the tiger."

But it's too late. His expression's so desolate that I put my hand to my chest and squeeze my shirt in my fist. Why am I so bad at this? If we were leopard and tiger I could rip my heart open and show him. Look, here's how I feel. Words are dead things, buried too deep. I can't find the right ones. I don't even know if the right ones exist.

The guard sticks his head around the door. "Let's go."

Cale nods. "I can only ask you once more, Rayne. Please pull out of the contest. Do it for me."

I can't reply. That's the one thing in the world I refuse to do.

He waits for longer than I expect, not giving up until it's clear I'm going to let him down. Then he picks up his suitcase and steps toward me. My heart pounds as I expect him to try and kiss me again. Instead he touches his band to mine. Here's my number." His voice is tight. Controlled. Then he turns and walks out. I can't even tell him he's given his number to a useless band, that I have no way to access it or call him.

I'm left standing in an empty room with just his warm, clean scent left behind, quickly fading.

My body trembles. It's like when Tori left, the feeling of losing something so precious I don't know how I can stand it. In the shelter, Tori was both my protector and best friend.

Cale is... even more.

But I failed him. If only I could go back in time, do things differently. I should have found the words to tell him how much he means to me. I should have kissed him back.

But now it's too late.

Chapter Twenty-Five

Early the next morning, I pace the hallway until the training room opens. I need to be the leopard so badly I have to fight not to scream at the guard until he unlocks the door.

Transferring into my leopard feels so incredible, I groan out loud with relief. It takes a while for me to float down to earth. By the time I do, the others are on the climbing wall.

I can smell the devil bear, but I don't look at him. I can't let myself think about him. Last time I was in this room, I almost lost everything. This time I'm not going to let anyone get the better of me. I don't care what I have to do, or how hard I have to push myself. I'm going to win, whatever it takes. No distractions.

The wounds Cale and Brugan gave me are gone, so either my leopard heals quickly by itself, or they worked on my Skin while I was at the hospital. I feel strong and fit enough to run circles around the others. Cale was wrong when he said I had no chance in the contest, and I'm going to prove it.

There are only three days of training left, and I'm going to use every second of time I have.

I spring toward the training wall. And stop.

I can smell the Tiger Skin.

It's Cale! He's padding out from his lab room. I almost trip over my own paws in my rush to get to him. The director must have let him come back after all. She must have—

I stop just short of him. There's something wrong. He doesn't smell like Cale. Underneath the tiger scent, instead of Cale's fresh, clean smell, there's a tang of something rotten. Like meat that's gone bad.

My stomach clenches when the tiger's top lip curls up to show more of its enormous fangs.

"You glad to see me, sewer rat?"

It's a rough growl, nothing like Cale's voice. My stomach heaves. I feel sick.

"Max?"

The tiger flicks its tail. "Hello sewer rat. I've been waiting for a chance to give you what you deserve."

Hearing Max's nasty voice coming from Cale's beautiful tiger makes me want to claw at my ears. I take off for the other side of the room, hoping he's too uncertain in his new Skin to follow.

Sentin's nearby, not on the never-wall, but standing back so he can watch Aza and Brugan. I drag in some deep breaths to try to calm down.

"Sentin, did you know about Max?" I ask.

He's standing on hind legs, and though his knees are bent in his distinctive reptile crouch, he's still taller than me. "Not until now," he says, dipping his neck to look at me.

"Why him? There must be scores of people lining up to compete. Why'd it have to be Max?"

"Does it matter?" He tilts his head to one side. "It's irrelevant who wears the Skin. All that matters are his weaknesses, and how he can be beaten."

He's right. I take another deep breath and try to force out my anger so I can think clearly.

"Max won't get used to the Skin in time," I say. "Not in just three days. He won't be ready."

"You're wrong. Look." Sentin motions at the tiger as it pads toward the never-wall. "Max must have used the Skin before. I suspect Director Morelle planned for him to step in if one of us couldn't compete."

He's right. The tiger leaps onto the wall and doesn't hesitate before springing to the next platform. It took Cale several days to be able to jump as confidently.

This is awful. The two strongest Skins are the tiger and the devil bear, and if either Max or Brugan get their claws on me, they'll do as much damage as they can.

"Sentin, can I ask you something? If you get hurt in the contest, are you afraid your human body might be injured?"

"I considered the possibility and conducted my own test." His voice sounds just as calm and even as it always does. "But it seems you're the only one who has that problem."

"All of you know that if you hurt me, it's for real. I can't imagine that'll stop you. It definitely won't stop Brugan."

His silver eyes blink very slowly, the eyelids coming up from underneath. "I plan to win, and I'll do what I need to, as will the others. If you'd prefer not to participate, I'm sure Director Morelle could arrange for another substitute."

"Not a chance." The suggestion I pull out now is so

unthinkable that funnily enough, it steadies me. I'll risk anything. The stakes are too high to do anything else.

And Sentin's right, as much as I hate Max, he's just one more obstacle to get past on my way up the tower.

Sentin turns to look at Max and a wave of color ripples across his scales. They turn from pure green to turquoise, but I've no idea if that's supposed to mean something. His scent never tells me much about the way he's feeling. He's almost as hard to read as the director.

"Who are you, Sentin?" I ask. "Are you in the army?"

"The army?" he repeats, and I don't need leopard senses to tell he thinks that's funny. "Not in the way you might imagine."

"What does that mean?"

"The battle hasn't started yet."

"What battle?"

"You'll see. After the competition, things will become far more interesting."

Fed up with his non-answers, I shake my head and ask the question that's been nagging me. "Is the competition rigged? Do I have a chance at winning?"

"I'm confident the contest result isn't predetermined. Although the probability of my win is extremely high, I can't predict everything that may happen. The element of chance makes the outcome uncertain."

My ears flick as I try to work out his meaning. "So you're saying I might get lucky?"

"Unlikely, but possible. And if you do, I'll need you to remember our bargain."

"Bargain?"

His scales change color again, silver rippling through them like water. "You know what I'm talking about, *Rayne.*"

I flatten my ears against my skull and resist the urge to growl. "What exactly are you asking me to do?"

"Maybe nothing. Perhaps a great deal. It hinges on the outcome of the contest and the events that transpire afterward."

"Can't you ever give me a straight answer?"

He drops onto all four reptile limbs. His sleek body is long, and lower to the ground than my leopard. He swivels his head to look up at me and his voice drops. "We both have secrets."

"You know mine. Now tell me yours."

His tongue flicks out for a second, long and blue, like he's tasting the air. "My skill lies in analyzing information and predicting future events based on historical data." He blinks, and I glimpse a second eyelid moving underneath the top one. "As I've already said, you're not my primary interest."

"Then who?"

His voice drops even more, so only leopard hearing could pick it up. "The contest is merely a diversion. She intends to start a war. I need to win so I can be close to her when that happens. It's the best way to influence the outcome."

I sit back on my haunches, confused. Is he saying the director wants to start a war with Deiterra?

"What are you talking about?" I murmur just as quietly.

"About ambition. Or more precisely, thwarting ambition. Sometimes the greater good calls for the sacrifice of individuals."

"I have no idea what you mean. But if it's me you're planning to sacrifice, I won't let you."

His scales get a little darker. "I'm afraid your sacrifice will be necessary. However, nothing is certain, and if I don't win, I'll need your help. Sooner or later I'll call on you to play your part."

"I won't let you win the contest." I'd need a hell of a lot more than a vague suggestion about stopping a war to do that. Anyway, if the Deiterrans are angry about the Skins, and the ambassador's son were really worried about it sparking a war, he wouldn't be competing at all. Him taking part in the contest is likely to annoy the Deiterrans most.

No, he's just trying to mess with my head.

"If my plan succeeds, you won't be able to stop me from winning," he says.

"Is that your version of trash talk?" I slap my tail against the floor. "I should ask my friend Tori to give you lessons, because you're not scaring me. I have a plan too."

Cale and I had our tactics worked out. Climb the outside of the tower. Let someone else get to the Kraken first, then slip past and get to the top. Maybe Cale thinks I don't have a chance without him, but I know better.

Stretching my limbs, I feel the strength and power in my muscles. "Get ready to lose, Sentin."

"I'm afraid I can't do that. However, I sincerely hope you survive the day." He says it straight, without any sarcasm. I think he means it. "And I find myself hoping you'll defeat Brugan," he adds. "With the extra practice you've had, you should be able to."

"You know about that?"

Another color change ripples over him. Darker green this time. "Aza wasn't reticent in relating how she caught you in here before the training room opened, but she doesn't know Cale was training with you."

"How do you—?"

The door opens and Director Morelle comes in. She

stops in the middle of the floor to let the five of us gather closely around her.

"The doctor has confirmed that Rayne's wounds were caused by a rupture in the cells implanted when her eye was replaced. A rare problem, but one that's not unheard of. I've been reassured that the timing was coincidental, and had nothing to do with the damage inflicted on her Skin."

Director Morelle's gaze is on me, so I nod like I agree. Doesn't matter if the others believe her story, they're not about to object.

"What's the schedule for the day of the competition?" asks Aza.

"You'll spend the morning resting, mentally preparing for the contest. After lunch, you'll be taken to the arena. Your Skins will be transported separately."

A whole morning in my human body. I'm already dreading it. If Cale were here, we could prepare for the contest together. His jokes would settle my nerves. The way he always looks at me makes me feel like I can face anything.

Do you know how much I miss you, Cale?

The others turn to stare, and with a shock I realize I must have sighed his name.

The director frowns. "Don't concern yourself with anyone no longer here, *Rayne*." Her emphasis on my name makes the hair lift along my spine. "I advise you to think only of doing your best in the contest." She lifts her hand, reaching for my face, and I have to force myself not to flinch as she strokes the tip of one perfect fingernail down my muzzle, following the same line as Brugan's claw. "You should be concentrating on that very hard indeed."

Chapter Twenty-Six

The noise is deafening. I'm in my Leopard Skin, stepping nervously from one paw to the other, in a small waiting room that leads onto the arena floor. This is it. The days of training are over, and the contest is about to begin.

My human body's here too, lying in a pod just like the one from my lab room. The roar of the crowd shakes the floor. Or maybe it's my legs trembling? Waiting with nothing to do but listen to the cheering and shouting of the crowd is torture. There are thousands of people watching, crammed into the rows of seats that circle the arena. From the noise they're making, it sounds like the entire city is here.

This waiting room is at the bottom of the arena, which technically means I'm in Old Triton now. The thought gives me some comfort though I've never been into the arena before, and this is nothing like the Old Triton I know.

Sentin, Brugan, Aza, and Max are also waiting in small rooms, probably just like this one. We've been spaced around the arena, so we'll all enter it from a different angle.

It doesn't help my nerves that after forcing myself to spend most of the last couple of days in the vReal, I still haven't made it up the tower far enough to see the Kraken.

"Ten seconds until the speech starts." The voice comes from the band of one of Director Morelle's red-uniformed guards. He's been stationed with me to guide me through the opening ceremony, whatever that's supposed to be, but he's just making me more nervous.

He touches his band. "Acknowledge." Then he nods at me. "Ready?"

I flick my tail in response.

The room has two doors, one behind me, and one in front that opens onto the arena. But the doors are solid and there's no window. I have no idea whether the arena's going to look like it did in the vReal game. What if it's completely different?

The guard says, "When it's your turn, walk a little way into the arena. You'll see the spotlight you have to stand in. Stop there and wait until the contest starts."

I turn to him in sudden panic. "How will I know when it starts?"

"You'll know."

The roar of the huge crowd dies suddenly and an eerie silence takes its place. The silence makes the fur on my neck rise. The entire world holds its breath.

Out booms a single voice, a man's deep, practiced voice that echoes in the sudden quiet.

"Ladies and gentlemen, it's finally here! The evening we've all been waiting for, the event of the century! Here to open the Morelle Corporation's Skin Hunter contest is someone who needs no introduction. It's the woman herself, head of the Morelle Corporation. The one. The only. Director Morrrrrrelle!"

"Good evening, citizens of Triton." It's Director Morelle's voice.

The guard moves to stand by the door, ready to open it. Any minute now I'll have to go out there.

"Welcome, everyone, to the Morelle Corporation's Skin Hunter contest." The director pauses for the cheers to die down. "And a special welcome to the esteemed ambassador from Deiterra." She pauses, but there's only a scattering of applause for the ambassador. He's probably here to watch Sentin compete while he decides how offensive the Skins are. What happens if he thinks they breach the treaty? Could he force the President to ban them?

Too bad if he does. When I win, I'll stay in my Leopard Skin permanently, no matter what anyone says. The President will have to kill me to get me out of it.

"The Morelle Corporation has always looked to the future and asked how we can make dreams into reality. As early as mid last century, my grandfather was working on nano-chip technology. He was a pioneer. A genius and a dreamer. Today his technology is used in every home. Every business. Every school and hospital."

Judging by what I can hear, the crowd's drinking up her speech. She pauses to let them go crazy.

"Edward Morelle passed his dreams to me, and I swore I wouldn't let him down. I started work to merge your telephone, computer, and holo screen into a thin, indestructible wrist band. A simple band you could wear, that would become an essential tool for communication, entertainment, business, security. Everything you need to make your life easier. A band impossible to steal. A band now so important to our everyday life that it holds our very identity."

More cheers. I swallow the sick feeling in my throat. How long is the director going to speak for?

"I swore we would never stop innovating. That my grandfather's company would not simply see the future, we would *be* the future. Since then the Morelle Corporation has brought you the gamenode and the mind-pad. We've brought you nano-tech and the vReal. We've helped to develop new surgical techniques and limb regrowth technology."

The guard frowns as I start pacing back and forth in front of the door, swishing my tail nervously from side to side.

"Many years ago, we at the Morelle Corporation had a truly revolutionary idea. What if we pushed the transmitter technology we were concepting for the mind-pad even further? What if we could use it, not to control applications, but to connect your brain with another body? And what if we designed that body to be stronger, faster, better than the original?

"Ladies and gentlemen, the contest you're about to witness is the culmination of that dream. You will see five prototype Skins perform physical feats far beyond the capability of any human body. You'll see those Skins fight, sustain injuries, even die. Yet the humans controlling them will remain completely unhurt. They're competing for the ultimate prize. Five million credits."

Another roar which quickly dies down. I imagine the director holding her hands up to conduct the crowd like an orchestra.

"And the winner of the Skin Hunter contest will become the proud owner of their Skin. The very first Triton citizen to own one!"

This time the noise is like thunder.

"It's my privilege to unveil these first prototype Skins to

you here today. The first Skin I'll introduce uses a small amount of human DNA combined with the DNA from a wolverine, bear, and wolf. We call it the devil bear. I give you... Brugan!"

I thought they were loud before, but now the whole waiting room shakes. It sounds like thousands of feet stomping above my head. Like the ceiling's about to cave in. Even the guard's eyes flick upward. The noise goes on and I imagine Brugan walking out into the arena. I bet he's flexing his muscles and showing off. Yeah, I can picture it.

The crowd chant his name over and over. "Brugan. Brugan. Brugan."

"And now for the next Skin." Director Morelle's voice again, cutting through the chants and silencing them instantly. The guard lifts his hand to the door and nods at me. My heart jumps. Me next? This is it. Finally, this is my chance to win all I could ever want, for me and everyone I love. If I can stay alive, the next few hours will change everything forever.

"Presenting the Clouded Leopard. Here she is... Rayne!"

The door opens. "Go," hisses the guard.

I walk out into a bright glare, through a wall of noise so thick it's like a physical barrier. A light shines on me, hot and blinding, making my sharp leopard vision blur. A spotlight. I stop, blinking upward. There's too much to look at, it's sensory overload. There are so many people here, the rows of faces go up forever.

A deafening chant starts up. "Rayne. Rayne. Rayne."

So many people, I can't believe it. I shift anxiously from paw to paw. What do they expect me to do, wave back? It's not as if I can.

"And now, presenting the Reptile Skin. I give you... Sentin!"

Through all the lights and noise and the blur of the endless crowd, my eyes adjust. In front of me is the tower I'll be racing up. I should be concentrating on the tower, but I can't believe how many people are here. The arena is layered with tiers and tiers of seats, and every tier looks crowded. The people shout, clap, and stomp their feet. They're chanting Sentin's name.

With an effort, I force my gaze to the tower. It's like the vReal version, only in real life it seems far more intimidating.

Close to the top of the tower are some huge air blimps. Spectator craft, I guess. Probably filled with rich people who want to get the best view. The sides of the blimps are covered with screens. Advertising? No, the screens are showing the Wasp Skin in close-up view as Aza leaps into the arena, wings outstretched and arms high. She must have just been announced. How the hell did I miss it?

Focus. I have to focus. Don't get distracted. Don't mess this up.

Through the dancing spotlights, I squint at the tower. It's not exactly like in the game. The struts are further apart and the gaps wider. What else will be different?

Did Director Morelle just announce Max? The crowd's chanting his name, so she must have. The noise bounces off the sides of the arena like rolling thunder.

Now the giant screens show all five of us. There I am, staring upward, tail twitching.

Is Cale watching? Even if he's not here, he must be in front of a holo. Where's a camera? I turn until I find one pointing at me, and stare into the lens, ears flicking back and forth in a private signal just for him. I want him to know I'm thinking about him.

I wish I could send messages to Ma and William and

Tori as well. Even if there were a way, they'd never believe I'm the leopard. But they'll find out if I win. When I win.

The crowd's gone quiet. Director Morelle's image appears on all the screens, her perfect face smiling her cold smile.

"I have a new dream. I want everyone to be able to wear a Skin. Imagine a world where you never have to fear any injury. Where you can experience a whole new level of freedom, without physical limitations. The Morelle Corporation is ready to open our first Skin store in New Triton. As soon as President Trask gives his approval, I'll make the dream a reality!"

Like the President's going to be able to stop it after this. If he were here right now, the crowd would tear him to pieces.

"Skins aren't a new form of entertainment, they're a whole new way of living. Skins aren't just progress. They're evolution!"

I've heard her say that before. The first time, I thought she was crazy. Now I don't know what to think. The noise in the arena is already deafening, but Director Morelle raises her arms, turning it up even more. She pauses, arms held high, eyes shining. Her lips are stretched into a wide, triumphant smile. She has total control of her audience. When she drops her arms, the roar snips off like she cut it.

"Let the contest begin. Are you ready to make history, contestants?"

My heart's thundering louder than the crowd can yell. It's time.

Chapter Twenty-Seven

The starter gun goes off. I race toward the tower and leap to the first ledge, gripping my claws into the metal. The platforms are further apart than in the vReal but I'm so hyped I could jump ten times the distance.

The others are hidden by the massive structure, but I'm alert for anything, even the smallest metal insect. My leopard senses are sharper than they've ever been, scanning for movement, totally focused on the tower. Next level. Adrenalin's fizzing through me, helping me leap faster than I ever have. I feel strong enough to bound all the way to the top.

Except that's wrong. I need to slow down, let Aza get to the Kraken first. *Don't mess up Cale's plan.*

Forcing myself to stop, I whip my head around, searching for danger. The crowd's cheering buffets my ears. Do they think I'm stopping so they can admire my Skin?

My leopard heart beats faster than my human one, and right now it's galloping. Every muscle screams to keep running. But I wait, frozen, scanning the tower. Where are the others? I can't see or sense them. No chance of hearing them over the crowd.

Metal bugs crawl toward me. I pinpoint each one, able at a glance to tell where they are and how fast they're moving. Other hazards go into my mental map. Chain on level five. A metal wheel rolling on level eight. A burst of fire on level nine. My route's planned out in an instant. My leopard senses have always been incredible, but this is a whole new experience.

All I want is to take off again, but I force myself to wait. A metal spider hurls itself at me, jaws gaping. I crush it under one paw then swipe a centipede away. Three more long breaths and I'm off again. I can't believe how easily I'm racing up the tower, how strong I feel. Like I could power straight through the Kraken.

There's Sentin. His shimmering scales catch the light before he disappears behind a girder, just above and to one side of me. Good. If he's ahead of me, Aza should be too.

Keep moving. Jump, run. I know what to do. Cale and I practiced on the never-wall for so many hours, I'm sure-footed even on the steepest beams.

The metal bugs stalking the platforms get bigger as I climb, and I'm going too fast to check where they are before I leap. I land on one, a nightmare creature like a praying mantis, as big as a dog. Its jagged metal jaws snap onto my leg. Howling with pain, I struggle to wrench myself loose, and when I jump away, I leave clumps of fur in its jaws.

My leg throbs. Shake it off, I've got to keep going. The bugs are as big as I am now, but there aren't so many of them. And when I sneak a quick look down, I'm higher than I've ever been. When's the Kraken going to—?

The tower shakes and I almost lose my grip. I dig my claws in, hanging on. Bolts drop past my head. A scorpion creature tries to stab me as it jolts off the platform and falls. When I crane my neck up, the rocking of all the tower's platforms makes me dizzy.

Is the tower collapsing? If it does, I'm dead.

Metal strikes against metal so hard that the noise reverberates through my body. It's the huge beam just above me, dropping, about to fall. Panic surges though me, kicking my heart and muscles into full alert. But there's nowhere to jump to. Nothing I can do to stop from being crushed.

Only the beam doesn't fall. It uncurls.

I gape at it, trying to understand what I'm seeing. It's a metal tentacle. The Kraken isn't appearing out of the tower. The Kraken *is* the tower. Piece by piece the metal pieces making up this part of the tower are forming themselves into a monster. Why didn't Cale tell me it'd be so huge? Maybe I picked the wrong side of the tower? Forget slipping past, it's too big for that.

Not all the tower has transformed into writhing tentacles. Some struts and beams and posts still hold up the upper levels, but it's hard to tell which bits aren't part of the Kraken. If I jump on a platform will it suddenly transform?

A tentacle swings toward me. I leap for my life, scrambling for a higher platform. No matter what, I've got to keep going.

The metal under my paws transforms, becomes a writhing tentacle. It bucks even harder beneath me as my claws dig in. Can it feel pain?

Sinking my fangs in as deeply as I can, I crush it in my jaws. At the same time, I bury my claws and twist. The metal tears apart with an awful screeching sound. The tentacle bucks harder, whipping from side to side, trying to shake me off.

A roar thunders from above, so loud it almost blasts me

loose. The monster's voice? Wincing, I hunch my shoulders. If only I could cover my ears. The sound is a blade stabbing through my head. All I can do is shut my eyes and hang on until it dies away.

When I can move again, I leap from the tentacle, heading upward, toward the middle of the tower. Wherever that roar came from, that's where I'm going. If the monster has a voice, maybe that's the place where it's vulnerable.

As I leap higher, metal crashes around me. I dodge bolts and rivets that whistle past. A heavy iron pipe smashes into a beam beside me and the next one hits my flank. It hurts, but I've got to keep going. I'm moving on instinct. My human brain withdraws as I let the leopard's skillful paws take over.

The higher I climb, the worse the shaking gets. There are more tentacles, more obstacles to dodge. Am I getting to the heart of the monster? The creature bellows again, but this time I scramble through the blast, ears pinned back as I haul myself forward.

From far above, I catch a flash of shimmering scales. *Sentin.* How did he get way up there? He's snaking up a vertical strut on the outside of the structure, and must be past the worst of the chaos. Which means he followed Cale's plan a lot better than I did. I didn't stick closely enough to the edge, and got caught in the thick of it.

There's no way I can catch Sentin now. But Cale said once we're past the Kraken, the tower will throw metal monsters at us to slow us down. Hopefully Sentin will bear the brunt of it.

When I start to climb again, there's a blur of red and black not far ahead. It's Aza, battling one of the tentacles with the stingers in her palms. She dodges and strikes in the same movement, so fast it's hard to follow. She's been hurt, there's a gash in one black armored leg, but she's not letting it slow her down. She tears into the metal, rips the end of the tentacle off, and sends it flying.

I leap, miss the next platform, and have to scramble. She turns and sees me. Her wasp helmet's filled with light, glowing from inside. She launches herself at me, hands outstretched, stingers aimed at my head. When I leap away, one of her stingers catches my back. My thick fur turns the killing blow into a scratch.

I spin as I jump, turning in midair to protect myself as she strikes again. The side of my paw thuds against her shoulder, throwing her off balance. She falls hard onto the metal beam, tumbling backwards.

I land heavily too, but recover fast. While she's still skidding backwards, trying to get her balance, I'm already springing away, ducking a swinging tentacle to grab hold of a sloping ramp. I scramble my back legs onto it, leap onto a horizontal beam, then spin around, searching for her. A thick pipe tumbles from above, catches her shoulder. She staggers, recovers. But she clutches her arm with her other hand. She's hurt.

We face each other in the chaos, metal clanging and falling around us, the struts shaking under us. I'm panting, my heart racing so fast I can't keep still. I've been moving defensively, trying to get away when I should be attacking.

She crouches, steadying herself on the ramp, helmet glowing as she stares me down. If she hurts me, it'll be for real. But by the way she's crouched, about to spring, she's going to try to kill me anyway. Winning's everything to her. It means more than my life.

She leaps, stingers outstretched.

Dodging away, I throw myself out of reach, twisting and rebounding. She lunges again, but I've learned the advantage four paws give me. I spring off a vertical wall, twist sideways and land behind her. She spins. Too late. My teeth snap shut on her black armor and I let the momentum carry us both forward. She falls and I drag her, my fangs tearing into her thigh. Screaming, she stabs her stinger into my face. Pain jolts through me like an electric current, but my jaws are clamped tight. Leaping forward, I use my momentum to fling her across the metal structure. Her head slams into a beam. The black helmet splits and blood leaks from the back of her neck.

She stays down, clutching her head. At the sight of her blood, my stomach convulses. *I did that to her*. But if I hadn't, she might have killed me. Besides, her real body should be okay. I'm counting on it.

Still, I hesitate for several long moments, tasting my own blood on my snout and wondering if I should do something to help her.

Giant metal creatures are already forming around her, emerging from the tower, putting themselves together as they lurch toward her. Entire portions of beams attach themselves together with nuts and bolts. They have sharp metal pincers, and gaping mouths filled with screws. They strut stiff-legged, and though they're only half her size, there are dozens of them.

"Get up," I yell, edging backward.

Aza doesn't move.

The metal monsters hesitate around her, as though they're waiting for a signal. Then they swarm over her.

I wince, backing away quickly.

Through the sound of crashing, thrashing metal comes a bellow from the crowd, their voices lifting together. They're chanting Brugan's name. Where is he? I strain my senses, searching with eyes and ears and nose, and catch a whiff of devil bear. When I climb one more level, I see him snarling and snapping, his claws tearing into a giant mass of metal. He's battling the head of the Kraken. Tentacles seethe and its mouth, filled with wicked spikes, snaps at him.

Looks like the devil bear's hurting it. Brugan's in close, tearing off pieces, his muscled shoulders hunched against its blows. He launches himself at one of its giant, cybernetic eyes and thrusts in one claw. The creature lets a cry so loud, the blast threatens to tear me loose. Without pausing, Brugan jumps at the other eye. He slashes and the monster's tentacles shudder and go still. Could it be dead?

Crouching, I get ready to leap past and chase Sentin to the top. But Brugan's got his back to me and he's not far away. A couple of big leaps and I could shove him off the tower.

No, bad idea. Better to get away before he sees me.

Too late.

Brugan turns, his huge chest rising and falling as he pants for breath. He's got a couple of nasty gashes across his chest, and his torso is slick with sweat and blood. His scent changes when he sees me, and his wolfish lips stretch into a smile.

I've got to get out of here. I leap and my paws barely touch metal before I'm springing off again.

Catch me if you can, Brugan.

Chapter Twenty-Eight

I'm stopped by a flash of something shiny that's moving fast. It's something new.

There's a fire burning nearby, blue-hot flames shooting out of a pipe. The metal of this part of the tower is pitted and rough, so the flames reflect off the shiny thing more than anything else.

It vanishes behind a pillar before I can make out what kind of creature it is. But when I jump to the next level, there's another one waiting.

The creature is huge, its shape human, but bristling with spikes. It lunges for me, slashing with spiked hands. The sharp tips of its blades rip through my fur as I leap away. It doesn't follow, but there's another one half-hidden behind a beam.

Every inch of the porcupine-creature is covered with blades, except for its eyes. As I meet its gaze, I feel a jolt of recognition. It's got the same cybernetic eyes I used to have. Same hideous model, cold and black. I'm looking into the nightmare of my old face. It gives me chills.

This one is injured. Its lower legs are gone, cut off at the knees. What could have hurt it?

A whiff of rotting meat comes from behind me. I spin around just in time. Max. The tiger hurtles at me, mouth open. His saber-teeth drip saliva. Cale's familiar tiger smell hits me hard, but underneath is Max's rotten stink.

Go!

Reflex kicks in, and I hurl myself away. This part of the tower's harder to cross. The beams are thinner, the gaps between them wider.

I make the next beam, then leap again. He twists to follow, and he's not far behind.

My back paw slips and I almost don't make the next jump. No time to hesitate or try to find the best way forward, I need to keep moving to stay in front of Max. I'm faster than him, but I'd better not lose my balance.

He growls so loud I feel the vibration through my paws. He must be close.

There's movement above me, glimpsed and gone again. Something's up there, hidden behind a sheet of mesh and a wall of hanging wires. Not Brugan or Sentin, or I'd smell them. A metal creature? I'm don't want to jump up there without knowing for sure, not with Max right behind me.

There's a beam up ahead. I could use it to rebound off and turn. The same move I used on Cale.

Launching myself at the beam, I land on four paws, then twist and fly back at Max. My claws sink into his flesh before we skid and tumble across the metal platform.

I catch the side of a beam to keep from falling right off the structure, and I'm back on four paws in a second, ready to flee.

Max lies groaning on the beam, his side red with blood. Should I attack again while he's winded?

Before I can move, my nostrils flare. I can smell the devil bear. Then Brugan leaps at me.

I try to jump sideways, but his meaty hand bowls me over and I smack hard into a pipe. I'm on my side, struggling to get up, when his weight lands on me, pinning me down. Gasping for breath, my nose fills with his stench.

He leans his weight on me, crushing me. I struggle and twist, and when I manage to get a claw free, I rake it across the open wound on his chest. He howls, slackening his grip, and I give a mighty jerk, putting all my strength in it, throwing him off balance so I can twist out from beneath him and scramble away.

When I've put a small distance between us, I turn to face him. Brugan's got bloody slashes all over him and blood clumps in his fur, but his wounds don't seem to be slowing him down.

Behind him, Max has managed to get back up. He's standing, sides heaving, blood dripping from his muzzle.

"Bitch," he snarls.

The word draws Brugan's attention away from me, and he edges toward Max. Maybe he thinks Max will be easier pray. Max mirrors his movement, keeping distance between them. I move too, not letting either of them get closer. We're circling, the three of us poised to react to any quick movement.

We're all injured. Warm blood's seeping into my fur, and my whole body hurts, especially my shoulder. The smell of blood is so strong, I can taste it deep in my throat. I'm not gulping in air anymore, but a mist of blood and sweat and adrenalin.

I don't know where Sentin is. Not on this level, unless he's hiding behind one of the vertical pillars. It's more likely he's above us, though there can't be too many more levels to the top.

The kraken has grown silent, but clanging and crashing sounds still come from above. A spiked limb drops, ricochets off the beam I'm on, and clatters down through the levels. Sentin must be a few levels up, fighting the shiny porcupine creatures. Perhaps they're easier to kill than Max or Brugan.

Brugan feints forward. I jump away, trying to make our wary circle bigger. Max is pacing, watching for his moment to attack. His eyes are hungry, burning up from the inside. When Cale was the tiger, his eyes were a beautiful gold. Now his eyes are glowing fires stoked with hatred and rage.

"She's mine," says Max, his gaze moving to Brugan. "I get to kill her."

Brugan's lips peel back again, this time in a gesture of contempt. "I'll carve you both into pieces."

Max growls, and Brugan answers with a loud snarl. Great. If I can get them attacking each other, maybe I've got a chance. But how, when I'm number one on both of their kill lists?

The crowd has hushed. They're watching the beasts circle. Waiting for one of us to attack.

I'm faster than Max or Brugan so I need to outrun them. To get higher.

As my eyes flick up, both Max and Brugan leap at me. I spring away, twisting to escape. Max gets close enough for my blood and sweat to spatter him when I leap. Brugan sweeps out to the side, trying to trap me between him and Max. The devil bear is moving faster than I thought he could, and if he keeps circling, I'll get stuck with nowhere to run. I need to go up, but if I jump too close to Sentin I could end up with all three Skins trying to kill me.

Get Brugan and Max together, that's my best chance. Risky, but I've got to try it. If they trap me I'm dead anyway.

Changing direction, I angle toward Brugan. I have to cut sideways which lets Max draw closer, but I keep ahead of him. Brugan turns so he's rushing at me, on a collision course. I stare into his eyes as he jumps, just two beams away now and moving fast. His mouth opens, his nostrils are flared, teeth bared in anticipation. Max is so close behind me he's about to plunge his claws into my back. Brugan right in front. One more leap and we'll slam into each other. What's below me? No time to look.

Instead of jumping, I drop.

Tumbling through the tower, I look frantically for something to grab hold of. Three floors of struts, platforms and beams plunge past as I twist in mid-air, reaching for anything to stop my fall.

My outstretched claws touch a beam, and I scrabble for it, almost managing to grab hold. My momentum yanks me free, and I slam hard into the beam below it.

The impact sends white-hot agony exploding through me. I lie frozen, unable to scream, fighting to pull air into my crushed lungs. If I were in my human body, I'd be dead.

My body's a twisted mass of pain, starting with the side I landed on and shooting through every limb. Judging from how much it hurts, I've broken a few ribs. It takes me forever to scrape myself off the metal and stand on shaky legs. If Brugan and Max followed me down, I'll be easy pickings.

Dropping out from between them would have left them on a collision course. Hopefully they're busy ripping each other to pieces right now, but I can't count on it.

Keep moving.

Legs trembling, I pick a close beam, an easy jump. It still takes huge effort. I move cautiously, scanning enemies. I'm so weak the last thing I need is to blunder into danger. Slowly I climb higher. Back toward the beam I dropped from, where the others are. They're still there. I can smell them now, the stink of devil bear and saber-toothed tiger. But mostly what I can smell is the warm, sickening stench of blood.

Flames flicker from below and spotlights play across the tower. Light dances and shadows jump. I keep my senses alert and my body hidden as well as I can, slinking along metal beams. Creeping quickly and silently, until I catch sight of Brugan's back.

The devil bear crouches over Max, his muscled, hairy back blocking my view of the saber-toothed tiger. But I don't need to see Max to know his life's draining away. His blood's splattered everywhere and I can hear rasping, popping breaths as he struggles to force air in and out of his lungs.

I ease forward, trying to see if Brugan's hurt. The devil bear's intent on his kill, on finishing the job. His claws are on Max's throat, crushing the last scrap of life from his body. Even with everything that's happened, Brugan's ruth-lessness still horrifies me.

I can't let him see me. The fall's made me too weak to be sure of getting away.

Something shiny catches my eye. One of those spiky creatures. Or rather, it's the creature's mangled body on a nearby beam. Three of its limbs are missing and half its face is gone. Did Brugan do that too, or was it Sentin? I glance up. Is the reptile still alive up there? Still fighting monsters?

My paw hits a piece of the creature, and metal skitters across the beam. I freeze. But the devil bear's already raising his head and turning toward me.

Chapter Twenty-Nine

B rugan growls and drops Max onto the beam. Brugan's front is thick with blood. His fur hangs in heavy, sticky clumps and his eyes look red and bloated.

Max gurgles. It's a horrible sound, wet and desperate. His paws twitch, scraping across the metal beam as though he's trying to get up.

Brugan keeps his eyes fixed on me, but bends his knees and thrusts one long, evil claw at Max, plunging it through his throat. Finishing him.

That could have been Cale. I'm so glad it's not I feel weak with relief. Doctor Morelle did me a favor when she kicked Cale out.

Sickened by Brugan's brutality, I turn my head away. Even the crowd is silent.

As soon as my eyes are off him, Brugan attacks. I jump away, forcing my tired, weak body to make the distance to another beam. Brugan leaps a moment later and lands heavily. For a moment I'm hopeful that he's hurt worse than I am. But as I jump again, so does he. He's gaining on me.

We're nearly at the top. So close. But I don't think I can get there without fighting Brugan, and I'm too exhausted, too badly hurt to win. He's too strong. I'm going to have to face him soon. What can I do?

I leap again, and almost land on a metal stick covered with spikes. The dismembered arm of one of the porcupine creatures. With my back paw, I flick the spiked arm across the beam at Brugan. A grunt of pain tells me I hit him, but he barely pauses.

I spin just in time to catch his arm in my jaws as he reaches me. I bite down hard. His momentum tumbles us both, but my jaws are clenched shut and I won't let go.

Hot devil-bear blood fills my mouth as I tear into his flesh with all my strength. He roars, and his free arm slams into my side. It feels like he's ripping my head from my body, but I lock my jaw. My fangs dig deeper, grinding against bone.

He rakes me with his claws, trying to shake me off, to get to his feet. He's so big, if he gets his balance he could crush me.

Planting my back paws, I throw my strength forward, grinding my teeth into his arm and keeping him down. But the shock of my first strike's gone. He's thinking now, counter attacking. His strength against mine. He drives me back and uses his free hand to push himself up.

Before he can stand, I let his arm go and launch my body weight at his leg. My teeth close around his knee. He falls back, howling, but both his hands are free now. He digs his claws into me. This time it's my flesh that's tearing, my scream of pain forced out between teeth still clenched in his furry knee.

His claws rake my sides, opening huge wounds. Pain sears hot. Unbearable.

My jaw opens and I let go, stumbling backward. It hurts so much I'm panting. All I want is to curl into a ball.

I back up, whimpering, while he lumbers to his feet, swaying and snarling. Blood cakes him from head to foot. He drags the back of one big hand across his eyes, wiping blood away.

I need to run. I shuffle backwards, hit something sharp, move around it, and come up hard against a metal post. Can't go any further.

Brugan steps forward, his bulk looming over me. There's nowhere to run. I can barely move, I've got nothing left.

It's over. We both know it. His lips peel back in a final, dreadful grin that shows his red fangs.

A piece of metal drops from above and glances off Brugan's arm. It's not big enough to hurt him, but he stumbles. It's not much of an opening, but it's all I'll get.

Without the strength to jump, I half lurch, half fall onto him. We tumble together onto the metal, but I'm on top, and somehow I grab his throat in my teeth.

He takes hold of my body with both hands. My teeth lock. If he tries to tear me away, he'll be tearing out his own throat. His claws rip into me again, but no matter how bad the pain, I can't let go. If I do, I'm dead.

I squeeze my jaw together, crushing his windpipe. Blood pulses into my mouth. His breath rasps. His arms beat against me as his body thrashes and jerks, desperate to throw me off. I squeeze my jaws tighter. I can kill him. I can survive.

He's getting weaker. Instead of clawing, his hands push against my face. My mouth and nose are clamped so tight I can't breathe. I scream through locked jaws, bite down as hard as I can, sinking my teeth deeper into his flesh. My throat is thick with blood. There's a loud roaring in my ears. The crowd cheers as Brugan's life drains away in hot, staccato bursts.

When his body goes limp, I pry my jaws open and gag. Then I push myself off him, moving slowly, painfully. Every step sends bolts of agony through my body. I'm half expecting him to get up again, but the devil bear lies still.

I look up. The top of the tower is close, just two more levels to climb. All I have to do is make it up there, step into the light, and I've won.

Don't think about Brugan. Don't think about anything.

This'll be over soon. Climb. Get to the top.

Every muscle's screaming, but I drag myself up to the next level. The beams here are narrow and spaced wide apart. My legs don't work properly and each time my left back paw touches the ground I scream with pain.

Keep going. I have to keep going.

There are more spiky limbs lying around on this level. A lot more. Pieces of the metal creatures are scattered all around the narrow beams. An epic battle's been waged. This is where Sentin must have made his stand.

Could he have survived? I don't see him. Nothing's moving up here, no creatures, no Sentin. They must have beaten him. His body must be here, unless they threw him off the tower.

I stare down, as though I might see his Skin lying on the ground a hundred and sixty floors below. Of course I can't see that far, there are too many crisscrossing metal beams. And looking down makes me queasy, so shift my gaze up instead. There are giant blimps floating up there. The screens are on the other side of the blimps, facing toward the crowd. I'm glad. I don't want to see myself.

The crowd's chanting my name. I ignore them. The

top level's just above me. Unlike all the others, the top level is a flat, solid piece of metal rather than just criss-crossing beams.

To get up to it, I need to make my way to the outer edge, where vertical beams are holding it up. With a broken leg I can't jump, so I dig my sharp claws into the metal and drag myself up.

It's too hard. My body hurts too much. So easy to let go. So easy to drop to the ground far below.

Tori speaks in my head, as clearly as though she were walking beside me. *"You think you have it tough? Some of the shifts I've done at the factory were a lot worse than this, and all I earned were enough credits for a crappy bowl of noodles."*

The thought makes me want to laugh, but I think that's only because I'm so close to passing out that I'm getting light-headed. Instead I pause, resting a second. Tori's right, the pain's nothing, it doesn't matter. I'm about to get everything I want. I must be the only one left alive, and I'm about to win the contest.

Cale, are you watching? I'm going to get your Skin back. And Ma and William will have a home again. Maybe even up in New Triton, in the sun. Yeah, Ma would like that. Tori, too. And I'll be the leopard forever.

I heave myself all the way up, managing to drag my whole body onto the flat piece of metal before I collapse. There are a couple of torn-apart metal creatures up here, too. A huge spiky body lies nearby, the biggest one I've seen yet. Still no sign of Sentin, so he must be dead. And there's nothing but dark sky and blimps above me.

I've done it.

A light shoots up into the sky, blindingly bright. The circle of light's coming from the center of the platform, and it's so close, all I have to do is drag myself over to it and I've won. The crowd's going crazy, cheering and stomping and clapping. When I haul myself back onto my paws they get even louder.

Every step makes my body light up with pain, but I limp forward, keeping my injured paw off the ground.

Ten more steps. Nine steps. Eight.

The crowd are shouting something. What are they saying? So many voices, it's hard to make out. Something about Sentin?

He bursts out from where he was crouched behind the fallen metal creature. His reptile scales are a dull rust color, crusted with blood. Sentin's on all fours and he's limping too. He's on me before I can think to react. When he rears up to his hind legs to shove me, I stumble, sobbing with pain. He keeps coming, determined, one goal in mind, and I can't stay on my paws.

I feel the edge of the metal platform. One last shove and I'm over it, plunging down, dropping backward off the tower.

I fall, tumbling toward the ground. Then slam hard into a metal platform.

Pain burns though my body, eating me up, taking me over.

Pain is all I am.

Consciousness floods in and out like waves. It takes a while for me to realize I'm screaming.

I force the pain down, swallowing it, holding it inside me as I lie on my back, looking up. I have to see what happens next. I need to see the contest end.

The light beams straight up from the top of the tower, projecting into the night sky. Sentin's up there. His image is in the light. He lifts his hands, stretching them up.

The bright spotlights that light the rest of the tower go out, leaving me in complete darkness. None of the other Skins matter now.

The shining image of Sentin's reptile lights up the sky. The crowd chants his name over and over. Sen-tin. Sen-tin. Sen-tin.

He's won. Sentin's won.

It's over. I've lost.

Chapter Thirty

M etal robots scrape me off the tower and carry me to the arena floor in darkness. I'm glad nobody can see me. The crowd's only looking at Sentin. That's good. Nobody hears me scream.

I'm battered and torn. My human body will be damaged too, but what does it matter? I lost. I may as well be dead.

When I refuse to transfer out of my Skin, a doctor injects me with something that paralyses me. It makes my sight darken and narrow so it's like I'm looking through a very long tube. My consciousness tears away from my leopard like bones breaking.

I can feel human limbs, my human body.

Pain.

I hear myself scream again, this time from a human throat. My clothes are too heavy. I can't bear the weight of them, pressing on my broken body. They're wet with blood.

Doesn't matter.

I lost.

My human body is being carried somewhere, and it hurts so badly I can barely think. Through the pain, I search frantically for my leopard, stretching my consciousness out to find it.

Where is it? There's a hole in my mind, a piece missing. I'd rather have lost an arm or a leg. The most vital part of me has vanished, lost forever. What's there to live for now?

A hand grips my arm, holding it still, then another needle slides in. A powerful painkiller, because the pain ebbs away and my head clears enough that I can open my eyes.

I'm in a small, white room that holds only a bed and a beeping machine that's probably measuring my vitals. A white-coated doctor frowns at me. She has dark red hair scraped back into a severe bun, and her expression is unfriendly. Over the stench of my own blood, I catch her scent. If I were still in my Skin, I'd say I can sense what she's feeling, that she's excited about something.

But no, it's my imagination. I'm clutching at the idea, because I can't stand that my leopard's gone.

And if she does smell, so what? Nothing matters now. Not the faint, muffled stamps and cheers above me that tell me I'm still in the arena complex, somewhere below ground level. Not the wounds that cover my human body, or the doctor tugging my bloody shirt off so she can examine the damage underneath. I don't look to see how badly I'm hurt. I don't care.

I'll never be the leopard again.

The crowd gives another muffled roar, and I imagine Sentin up there, parading in front of the crowd. Raising his elongated, shimmering arms to the sky, reveling in his win.

The doctor sprays something over my torso to seal my

wounds. The cold liquid hardens as it hits, and my flesh tightens underneath. She makes me roll over so she can do my back, then she snaps, "Bring some clean clothes," at someone, and I realize that somehow I already knew there were two people standing by the door even though they're behind me.

It's only because I'm half naked that I summon the energy to look who's there. A red-uniformed guard is standing at attention beside the door while another guard disappears out through it, his heavy boots making every step loud.

Everything's in sharp focus. I'm suddenly aware of every smell, every tiny movement, every sound. They're not as clear as when I was the leopard, but far sharper than my human senses have ever been. Over the last few days I've noticed my senses were getting better, but nothing like this. Whether it's because I'm still pumped up after the contest, I'm not sure. But I *can* smell the doctor's perspiration, and I'm sure she's excited about something.

The doctor tries to strip off my jeans, and I grab hold to stop her pulling them down. She's not going to get me naked. Not in front of the guard.

I hear more footsteps. A pair of heavy boots in the hallway outside. Without a shirt on I'm not turning around, but when the door opens I know by his scent it's the guard she sent away. The doctor takes some clothes from him and hands me a clean shirt. I sit up to put it on, amazed I don't feel worse. Surely the painkillers she gave me can't be that good? Is it another unexpected improvement, my body recovering extra fast?

"Here." The doctor gives me a clean pair of jeans. "Take the dirty pair off and I'll treat the rest of your wounds."

The shirt is long enough to give some cover, and my jeans are a nasty black color, heavy and dark with blood, so I do what she says. It takes me a while, first to get my shoes off, then to tug off my heavy, sticky jeans, even with her help.

When I've finally stripped them free, she sprays the cuts that cover my legs. There's only one that's really nasty, a deep gash in my thigh that she frowns at before she sprays.

The ankle's puffy. "Not broken," she says once she's scanned it. "Torn muscles. You'll heal."

When she's done, I tug on the clean pair of jeans and put on the shoes she gives me.

The doctor looks me over before nodding in approval. "Wait here," she says, then leaves.

Watching the guards, I ease myself back onto the bed. What happens now? They've cleaned me up, but only on the surface. The doctor didn't do a great job of cleaning or treating my wounds. I'm being held together with temporary spray and painkillers, then clean clothes to hide the damage.

Guess the Morelle Corporation has officially stopped caring. Any minute now they'll kick me out, back to Old Triton, which will probably mean a long, slow, miserable death. With Rayne's band I've no chance of getting work or being able to stay in a shelter.

The door opens and Director Morelle comes in. What's she doing here? From the thumping coming from above, it sounds like the crowd are leaving the arena. Is the whole event over?

"Wait outside," she tells the guards. She looks at me like I'm a nasty bug that just crawled into squashing distance. If she's glad I survived, she's hiding it well.

"Hello, Rayne. Your parents insisted on seeing you as

soon as the contest was over." Director Morelle inclines her head toward the door. "They'll be here in a moment."

"My mother?" I croak.

The director shoots me a scornful look, and my chest contracts.

"You mean Rayne's parents?" I ask. Is she crazy? She knows I'm not Rayne, so what kind of game is she playing? Damned if I'm going to stick around to find out.

I push myself off the bed and up to standing, but Director Morelle steps forward and grabs my upper arms, forcing me back onto the hospital bed. I wasn't expecting it, and wouldn't have believed she could move so fast. Too late, I struggle. It's like fighting back against a statue. When I throw all my weight forward, she doesn't budge, doesn't even flinch. How could she be so strong? New Tritoners often have nanobots injected to give them extra strength, but this is way too much. Is there some other kind of strength tweaking I don't know about?

She brings her face close to mine, and it shows no sign of strain. Not the smallest bead of sweat, not a wrinkle, not a hair out of place. I can't smell perspiration, and I could never detect a hint of emotion in her, not even when I was the leopard.

Is she even human?

I freeze as the thought crystalizes and becomes so obvious I should have realized it earlier.

Could *she* be a Skin?

Bringing my face close, I take a deep breath, dragging in her scent. Human flesh and blood? I think so. But underneath the flesh, deep inside her, there's something else. It's not my imagination. It's a core of carbon fiber. I can sense it. I know I'm right.

She's a Skin.

But there are only supposed to be five Skin prototypes, the five for the contest, and humanoid ones are illegal.

The door opens.

Director Morelle lets me go and turns in one smooth motion. It's a man and a woman, their worried expressions turning to frowns of dismay when they see me. They have the perfect features of floaters, and skin that's a rich, dark brown. Rayne's parents.

The man turns his frown to Director Morelle. "This isn't our daughter."

Rayne's mother stares at my wrist, her eyes widening. "Why are you wearing Rayne's band? How did you get it? What have you done with her?"

The scent of their shock and worry fills the small room, so strong it makes my head swim.

"I don't... um…" I get up, my heart racing, and flick my gaze to the door. Should I run?

Director Morelle speaks up, sounding surprised. "I had no idea this girl wasn't Rayne."

"Where's our daughter?" The man's face is going red. His fists clench and unclench and when he lurches at me, I'm sure he's going to attack. "Where is she? What have you done with her?"

"I haven't done anything. I swear."

"Where did you get her band?" He tries to grab me but I pull away, fending him off though he's much bigger than me.

"I saw her in the shelter, but they killed her. The sharks did, I mean. Not me." The more I back up, the further I get from the door. I raise both hands, trying desperately to show that I'm not dangerous. That I'm no killer.

The man freezes, and the woman goes pale. She lifts both hands to her mouth. "What?" she whispers.

"Some men were trying to rob her. One had a blade." I suck in my breath, hating that I'm the one to tell them their daughter's dead. Hating myself for taking the band from a dying girl. "He killed her and I took her band. I'm so sorry. I swapped it with mine."

"That's not true." The man deflates, his arms sinking by his sides. He looks smaller than he did a moment ago, as though he's shrinking before my eyes. "You're lying. She's not dead."

"If she stole your daughter's band, it's likely she killed her so she could take her place in the contest." says Director Morelle.

The woman's eyes fill with tears. "Where is she? Where's Rayne?"

I've no idea what she means. Does she want to know what happened to her body, or does she not believe that Rayne is dead?

"Security!" At the director's yell, the two guards come rushing in. "Take her into custody."

They grab me, one on each arm, their fingers digging into my flesh.

"She needs to tell us where our daughter is," says the man in a broken voice.

"Rayne's dead." Director Morelle waves at the two men, gesturing them out. "I'll turn her murderer in to the police and they'll find your daughter's body." As the guards drag me toward the door, the director glances down at her band. "We must go. There's been an explosion outside. They're saying it could be a terrorist—."

"Where is she?" Rayne's father cuts off the director, his shout filled with desperation. I still don't know what he means.

"I didn't kill her," I call as the guards drag me out. "Please believe me."

Outside the door, the red-haired doctor who treated my wounds is waiting, hypodermic in hand. She jabs the needle into my arm and my vision blurs. When I try to protest, a nonsense sound slurs slowly out of my mouth.

The world goes dark.

Chapter Thirty-One

I wake up with my arms strapped down. I'm lying on a bed in a lab room. My brain is fuzzy. I can't think straight.

A woman is speaking, her voice muffled and far away. "…changes at the cellular level," she says. "A sympathetic reaction to extreme stimulation of the neural cortex. The surgeon reports a further improvement in eye function, far beyond the normal range."

A machine beeps next to me and I manage to turn my head enough to see it. Wires run from the machine to my head. Hard things are attached to my skull. They itch, and I wriggle my forehead trying unsuccessfully to shake them loose. Numbers run across the machine. I blink at them, but they blur into each other.

"Yes, director," says the woman. "She's waking up now,"

Whatever drug they've given me has made my vision blurry. I try to tug my wrists free of the straps that hold them to the bed, but the straps hold firm.

Am I in hospital? In prison? I'm wearing a smock, so

hospital seems more likely. But the room's ceiling is the same color as the ceiling in the room they gave me at the Morelle scraper. Could I be there?

I hear footsteps coming closer, then the woman says, "That's it, Milla. Wake up." Blinking at the white-coated doctor, I see it's the same red-haired, hard-faced woman who bandaged me up after the contest. But behind her is another shape. I blink harder, trying to make out what it is.

Could it be—?

A sharp jolt of hope fights through the fuzziness in my brain.

My Leopard Skin.

It's lying down, strapped to a large gurney. So many thick webbing straps tie it down that only its head is clearly visible.

"What have you done to it?" I whisper, closing my eyes. I squeeze them as tight as I can, trying to transfer into my leopard. *Transfer, dammit.*

My head is too stuffed with wool. My consciousness is trapped inside my own tied-down body.

The doctor's hands on my head make my eyes flutter back open. She's adjusting the hard things—electrodes—on my skull.

"What's going to happen to me?" My voice sounds as fuzzy as my brain.

When the woman doesn't answer, I jerk my head away from her hands.

She clicks her tongue, reaching for the electrode she's trying to adjust. "It'll be easier if you don't fight."

"Tell me what you're going to do." I jerk my head again.

Her mouth presses into an annoyed line. "The director wants to know why your body reacts to wounds inflicted on the Skin. We're going to measure exactly what's happening inside your brain as we—"

"As you what?" But I already know. That much, at least, is filtering into my woozy mind. "You're going to damage my Skin? On purpose?"

The thought is so horrible, I jerk the webbing holding my wrists again, fighting to get free.

"The sooner we get the data we need, the sooner this will be over. So please hold still and do what I tell you."

In spite of the fuzziness in my mind, my body isn't sore and as far as I can tell, my wounds have healed. My Skin's wounds, too. Though the straps holding it down look so tight they're digging into its flesh, I can't see or smell any blood.

Last thing I remember, the director said she was turning me in for Rayne's murder. But that little scene she organized was obviously just an act for Rayne's parents.

"How long have I been knocked out?"

"Long enough to heal." She sounds distracted as she checks some numbers on a tablet.

I blink hard, trying to clear my head. Long enough to heal? Sounds like I could have been out for days. The director didn't turn me in to the police. She's kept me here.

I'm officially not Rayne anymore, and nobody's looking for me. The director can do whatever she likes with me. There's nothing to stop her if she decides to cut open my head and dissect my brain.

Worse, she can take my leopard apart, piece by piece, and there's not a damn thing I can do to stop her.

"Don't hurt my leopard," I gasp. "Please."

The doctor turns to a tray of instruments. "We have no choice. You're the only one who's exhibited those kinds of symptoms. We need to find out why." She picks up a hypodermic. "When I inject you with this, you'll be able to transfer into the Skin."

The needle stings as it slides into my arm.

My fuzzy brain clears and I squeeze my eyes closed. I want to transfer into my Skin so badly I'm shaking. My fists clench and it's all I can do not to transfer.

But awareness is rushing through me. A brilliant clarity that's come from whatever drug she injected me with.

And with the clarity, comes a realization.

I can smell the alluring feline scent of my leopard, making it even harder to resist the transferal. But over that, the scent of the doctor is clear. There's excitement in her smell, and I can sense it as clearly as if I were in my Leopard Skin. With my eyes closed, I can tell exactly where she's standing. I can hear her starched coat rustle and detect the movement of her hand through the air.

And I feel *strong*.

I have no idea how long she kept me knocked out, but my body has done more than just heal. My veins feel like they're on fire. I feel almost as good as I did when I was the leopard. Somehow, I have my leopard's sense of smell and hearing. Could I have gained its strength?

She's tied me down with a webbing strap around each wrist. Am I strong enough to break the straps?

Though I'd give anything to be able to transfer into my leopard, it's trussed up so tightly it won't be able to get free. She knows how strong the leopard is. But she hasn't tied my human body up as securely.

I focus everything I have on my wrists, pulling against the straps with all my strength. As I feel them start to give, a cry of effort squeezes from my lips. I feel the veins pulse in my neck as I strain.

The doctor makes a shocked sound. "What are you doing?"

My restraints tear open.

As I leap from the bed, the electrodes rip free from my skull. The doctor staggers backward, her eyes wide. Glancing down, I see how thick the broken straps dangling from the bed are. No normal person should have been able to break those straps.

I'm not sure I'm entirely human any more.

That's okay. I don't want to be human. There are better things to be.

The doctor scrambles backward, away from me, but I grab her by the shoulders, swing her around, and press her onto the bed I've just vacated. The broken straps are useless, but I jerk some of the machine's wires free and use them to tie her hands to the bed. It's not as secure as I'd like, but she's deathly pale, and her excitement has turned into a fear is so strong I can taste it. She's not going anywhere.

Grabbing a scalpel from the doctor's tray of instruments, I turn to my beautiful leopard.

The straps are so thick around its body, I don't know how long it will take to cut them off. Frantically, I start sawing. Once it's free, I can become the leopard and carry my human body out of here. It can dangle from my jaws.

There's a noise from a long distance away, only audible because my hearing is sharper than it should be. Boots are pounding down the hallway. Stompers' boots, getting closer. At least four stompers. No, six.

Of course, there must be cameras in here. They saw me get loose. And I don't have time to get my leopard free before they'll burst in here.

Shit.

I hesitate for several precious seconds, staring at my leopard, my hand in its fur, desperate to find a way out of this without leaving it behind.

The boots are getting closer.

No time.

Sobbing with frustration, I slam out of the lab room, turning away from the oncoming stompers. A hallway stretches out in front of me. I have no idea where I am. All I can do is run. My legs pump hard as I fly down the corridor. My feet are bare and all I have on is a hospital smock. Still, I'm faster than the stompers. Not nearly as fast as my leopard—

I push the yearning for my Leopard Skin away. No time for regrets now. If I make it out of here alive, I can figure out a way to get my leopard back.

The thumping of the stompers' boots gets more distant as I race past more lab rooms, most with glass doors. Inside, I catch glimpses of terrible things. An ugly dog creature the size of a horse. A metal animal skeleton with a human face that turns to look at me as I run past. What looks like a human heart in a jar. It's pumping, and wires snaking out of it connect to a pair of hair-covered legs.

The lab rooms are filled with doctors or technicians wearing white coats. I even push past some doctors in the hallway, but they're too startled to try to stop me.

Sliding around a corner, there are windows in front of me. The ground looms far below. I'm too high up to jump, even if I could get the window open. I must be inside the Morelle scraper, higher than I've ever been, on a much higher floor than when I stayed here.

From up here I can see the streets of New Triton laid out in neat rectangular shapes. Through the holes in the center of the rectangles, Old Triton looks dark. A buried city. And there's the wall between Deiterra and Triton. I've never seen it so clearly, but I don't have time for more than a glance before I turn away. The stompers will be on me in no time.

A blinding flash of light from the window makes me duck. BOOM! The sound is so loud, it rocks the building. I brace my feet against the shaking, and hear glass crash in a nearby lab room.

Somewhere on this floor, people start screaming. Straightening, I see thick black smoke pouring from a nearby scraper. What the hell? Could a bomb have gone off in New Triton?

Was it the Fist? No, it couldn't be. That was a massive explosion. The Fist can't possibly have bombs that size.

Sirens shriek, and I clap my hands over my ears. Men and women in white coats pour out of lab rooms, hurrying toward a door marked with green.

I stare, perplexed, as they file through it. Beyond, I catch a glimpse of a stairwell. Is that the exit?

Making a snap decision, I rush for it, overtaking workers as I hurtle through the door. I run down the stairs, shoving through white-coated workers. Some are babbling about a Deiterran attack, but surely that has to be speculation.

More people are pouring into the stairwell from lower floors, filling the staircase and making it difficult to push my way through.

I could easily get trapped in here.

The next door I get to has the number 25 on it, so I must be on the twenty-fifth floor. Struggling down that many flights of stairs through all these people will take too long. Long enough for stompers to be waiting for me at the bottom.

A bunch of workers are streaming through the door, joining all the others descending the stairwell. I shove against the tide, working my way through them. They shout and protest, but I push with my head down and manage to struggle out the door.

The hallway on this floor is similar to the one above, with more lab rooms coming off it. But at the end of the hall, I spot a sliding glass door leading out to a balcony. I run and tear the door open. Outside on the balcony, I can smell smoke from the burning building, and hear the wails of fire engines, competing with the alarm still sounding inside the Morelle scraper. Flames lick the side of the scraper the explosion came from.

The wind whips up my hair and the hospital gown as I lean over the chest-high rail, peering down.

The ground is so far away, it makes my legs weak. But below me, on the next floor down, is another small balcony. And below that, another one. There are no balconies above me, so this must be the highest floor that has one. But from this floor down, there's one on every level.

Even as I climb over the rail, I'm afraid I'm making a terrible mistake. It's a long drop to the balcony below, and it'll be tricky to land inside the balcony rail. If I miss, I'll fall twenty-five floors, and bits of me will splatter all over the street.

If I still felt completely human, I wouldn't even attempt it.

Taking a deep breath, my heart thumping, I lower myself over the side of the balcony. I dangle for a moment, then drop, twisting my body toward the building as I fall.

I land as well as I could have hoped for, though the force of the drop jars through my bare feet. But there's no time to celebrate. I have twenty-four more balcony jumps to survive.

By the time I'm at the last balcony, looking down to street level, an ever-increasing crowd throngs the sidewalk. Seems like the entire population of New Triton is standing outside, gaping at the building that's on fire.

A few are staring and pointing at me. They must have spotted me dropping from balcony to balcony. But there's no sign of stompers, or of the director's red-uniformed guards.

As I dangle from the last balcony, I crane my neck, peering down to see the people below pushing and scrambling to get out of my way. I drop onto the sidewalk, conscious of how strange I must look to them in just a hospital gown, with my hair blowing messily around a face that looks nothing like theirs.

But the thick crowd is a blessing. I can disappear into the throng.

Dashing through them, I keep my head down. My blood is pumping, and I know I can run faster than I used to.

A big guy just ahead is holding a raincoat. I come up behind him, jerk it out of his hand and take off. He shouts and tries to come after me, but I lose him easily.

The coat's so big, it hangs to my thighs and covers my hands. Good. I pull the hood up so it flops over my eyes and hides my face.

On the other side of the street is a glass barrier. It's there to stop people accidentally falling into Old Triton. But that's exactly where I want to go. Though I've already dropped twenty-five stories, I have another twenty-eight to descend.

Climbing over the barrier, I find a foothold underneath the street. Thick metal beams hold up the road, and below the beams is a building. Old Triton is twenty-eight stories high, and almost all of our buildings are exactly that tall. Every inch of Old Triton's space is used. Our city is overcrowded, dirty, and dark.

Perfect for hiding in.

The side of this Old Triton building is brick. There's a

fire escape a little way along, and I inch across, hanging on to the metal beam that holds up the New Triton street, until I'm above the fire escape. I should be used to dropping from heights by now, but this fall is the scariest one yet.

Heart racing, I let go of the beam and drop. I grab hold of the top of the fire escape, cutting my hands on the rusty metal. Then all I need to do is climb down the ladder.

Once I'm finally at ground level, the Old Triton gloom feels like a comforting blanket that wraps around me to hide me and keep me safe. I take off down an alley that leads to exactly the kind of place I need, a long underpass where a solid section of New Triton stretches overhead in all directions, turning the dimness into pitch black.

From the buildings around me, faint lights shine halfheartedly out of grimy windows. A few weeks ago they would have been barely bright enough to guide me, but now my night vision's sharp and I move fast, sure of every step. I've spent my whole life in Old Triton, in darkness. This is *my* arena.

I can hear the tiniest sounds, detect even the faintest scents. In one apartment, an old man is frying food with the window open, and his sweat stinks even more than the charred meal. He calls to a woman, but I can hear her snoring. Next door, canned laughter comes from a holo. Above them, a mother shouts at a child. Washing lines are strung from windows, the clothes stinking of damp, of never drying completely. These people live too close and work too hard. They're people of darkness. My people.

We've let ourselves be pushed down for far too long.

In a boarded-up doorway, I find a place to catch my breath. I sit with my back against the boards, waiting for night to fall and for New Triton to get as dark as it is down here before I go back up there.

From the moment I walked through her door, an impostor wearing a stolen band, Director Morelle must have known she could use me however she wanted. I was her private science experiment. Cale too, probably. No wonder she didn't stop us training at night. Much better to watch and see what happened. Easy enough to get rid of us afterward.

But without knowing it, she gave me exactly what I needed. I don't know how I have the leopard's abilities, but maybe it's because I refused to give them up.

For the first time in my life, I'm *strong*.

The only question is, what am I going to do with what I've gained?

For too many years I've let myself, and the people I love, be pushed around. We've been bullied, relocated, assaulted, and beaten. I've let everyone I care about be taken away.

No more.

Curling my hand into a fist, I clench it hard. It's time to stop being a victim. I'm going to fight back, and I know exactly what I want. I'll save Ma and Tori from the director's factories and shelters, and William from her academy. And I'll get my Leopard Skin back.

Without a working band, there's only one place I can go for help. *133 Birchel.* As soon as it gets dark up top, that's where I'm headed, to the address that Doctor Gregory gave me. The doctor will know where Cale is, so I can find him too.

Rescuing the people I love won't be easy, but for the first time, I think there might be a way. One thing for sure, I'm done with running from the director. Now I'm ready to show her just how sharp this leopard's teeth really are.

Whoever I am now is up to me to decide. What matters most is that I'm very much alive, and somehow the leopard's alive in me.

So watch out, Director Morelle. You think I'm unpredictable? You won't even see me coming.

Afterword

Dear Wonderful Reader,

Thank you so much for travelling into Milla's world and trying on her Skin!

Milla's determined to get her family and her Leopard Skin back, but it won't be easy. Without a working band, she's going to struggle to survive, let alone fight the most powerful woman in the world.

She's also about to find out why parts of Triton are being bombed. Is it war with Deiterra? Is it the Fist? Either way, the people she loves are in terrible danger.

Maybe Cale will be able to help. Or will he walk away when he discovers Milla's been lying to him about who she really is?

Milla's journey continues in book two of the series: *Skin Rebellion*. I hope you'll come with me for the rest of this wild ride.

- *Tania.*

CPSIA information can be obtained
at www.ICGtesting.com
Printed in the USA
BVHW031101070519
547581BV00001B/134/P